JONNY THOMPSON

The Limestone Manor

To my Hometown.
The Town Worth Living In.

1

Cliff Shaw rubbed his knee for what felt like the umpteenth time this trip, though he never really understood why. It's not like it helped the pain for very long. Painkillers might have been a good option, though he had decided sometime in his sixties that *I'll be damned if I ever take meds.* Apparently, between pain and stubbornness, stubbornness would prevail.

"Sir, can I offer you a coffee, water, soda?" asked a woman in her early thirties with a name tag that read something like Natalie or Natasha, not that Cliff was able to make it out without his glasses and those were tucked somewhere in his bag.

"Does it come with the ticket?" Cliff asked absently.

"Sorry, sir, drinks are extra."

"Of course, they are. Along with bags, knee space, and I can only imagine, urinating is as well?"

"Actually, not that last one sir." She smirked.

"Well, bless that, then," Cliff said giving his knee another rub.

"So? No drink?" she asked, her smile annoyingly spread across her face.

"You know there was a time when trains were a luxurious way to travel. People wore suits and drank martinis and enjoyed the passing countryside. Now it's neither convenient nor cheap. For example, my train was supposed to go through Stratford this morning. Then, at the last minute, they redirected us through London, which is very much not on the same path, and they didn't give so much as an explanation." Cliff looked at the young woman for some sort of response, but after a couple of empty beats, he supposed he wasn't going to get one. "So anyways, I have to ask myself what's the damn point?" Cliff added shaking his head.

"Aww, the good old days," Nat-something said, looking off at some distant image in the sky.

Cliff let out a short burst of air that could have been a laugh. "Good old days? I watched friends die in a war, from diseases that don't even exist anymore. We were lucky to make it out in one piece, or even with just one piece missing. If you think for one moment I wouldn't take a flu vaccine, endless communication with my friends around the world, and convenience of travel, then you are sorely mistaken, young lady."

"So what's your point?" she said in the unappreciative way a young person speaks to someone older than themselves.

"The point, young lady, is, what was the point of all that suffering, if, after a hundred years of trains, we not only haven't made them move any faster, but we've made them more expensive as well? In fact, I believe this is the same train I was on fifty-four years ago when I left this godforsaken town."

"I see your frustration," she said, nodding slowly. "So, that's no to a Coke?"

"No! I don't want a Coke. Aren't you the least bit curious as to why I left fifty-four years ago? Or what godforsaken town I'm referring to? Or why in heavens I'm going back?!"

"To be honest, you don't really seem like you want to talk to me," Nat said quietly.

"True. I don't, but now that I've started, it seems a shame to give up halfway."

"So, you do want to talk?"

"Are you trying to make me feel senile?"

"No?" Nat said, hesitantly, though unable to not make eye contact with Cliff.

"Good." Cliff looked away for a moment to rub his knee.

"Do you want an Aleve?" Nat asked.

"Pain or stubbornness," Cliff whispered to himself.

"What's that?" Nat asked, leaning in.

"Nothing."

"So, where you off to?" Natalie asked, sounding unsure if she should stick around or keep walking.

Cliff let out a deep sigh. "Have a seat, Nat. Do you mind if I call you Nat?" Cliff asked as she sat down across from him.

"It's Sarah?" Nat said, taking a moment to examine her name tag, before having a good laugh. "This is Natasha's shirt."

"Well, you're Nat now, 'cause I've already put that in the old noodle." Cliff tapped the side of his head thoughtfully. "It can be like a nickname or something." Cliff smiled.

"Sure," Nat said.

"Do you know what the problem is when you ask where someone is going?" Cliff turned sideways to face Nat, who was shaking her head cautiously, as if half expecting Cliff to berate her again. "It's that you don't get the why. And the why's all that matters. Who cares where I'm going, it's a non sequitur, it ends. Do you understand?"

"Not really."

"For instance, where are you going?"

"Montreal, then back home."

"Where's home?"

"London," Nat answered, and Cliff remained silent for a long time.

"You see, it ends. It's boring. We got nothing. But if I asked you, why did you join Via rail?" Cliff lifted his brows expectantly.

Nat tapped her chin thoughtfully. "I guess I wanted to travel."

"Where did you want to travel to?"

"I'd never been much further then London before, so I guess Montreal, Halifax, Regina. Anywhere, really."

"And did you?" Cliff asked, giving her his first genuine smile of the trip.

"All of them! I was a little nervous at first, about being on the train for so long, but it's given me a lot of time to read and work on some of my writing," she added excitedly.

"So, you're a writer?"

"I try to be when I can." Nat gave Cliff a broad smile.

"Good for you. May as well try and be what you want to be. You're going to die either way." Cliff laughed as he leaned back in his seat. "You see how much better the why can be?" He gave Nat a little wink before leaning his head back and closing his eyes.

Cliff could feel Nat's presence across from him, and he didn't hear her trolley rolling away like he would have expected.

"What?" he asked, not bothering to open his eyes.

"Aren't you going to tell me why you're going to wherever it is you're going?" Nat asked, sounding a little frustrated.

"You still haven't asked me anything," Cliff said smugly. "I'm not in the habit of spilling my life's story to people who haven't asked. I'm not that kind of old."

"Okay, well then, why did you leave..." She paused for a moment. "St. Marys!" she said, her excitement causing Cliff to open one of his eyes.

He caught her smiling as she read the ticket he'd left on the edge of the table. *Must have left that out when the conductor swung by.*

"Good eye, kid," Cliff said, tucking the ticket back in his pocket. "For that, I'll give you an answer." Cliff leaned towards Nat conspiratorially, resting his arm on the armrest and kicking his legs out a little into the empty seat beside him. The extra extensions for his knees felt good. "It was a woman," he said.

Nat looked almost disappointed as she slouched back into her chair.

"What? Not the answer you were looking for?"

"Just feel likes a lot of work to run away from a woman for fifty-four years, what with all the wars and dying and all," Nat said.

Cliff gave her a broad smile. "Maybe, but as I always say, pain or stubbornness. Stubbornness always prevails."

"So, you've been this stubborn for…ninety years?"

"Eighty-two, thank you very much. And yes, it's a gift." Cliff watched Natalie stare up at the ceiling of the train for a moment.

"Eighty-two?" she said after a moment "Are you telling me you joined World War II when you were nine?"

Cliff held up his hands in surrender. "You caught me. Thankfully, I only lived through one, but that doesn't mean I didn't lose people."

"I'm sorry to hear that."

"It was a long time ago, kid." Cliff's mind filled with faces of people he'd not thought about in a very long time.

"So why did you run away?"

"What makes you think I ran away?"

"Well, you left, and she didn't…I suspect," Nat said, narrowing her eyes at Cliff. She must have seen his answer somewhere in his face as she gave him another wide smile. "Which means you ran away, because no one can run away staying where they are." Nat laughed.

"I would beg to differ," Cliff corrected absently. "But you'd make yourself a fine detective. In this situation, you are, in fact, correct. I left. We wanted different things. Like she wanted to stay, and I wanted to not stay. It's all extremely underwhelming."

"But now, after years, you finally reconnected, and you are going back to St. Marys to be with your one true love!" Nat said clapping her hands together triumphantly.

"Should have stopped while you were ahead. That is utter nonsense, I'm not even sure she's alive, or in St. Marys." Cliff waved his hand at Nat.

"So why are you going back?"

"Truth be told, Toronto was getting a little too big for me on my own. Don't look at me like that." Cliff swatted a hand towards Nat's nearly pouting face. "I enjoyed being alone. I'm good company."

Nat let out a little giggle but stopped when Cliff shot her a look.

"The point is, I like me, and that was working out fine for a long time. But as life would have it, the world these day is not designed for a solo octogenarian, and to my chagrin, I have found myself needing to slow down."

"Well, you're going to the right place."

"You've been?"

"To swim in the Quarry when I was a kid, but I think I got the gist when we drove through it." Nat laughed.

"People still swimming in that oversized fishpond?" Cliff scoffed.

"As far as I know." Nat shrugged.

"Don't you have other people to serve?" Cliff said, looking down the aisles and seeing the odd head pop up above the seat backs.

"This is a train, sir."

"Call me Cliff. My mother was a sir." Cliff saw the confused look on Nat's face and added, "It was a joke, kid." Cliff chuckled to himself.

"Okay, so if it's not for love, why are you going back here? I mean, from what I can tell, you would seem pretty happy to die just about anywhere else." Nat shrugged.

Cliff gave her a wary look.

"It was a joke, Cliff." Nat laughed.

Cliff tried to keep his face stern, but regrettably, a smile snuck out on him. "I got a letter from an old friend. He mentioned he had a room that had just opened up for me at an inn he recently bought. Some place called the Limestone Manor, named like everything else in the damned town. He said it would be perfect for me and that I should come down for the year and give it a try. Even told me he'd only charge me half price till then. Figured what the hell." Cliff leaned back in his chair. "You got any tea?" he asked eyeing up the cart.

"Now you want a drink?"

"You got me doing all this talking, and my throat is parched." Cliff rubbed his throat, as if to emphasize his point.

"Herbal or black?"

"Black with milk and sugar," Cliff said, tapping his throat again when she shot him a look.

"Coming right up." She grabbed one of the packets of tea and ripped it open, then placed it into a small paper cup.

"How much is this going to set me back?"

"Three dollars," Nat said, filling the cup and leaving the teabag to sit for a moment.

"Three dollars! What are we, at war? Last I heard, a bag of tea is still roughly thirty-five cents. Is the water mixed with gold?"

"I didn't make the prices." Nat shrugged.

"I suppose not."

"Next stop St. Marys," said the conductor over the speakers. "However, we're experiencing some delays at this stop for anyone continuing on with us to Stratford, and we apologize for the inconvenience."

Cliff looked out the window, catching a glimpse of the countryside passing by. Green pastures with little calves running up along the fence on awkward legs, and golden wheat fields blowing effortlessly in the wind.

He was no longer in the concrete jungle of millions of people wandering around at all hours of the day, filling the streets with an energy that had once frightened him but now gave him life. A life that he'd just left for this.

Hearing them call "next stop," made his heart beat a little faster than he'd imagined it would have. That same nervousness he'd felt as a young man, going to live in the city for the first time, had returned. But, this time, it wasn't the streets that made him anxious. It was the nothingness that seemed to loom as his eyes drifted from field to field without so much as a hint of human life.

"You okay? You look a little pale," Nat asked, handing Cliff the hot tea, now filled with sugar and milk.

"Fine. Just hit with the reality that I no longer live in the city." Cliff sighed.

"Aww, come on, you'll be fine. A little R&R never hurt anyone." Nat plopped herself down on the seat across the aisle from him again.

"Hurt, no. Killed. Yes. Some people aren't built for it. Why do you think so many people die when they finally retire? Not enough stimulus." Cliff shook his head.

"Come on, you're trying to make me believe you only just retired?"

"Not at all." Cliff took a sip of the hot liquid. "I had the best of both worlds. Retired in my full-time job, took a part-time job, then moved on to do *that* part time. Up until two years ago, when I quite cold turkey, once the stress got to be to much."

"You have a funny way of answering questions without actually answering them," Nat said, taking a Diet Coke from the trolley and cracking it open.

Cliff narrowed his eyes at the silver can.

"What? My throat was parched." She tapped her throat and laughed loudly.

"You have a funny way of not actually asking the questions you want answers to," Cliff said, raising a brow.

"Okay, fine. What did you do while you were working, then partially working. Then partially working the partial job?" Nat tilted her head in confusion at the last part, though in the end, she seemed content with the final wording. "Oh," she added, sticking up a finger. "And what's the big deal about St. Marys, if you've been retired for two years anyways?" She waved her hand as if to say, *Your turn.*

"Firstly, I don't agree with this line of questioning, but if you concede to giving me this tea on the house—" he raised a finger to stop Nat's protest, "—I agree to answer your questions, and, for the sake of time—" he looked outside the slowing train, "—I agree not to sidestep those questions. Deal?" Cliff stuck out his hand.

"Deal," Nat said, grasping it and giving it a firm shake.

"I was a detective in the Toronto Police Department. Then I went off and did some private detective work on my own, and then did a little bit of side detective work at the end, but mostly for old friends. Just the odd job to make a few bucks. As for your question about why St. Marys is such a big deal…well, Toronto always had people. Lots of them, and with that comes a level of anonymity, which I enjoy."

"Interesting. So, you were a detective. Explains your fascinations with the 'why,' I suppose," Nat said, which earned her a nod and a wink from Cliff. "But…"

Nat stopped as the train slowed down before coming to an abrupt stop, causing Cliff to spill a little of his tea on his pants. He frowned as he used a napkin to dab at the spot before he turned and spotted the same small multi-shaded red brick building with a cedar shingled roof that he had seen when he left the town all those years ago. Like so many things in the town, it was over a hundred years old, yet it still maintained a certain appeal to it, that had the ironic twist of making Cliff want to stay onboard and keep going.

"You were saying?" Cliff asked, as he suddenly found himself unable to stand up.

"Don't you want to get your things?" Nat pointed to the modestly sized black bag Cliff had put at the foot of the window seat he'd hoped would never be occupied.

"I'd love to hear what you were going to say," Cliff said, trying to hide his nerves.

"Look, if you're trying to delay getting off, I hate to break it to you, but the entire train is delayed. So, you'll be having to work pretty hard." Nat laughed.

"I'm not..." Cliff started to protest, but then sighed. "Is it that obvious?" He looked over at Nat, who offered a sideways smile and a nod.

"Fair enough. May as well bite the bullet." Cliff stood and lifted the extendible luggage handle, wiggling his bag out from between the seats. "Do you have a garbage?" he asked as he finished the last of his tea.

Nat pointed to the bin on the side of the trolley, and Cliff tossed it inside. Noticing the clipboard she'd left out on the trolley, he picked it up and looked over the sheet. Pretending to read over the contents as he tucked a tip into the clip.

"This stuff is expensive," he said casually, setting it back on the counter facedown, so as to hide the amount he'd left for his new friend. It was a habit he'd picked up when he realized he had no reason to keep his money. He wouldn't be able to be buried with it, and he had no family to leave it to, which meant he could give it to those people who surprised him most. And Nat was most certainly a surprise.

"What was it you were going to say, Nat?" Cliff asked as he walked towards the train door with Nat following close behind him with her trolley.

"Right! It was that, in my experience, the only people who like anonymity are those who don't like to be held accountable for their actions. In a small town, you have no anonymity, and you also have a town full of people ready to call you out on your shit," Nat said with a shrug. "Pardon my language," she added with a blush as she tucked her trolley into a small closet and locked the door.

"Fair point. But I thought you said you were from London?"

"I am. But I grew up in Mitchell." Nat laughed. "Being a detective, you must have loved the anonymity. It meant you could bury yourself in work. But here, in a small town, you can't, because nothing ever happens," Nat said as she stepped off the train to greet the awaiting passengers.

Her jaw gaped at the sights around her. "At least not usually," she added, as Cliff stepped off behind her and was immediately surrounded by the police.

2

"Guess we know why your train was redirected," Nat said as she let out an awkward kind of laugh.

"I already told you, Jan, we're not answering any questions. Now beat it!" said a particularly gruff individual with an OPP hat tucked under his left arm. The young man, in his midtwenties, had short blond hair underneath a beige Tilley hat, and he was tucking a small notebook into a brown leather satchel. He scurried off and out through the green gateway towards the main parking lot but stopped when he spotted a decidedly important man as he stepped into the train's courtyard.

"Mr. Mayor, care to comment on what's going on here?" the man named Jan said, stopping mid-exit.

"No, I do not, Jan. I think it's more important we let our fine friends here at the Ontario Provincial Police do their job, rather than us getting in the way," the mayor said, giving a big smile. "Wouldn't you say, Captain?"

"Mr. Mayor, what a surprise to see you down here. You shouldn't have." The captain turned to a young officer behind him and whispered something in his ear, which the younger man must have found funny.

"I wonder what happened?" Nat said to Cliff as she stepped off the train onto the concrete landing. "I didn't realize St. Marys had so many police."

"They don't," Cliff said, pointing out the OPP stripes on their uniforms as he stepped behind her, trying to ignore the conversations around him but finding it difficult. "Looks like someone fell off the tracks into the creek." He scanned the area, taking in the scene unconsciously.

"What makes you say that?" Nat looked around aimlessly, as if trying to see the telltale signs of whatever Cliff had noticed.

"Well, whatever it was stopped the train schedule, which means it likely has to do with the tracks or the train. Since the tracks look clear…" he said, pointing ahead of the train across the bridge, "and they have officers out there looking over the edge, I'd say someone or something was found at the bottom."

"Not bad, Detective." Nat put her hand on her hips in surprise. "But I hope whoever it was is okay."

Cliff cocked his head.

"What? Can't a girl have wishful thinking," she added, shooing him away.

"In my experience, you don't have this many police when everything is okay," Cliff said morbidly, starting towards the large metal gates that led out towards the parking lot. "Thanks for the conversation Nat." Cliff tossed a hand in Nat's direction. Glancing upward, he stopped and caught the shining steel siding of the water tower looming over him, with the giant black letters spelling out "St. Marys" across it. He let out a rather weak groan.

"How about a picture with the captain, Mr. Mayor?" Jan yelled as he pulled out a camera that had been strapped around his back. He held it up to take a picture.

The mayor was already prepping his biggest smile, while the captain seemed ready to strangle everyone.

"Officer Thomas, would you please show Jan off the premises," said the captain to the young man beside him, who seemed all too willing to put his power to use.

"Come now, Jan. Time to let the big boys work," Officer Thomas said, shooing the reporter away.

"I have a right to let the people know what's going on," Jan said.

"You want a story?" Officer Thomas said. "How about 'Mayor Greets New arrivals at the Train Station'?" He laughed and gestured at Cliff still stopped on the platform.

Dear God no.

"I like it," the mayor said, moving in beside Cliff and putting his hand out to shake his hand. "I'm Mayor Whitten, welcome to St. Marys!" He reached out to shake Cliff's hand.

"I'd actually prefer—" Cliff started, but was too slow. The mayor had already reached for his hand and turned to face Jan.

"Smile," the mayor said to Cliff as Jan began taking photos.

"That's enough," the captain said, turning to face everyone. "Officer Thomas, would you please escort Jan off the premises. Mr. Mayor, I'll reach out to your offices once I have a better idea of what is going on."

The mayor, without batting an eye, released Cliff's hand and smiled at the captain. "I look forward to your call, Captain. As you were!" He left, following Officer Thomas as he escorted Jan out.

Cliff, who was still a little dazed by everything that had just happened, watched the entire scene unfold and now stood in the middle of the train platform, more confused than ever.

"I'm going to have to ask you all to keep moving, sir," the captain said gruffly.

Cliff could tell that, not only was he annoyed at the most recent interruption, he was also rather warm in his multilayered uniform, which seemed to be trapping in all the hot air. It was made all the more noticeable by the large bead of sweat dripping down the man's forehead.

"What happened?" Nat innocently asked the large man as she stared down the tracks at the collection of officers preventing the train from moving forward. He didn't look too pleased to be asked any more questions.

"There was an incident on the bridge," he said, making to turn away, but Nat was quick.

"Did someone…you know…" She made a gesture, using her fingers, of jumping off the palm of her hand, with a particularly unpleasant look on her face.

The big man stared at her for a long moment before she added, "jump," in a hushed whisper.

"There was an incident," he said bluntly.

"I think you might be right about the jumper, Cliff. Such a shame," Nat said to Cliff, who hadn't been able to make it through the metal gates yet, although now he wished he had.

"What do you know about it?" the large man asked, turning to face Cliff. He couldn't see what his name tag said, just captain something.

"Nothing, Captain. I just got off the train, and I made some assumptions," Cliff said dismissively.

"Cliff was a detective," Nat said, and Cliff shot her a look, although it didn't seem to bother her one bit.

"Ohhhhh, a detective were you? Had a lot of these situations, did ya?" the captain added pompously.

"One or two," Cliff lied. He'd likely handled more jumpers and murders in his career than this smug bastard had days in the force. Not that he was willing to say any of this to him. From Cliff's experience, guys like him only wanted one thing, to be superior. So it was best to always use the path of least resistance.

"Where abouts, old timer?" the captain continued, taking another step closer, plopping his hat back on his head, as if to highlight his current station in life.

At the closer proximity, Cliff could now make out the last name on the badge as Marks. But something in his gut told him Captain Marks enjoyed the "Captain" part of the title most.

"Toronto PD. I moved around a bit over the years." Cliff gripped the handle on his luggage a little tighter. *Why didn't I leave?*

"He was also a private investigator," Nat added with a nod as if to say *you're welcome.*

Cliff cursed himself for ever allowing himself to get into a conversation with her and was also beginning to regret the tip he'd left for her in the cart.

"Thank you, Nat," Cliff said tightly. "But that was a few years ago now. I'm sure you and your team have it all covered here. Thank you for the conversation, Nat. Captain," Cliff said, giving them each a short nod before making his way to leave.

"Where are you off to? Queens Hill?" the captain asked with a smirk.

"What the hell is a Queens Hill?" Cliff asked.

The captain pointed just up over the Queen Street Bridge towards a tall, red brick building Cliff had never seen before. "It's the retirement home."

"I'm not going there. I'm going to a place called the Limestone Manor," Cliff said, barely stopping to turn back around to create enough space for him to be away and on his own again.

"Do you know where it is?" the captain asked.

"I'm sure I can find it on my own."

"I'll have one of our officers get you there safely," the captain offered with a big annoying smile, which Cliff caught as he stopped and turned back towards the large man.

"No, I'm sure you need all hands—"

"Nonsense, we can't have one of our own wandering aimlessly around town. Take Lou with you. Honestly, you'd be doing me a favour." Before Cliff to protest, he called out for Lou.

As it happened, Lou was a tall woman with dark eyes and olive skin.

Her long neck popped out of her standard navy blue and gold uniform that, given the June heat, didn't seem to bother her as much as it did her sweaty-browed captain.

"Yes, Captain," she said with an almost giddy bounce in her step. Though Cliff guessed that would fade when she discovered why she'd been called over.

"I need you to make sure this man gets home safely."

"But, sir—" She attempted to protest, but Captain Marks quickly raised a finger to stop her.

"He's one of our own, former Toronto PD, and we need to treat him with the respect he deserves." He said this with a definitive tone that left little room for protest, no matter how obvious it was that she wanted to.

"Yes, sir," she agreed reluctantly. "Where are we going, sir?" she asked Cliff, stepping up to him as both their shoulders seemed to deflate.

"Limestone Manor," Cliff said, equally reluctantly, before he started to walk out through the gates.

"Bye, Cliff! Nice chatting with you," Nat called before turning to run back to the train.

Cliff threw up his arm to give her a wave, trying to figure how he'd somehow managed to trade one unwanted companion for another.

"I've got the address up on Google maps, sir—"

"Call me Cliff," he said, making his way past the parked OPP cars in the parking lot, his little suitcase in tow.

"I have a car, si— Cliff. If you would prefer to drive," Lou said, running up beside him, pointing to one of the cars in the parking lot.

"God blessed me with two working legs, and I plan on using them until either I, or they, give out." Cliff didn't bother to look back at her as he continued up the little hill towards Queen Street. It seemed that Queen Street was the unoriginal name given to every main street in every small town in Canada.

He reached the top of what, if he remembered correctly, was the first of many hills he was likely to encounter on his walk to wherever this place was. He paused, taking a moment to look back up at the water tower again, which, after that short walk, now seemed directly overhead.

"'The town worth living in.'" Cliff scoffed at the words written on the water tower.

"Doesn't sound like you're too happy to be coming here."

"Do you find most people happy to be in this miserable town, Constable?"

"Please, call me Lou. And yes. I usually do," Lou said with a small laugh.

"You're joking," Cliff muttered.

"Don't look so surprised," Lou said, seeming to catch the look of disbelief on Cliff's face. "Not everyone shares your dislike for this small town."

"Ha! If you can even call this a town. What sort of town doesn't have a highway through it? Umm? Name one other town that doesn't. When I lived here, Highway 7 went straight through. It brought people here. Now it just goes around it, so why would anyone come here?" Cliff looked around, trying to figure out which way he should be going.

"People looking for the Quarry, or the baseball hall of fame—"

"*Canadian* Baseball Hall of Fame," Cliff corrected, raising a brow. "What's that bring to town? A hundred people a year? I stand corrected…it's a mecca."

"It's quiet."

"Shoot me now," Cliff jested.

And Lou started to laugh but seemed to catch herself. "So, you used to live here then?"

"A long time ago, though I have to imagine things are a little different here now."

"I'd say so. Sounds like people might actually *want* to live here now." Lou smiled.

"You know, I'm perfectly capable of finding my own way, despite what your captain might think," Cliff said, looking down towards the downtown core. He tried not to think about the last time he'd stood on this corner, making a completely different decision. A decision that would carry him through the rest of his life. Although the town looked a little different, he could still make out the outline of the place he'd left behind, buried underneath updated streets and refurbished buildings.

"I'm sorry about him. He can be…"

"A dick?" Cliff inserted.

"Yes, actually." Lou laughed.

"Not hard to figure out that, Lou. Though I suspect you deal with that often."

"How'd you guess?" Lou let out another awkward little laugh, and Cliff gave her a sympathetic look and raised his brows. "Fair."

Cliff turned right, heading towards downtown, the looming water tower now at his back as he slowly made his way down Queen Street.

"Are you sure you know where you're going?"

"No, but I figured how difficult could it be to find a house in this town?" Cliff said, pulling the rolling suitcase at his heels.

"I think you might be underestimating the size of this town, Cliff." Lou let out a little laugh.

Cliff scoffed at her and gave a quick look around. He had to admit, it had been a while since he'd been here. As he glanced around at the buildings, there was still a lot he recognized, but it was mixed in well with a lot more he didn't.

He stopped suddenly, causing the tailing Lou to bump into his suitcase.

"Well, then, if you're going to follow me like a child, why don't you make yourself useful and use that gadget of yours and get us moving in the right direction?" Cliff pointed indifferently at Lou's pocket, where he suspected she had a cell phone. Just like every other person her age in the world.

"Right, yeah, sure." Sure enough, she pulled out a large, black-encased phone from one of her many pockets. "What's the name of the place again? Limestone…"

"Manor" Cliff finished for her.

She opened it up and mumbled the name to herself as she scrolled along the screen.

"Aww, found it. Odd," she said as a smile cracked the side of her mouth.

"What?"

"Nothing. The good news is, it's close by."

"Of course, it is," Cliff mumbled.

"Follow me." Lou sidestepped over the luggage bag and out onto the road. She put her hands up and began stopping the cars, to Cliff's utter disbelief.

"What are you doing?"

"We need to cross the street," Lou said, waving Cliff onto the road, a backlog of two cars now in either direction, with drivers looking confused.

"And we couldn't have just waited for an opening like normal people?" he hissed. "You had to make me cross in front of a bloody audience?"

"I thought this would be easier," she said innocently.

"One day, I hope this happens to you, and although I'll be long dead by then, I want you to know, wherever I am, I will be laughing at you," Cliff grumbled, trying to cross the road as quickly as he could on his bum knee, though it would never be quick enough for him.

When he finally reached the sidewalk, Cliff tried to ignore the eyes of the people who'd been observing his journey across the street. He didn't look at them, but he could feel them on him nonetheless.

"Just down here, then up Peel Street," Lou said, glancing down at her phone before walking forward.

"That's new." Cliff pointed to the Tim Hortons across the street, which had a steady line wrapped around the drive-through.

"I heard it's had a lineup since it opened," Lou mused.

Cliff looked at the steady flow of people walking in and out, as more cars pulled into the drive-through line. A group of elderly people were tucked in under the shade of the trees in their lounge chairs. All their eyes had drifted over towards Lou and Cliff, giving him a thumbs-up as they laughed amongst themselves.

"Looks like a hub. I imagine it's already littered with rumours about what's happened up at the tracks," Cliff said absently.

"Well, I'm sure that's all they are. Rumours," Lou said passively, and Cliff shot her an amused look. "What?"

"You think, in a town this small, those rumours won't have a little truth in them?"

"You can't tell me you actually take any stock in that, do you?"

"Some of my best leads came from rumours. I'm not saying you should believe everything, but it never hurts to know what the word is on the street. You just have to remember to trim away all the fat," Cliff said, standing on the corner as he looked up from the foot of the Peel Street sign. "Good Christ, you couldn't have found a route without a damned hill?"

"You want to go somewhere in town that doesn't have a hill?" Lou laughed. "I think you might be in the wrong town. Here give me that." She took the handle from Cliff, who was reluctant to let her have it. But seeing the mountain in front of him, he conceded.

"How did you get stuck walking an old man to his house anyways?" Cliff said, taking one tiresome step after the other. He was fortunate enough to have all his parts still working, but after the two-and-a-half-hour train ride, sitting with limited leg room, he had to admit this was not what he wanted to be doing.

"I'm the newest recruit, I guess. Only got to this area a few months ago," Lou said trekking up just behind Cliff.

"Where you from?"

"Grew up in Winnipeg. Mom's still there, but my dad lives just outside of Thunder Bay now."

"Jets country," Cliff said with a smile.

"Blue Bombers country," Lou said proudly, which made Cliff laugh.

"So how did you end up here?"

"OPP pretty much sends you anywhere in Ontario. I would have preferred to be more west, to be closer to my folks, but what can you do?" Lou said with a shrug.

"Instead, you're here, walking an old man to his apartment, instead of trying to figure out what happened to that young man," Cliff said, glancing up towards the crest of the hill, which still seemed like mile away, despite them being two-thirds up the hill already.

"Who said anything about it being a young man?"

Cliff turned around, letting out a big grin at the puzzled expression on Lou's face. "No one." Cliff laughed.

"Oh shit. I mean…please don't tell anyone I told you. We're not supposed to be releasing any details yet."

"Please, I'm willing to bet half the town has heard at least one version of what's going on already. But you don't have to worry about me. I know enough not to speculate." Cliff stopped briefly to take in a deep breath.

"You okay?"

"Peachy." Cliff didn't bother to turn around, but started walking again, making his way up the last little climb of the hill. "Where we going now?" He looked around, trying to get a sense of where he was. He turned back around, and looking past Lou, he could see the peak of the spire at Holy Name of Mary Parish just over the trees.

"Only a couple of blocks up the road, it looks like," Lou said taking another look at her phone.

"God bless that." Cliff did an about-face and continued up the road. "So, tell me about the kid? Is he a local?" He turned back and caught Lou narrowing her eyes on him. "What? We can either carry on with pointless small talk—which I've had enough of for one day—or we can discuss what it is we both really want to be talking about."

"I told you, I can't."

"Correction, you can't give *specifics* about people. Nothing to say you can't give general details."

"That's *exactly* what I can't do!"

"Come on, would you rather me ask the gang down at Tim's?" Cliff asked, pointing down the hill to the group still in view, happily talking amongst themselves.

"Okay, fine. But you can't go blabbing about it around town."

"Do I look like the kind of person who has anything to say to anyone in this town?" Cliff laughed, but he could sense Lou's hesitation.

"He's not from town. Likely just some guy visiting, who got drunk and thought it would be fun to wander over the bridge."

"Possibly," Cliff said thoughtfully.

"What?" Lou's voice dropped conspiratorially.

"Nothing. It's just curious is all," Cliff said with a shrug.

It was Lou's turn to be annoyed. "You're the one who wanted to talk about it."

"It just doesn't add up."

"What doesn't?"

"There's what, six thousand people in this town?"

"Maybe closer to seven."

"Still, it's small. If the person wasn't from town, they were most likely here visiting someone. If they were drunk and missing, you would think someone would be asking about them."

"Maybe they don't know they are missing?"

"Perhaps. But my guess is, you didn't find the body, which means someone else did, and between them calling you and you arriving, they called half a dozen people to tell them what they found. Which means everyone in town knows that a young man's body was found near the train tracks. If you had a friend visiting who was missing, and a body was found even hinting at the same age, wouldn't you be going straight to the police?"

"But this all hinges on the idea that information is going around about the body," Lou protested.

Cliff laughed. "Please. People like to gossip. And how many dead bodies have turned up in this town in the past…twenty years. Maybe a dozen? Less? Try and tell me this isn't wildfire." As if to prove his point, a young couple walking some sort of black poodle-looking dog rounded the corner, and Cliff managed to catch the tail end of the woman talking.

"I heard at the grocery store he was found in the creek or some-thing…" Her words trailed off as they caught sight of Lou in her OPP uniform, behind Cliff, lugging a suitcase. The couple carried on down the street as Cliff turned to offer Lou a smug smile.

"Okay. Point taken," Lou said with a sigh, before looking down at her phone again. "This should be it on the left." She pointed to the house beside them.

"This is the Limestone Manor?" Cliff asked skeptically, pointing up at the large, yellow-bricked house with a Victorian turret-peaked top on one side and a double wide and tall chimney rising out beside it.

The house was tucked in behind a gated wrought-iron fence and a well-manicured garden. A beautiful wooden porch appeared to wrap around at least two sides of the house, overlooking the gardens. However, despite having numerous places to sit, and the weather being rather nice, the house appeared empty.

"That's what it says," Lou said, pointing at an old cast-iron rod with a wooden sign hanging by the side door that read *Limestone Manor*.

"Was Yellow Brick Manor taken?" Cliff mused.

"It looks nice," Lou said, admiring the curved pathway through the gardens.

"It looks like it has a ton of stairs," Cliff mumbled, before letting out a big sigh. "Well, thank you for getting me this far, but I'm sure I can cover the last twenty or so feet on my own." Cliff stuck a hand out for his bag, but Lou held tight.

"Not so fast," she said, resting the bag on its wheels at her side. "If it's not a drunk accident, what do you think it is?"

"What?" Cliff said, more than a little confused.

"You seem to think it wasn't an accident. So, what was it?"

"I would have thought that was obvious."

"You mean to tell me you think this is a murder?"

"Correction. I'm not telling you anything. I'm just looking at the information that's in front of me. An unknown body in a creek, with no ties to the community that you can see?" He raised a finger before Lou could interject. "That feels obvious to me."

"But this is St. Marys. Not Toronto."

"True. But don't be mistaken. Just because something doesn't happen all the time, doesn't mean it never happens." Cliff stuck his hand out for his bag again, and Lou reluctantly handed it over.

Cliff turned to make his way up the driveway. In one of the parking spots was a beaten-down grey sedan, and when he reached the front door, he saw it was wide open. Cliff shook his head, ready to admonish his old friend, when he caught a glimpse of the note taped to the front door.

Cliff, at the cemetery back around 2 p.m. Hans.

Cliff looked at his watch. The hands pointed to 12:48.

"Lou," he called out calmly, turning back and catching Lou's attention just as she was rounding the fence on her way back to the train station.

She stopped and turned to face Cliff, standing by the door, waving a hand for her to come back. She looked confused but returned to his side on the porch.

"What's—"

Cliff put his finger to his lips and pointed to the note on the door, specifically at the time. Hans wouldn't have left the door open if he wasn't expected home for another hour.

It wasn't long before Lou pieced together what Cliff was getting at. She pulled the gun out of her holster and proceeded slowly into the Limestone Manor.

3

Cliff followed a few steps behind Lou, despite her insistent hand-waving indicating he should stay outside. The two moved quietly through the large entranceway, which opened up into four options. Two options looked like sitting rooms on either side of the front entrance, a set of stairs lay up ahead of them, and finally, a narrow hallway led into the belly of the house.

Neither sitting room gave any indication that anyone was home, and the only noise was coming from down the narrow hall, where they heard what sounded like a plate scraping across a tabletop. Lou moved through the house with her gun raised towards the sound, with Cliff hot on her heels.

Someone was definitely in the house, as more sounds clattered from inside what Cliff now assumed was going to be the kitchen. This was confirmed by the closing of a fridge door. Cliff and Lou exchanged confused looks.

Lou put a finger on her lips as she leaned against the wall outside the kitchen. She sucked in a deep breath and rounded the corner.

"Drop it!" she shouted, pointing her gun towards the only moving body in the room, which promptly dropped a glass plate, that shattered as it hit the ground, followed by the plop of what appeared to be a peanut butter and jelly sandwich.

A shrill, muffled cry came from the young man who stood in the kitchen, knees shaking and his mouth full of a partially chewed bite of sandwich. He stared at them, looking to be deliberating whether he should continue to chew or not.

"What are you doing here?" Lou asked, relaxing her arms and dropping her gun slightly. She must have recognized the man, because she seemed to relax a little as she scanned the rest of the kitchen, not noticing any real threat.

"Wha're you 'oin' 'ere?" the man mumbled, his mouth still full sandwich.

"What?" Lou asked, shaking her head in annoyance.

The young man tried to speak again, but put his finger up to signal he needed a minute as he started chewing aggressively.

"Wadder," he mumbled again, pointing to an empty glass on the counter.

Lou waved another annoyed hand in the man's direction.

He grabbed the glass and filled it up and took a quick sip of water. He finished chewing and swallowed, licking his gums and taking another sip of water as he tried to get the last of the peanut butter off his teeth.

"I said, what are you doing here?" he repeated, after taking another sip of water.

Cliff began to recognize the kid as the reporter, Jan, from the train station, who had been run off by the captain. Lou must have recognized him as well, as she shook her head, tucking her gun back into her holster.

"I asked you first, Jan," Lou said hitting the soft J sound of the dutchman's name.

"I was trying to eat a peanut butter sandwich," Jan said, nervously glancing in the direction of Lou's holster.

"I can see that. But why are you here? In this house?" Lou shook her head at the tall scrawny man.

His face was still pretty white, and it seemed as though he wanted to say something but couldn't find the words. So Cliff found them for him.

"Your Hans's grandson, aren't you?" Cliff asked, getting an affirmative nod from the young reporter.

"How did you know that?" Lou asked.

"Hans mentioned his grandson, Jan, before. I only just pieced it together."

"You must be Cliff," Jan said, stepping tentatively toward Cliff, trying to avoid the broken glass as he extended his hand. He paused when Cliff didn't enter the room. Looking down at the glass on the floor again, he smiled. "I should clean this up." He tiptoed around the shards of glass towards what Cliff assumed must be a broom cupboard.

"I still don't see why you're here, Jan," Lou said. "I thought you were robbing the house. For Christ's sake, I could have shot you."

"Well, after your boss yelled at me, I got frustrated," Jan said, sticking his neck out from behind the cupboard door. He quickly buried it back in again when he spotted the irritated look on Lou's face. "And when I get frustrated, I get snacky, and Opa has the best snacks." Jan continued banging around in the cupboard, as if he was digging through an antique store.

"It was a peanut butter sandwich," Lou chastised.

"A free, peanut butter and *jelly* sandwich," Jan retorted from the cupboard. "Ah-ha!" He said at the sound of maybe a plastic bucket hitting the floor.

Jan stepped out with a red broom and matching dustpan.

"Well, since you're not robbing the place, I think I can leave." Lou looked around to check on Cliff, who'd found a seat at the table in the corner. "You all good?"

"Still kicking, if that's what you're asking." Cliff put a hand on his chest making a show of feeling for a heartbeat.

"Any chance you would be willing to give me a quote for *The Gazette?*"

Jan asked, looking more than a little disappointed at the partially eaten sandwich now resting atop a pile of broken glass.

"Sure," Lou said, which came as a big surprise to Jan. "Local idiot drops sandwich during fake burglary." Lou grinned.

"Ha ha." Jan dumped the contents of the dustpan into the garbage. "Come on, Lou, the people deserve to know. You want the rumour mill going wild in this town?"

"I think that train's already left the station, big guy," Cliff said with a laugh.

"See, Lou! Come on. What do you have to lose? I mean, you did pull a gun on me," Jan said, flinching nervously at Lou's glare.

"First of all, I didn't pull a gun on you, I had the gun pulled when I entered. Second, you know I can't go against the captain's request, or else I could lose my job." Lou said. "So, if you'll excuse me, I need to get back to work." She tucked her thumbs in her belt as she turned and walked away. "Nice to meet you, Cliff." She added with a quick wave in Cliff's direction which he returned.

Jan looked as though he wanted to call out after her but managed to stop himself, looking a little disappointed at having not said anything. Instead, he just finished sweeping up the floors and dumped the remainder of the glass in the garbage.

"Sorry about the scare," Jan said, tossing the broom and pan back in the closet before heading back to the counter and pulling out two more slices of bread. "Want one?" Jan asked turning to look at Cliff in the corner.

"Sure, why not?" Cliff leaned back in the chair as he watched Jan pull out two more slices. "So where is Hans?"

"Up at the cemetery still, I think," Jan said with a shrug. He took a generous helping of peanut butter and began smearing it on two slices of bread.

"Didn't realize he'd moved," Cliff said as he watched Jan repeat the process with jam.

"He didn't…" Jan looked white as a ghost, eyes wide, as he turned, holding a partially jam-covered piece of bread. "He's not…you know…"

"I'm messing with you, kid. I talked to him the other day, though these days, that seems like ample time."

"You shouldn't joke about that stuff," Jan protested, putting two slices of bread together and handing it over to Cliff with a smile, and repeating the process for himself.

"You shouldn't take that stuff so seriously, kid."

"But death isn't funny."

"Sooner or later, everything is funny." Cliff took a bite of the peanut butter and jam sandwich, thinking about the last time he had had one.

"'ood, wight?" Jan said, swallowing a mouthful in a way one can only do when they are young and thoughtless. "Opa just picked up the jam the other day at Maple Hill's." He took another big bite.

"Not bad," Cliff said, taking slightly smaller bites, not wanting to risk his teeth against the Skippy. "That your car out there?"

"Yeah, why?" Jan asked. Polishing off the last of his sandwich, he made his way to the fridge and reached in to grab a ceramic jug with a depiction of a cow jumping over a sunny wheat field. Then he took a glass from the drying rack beside the sink and poured a small glass of milk. "Want some?"

"I do now," Cliff said, realizing how difficult it was to swallow peanut butter.

Jan picked out another glass and pulled the now-empty bag of milk out of the ceramic jug and tossed it into the garbage. Opening the fridge again, Jan pulled out another bag of milk and plopped it into the container. Then using one of the fridge magnets, he sliced off one of the corners of the milk and poured Cliff a small glass.

"Thanks." Cliff took the glass from Jan and slowly sipped the milk, which seemed to marginally help the sticky feeling the peanut butter had left on the roof of his mouth. "Any chance you'd be willing to give me a ride to the cemetery?" Cliff asked Jan, who'd already finished his glass and was pouring a second.

"Of course." He put the jug back in the fridge, threw together a third sandwich, and wrapped up the sandwich in a paper towel.

"Ready?" he asked, his lanky arms swinging as he made his way towards the front door.

Cliff put his empty glass in the sink and followed Jan outside.

"So, you're a reporter?" Cliff said, shutting the door behind him as they left the house.

"I want to be. But, truth be told, I mostly handle community events, hockey tournaments, Hall of Fame Induction Week, the teddy bear parade, that sort of thing." Jan pulled hard on the door handle of his old Pontiac. "Door's a little stuck," Jan said, nodding to Cliff who discovered just how stuck it was as he used most of his strength to pull it open. "Hoping to get that fixed soon," Jan said, with a smile that said he was likely never getting it fixed.

"Can't imagine a lot happens around here."

"You can say that again. The worst thing that's happened in these parts is someone keeps stealing licence plates. I'm not even sure why anyone would want them, but there's been, like, ten stolen in the last month alone. Then when something finally does happen, the police won't even talk to me. It's ridiculous."

"Insurance fraud," Cliff said, clicking his seat belt into place.

"What?" Jan frowned in confusion.

"You said you didn't know why anyone would want to steal licence plates. Either to hide a vehicle in plain sight or insurance fraud," Cliff said, casually.

"Interesting. How would you know that?"

"I used to work in the industry."

"A thief?" Jan's eyes shot wide.

"Worse. A detective," Cliff said, which seemed to leave Jan more puzzled than anything. "It's a joke, kid," Cliff offered up, his dry tone clearly doing little to ease Jan's awkwardness, despite him letting out a tight laugh.

"Wait, is that why you were with Lou? Are you some sort of consultant on the case? Do you know what's going on?" Jan pressed.

"No to all of that. I'm just an old man who wanted to be left alone."

Jan pulled out of the driveway, taking the first two lefts as he headed down Elgin Street East. Cliff caught the back side of both the Anglican and United churches, their pointed peaks raised high in the sky above all of the surrounding buildings.

Cliff remembered going into the Anglican Church every Sunday with his parents, whether he wanted to or not. Even as a boy, he was amazed at how impressive not just his, but all the churches in town, were. They acted like a beacon to their followers as they sat atop the hills along Church Street.

Cliff turned to spot Jan chuckling to himself.

"What's the matter with you?" Cliff asked.

"I'm just thinking about what you said."

"What did I say?"

"Just that you're looking to be alone."

"What's so funny about that?

"Nothing." Jan shrugged. "Just funny that you would move in with Opa if that's what you're looking for."

Cliff's stomach dropped when he spotted the amused looked on Jan's face. "Why wouldn't it be a good place?" Cliff asked, the words coming out slowly.

Jan chuckled to himself. "You'll see." He laughed as he pointed up the road. "Cemetery is just up here."

Jan drove along the tiny black fence separating the sidewalk from the weathered tombstones housed on the other side. In the distance, Cliff could make out a small group of people gathered around a tiny hole in the ground. Cliff's eyes weren't what they used to be, but he caught the unmistakable height of his old friend Hans. Even at eighty-three, he stood a good head over everyone else around him, even with his head bowed.

Jan drove past the group to the main entrance, taking a right as he pulled into the narrow roadway. Jan drove slowly up the road, stopping about fifty metres from the tiny group. Hans looked up from the pack, spotted Cliff as he stepped out of the car, and nonchalantly waved for him to come over.

Cliff, who hardly felt dressed for the occasion, in brown khakis and a blue button-down shirt, thought it would be better to stand off to the side to wait for the ceremony to finish, but Hans seemed insistent with his waving, as though he might not actually stop until Cliff came.

"Nice to meet you, Cliff," Jan said. "I'm sure I'll see you around."

"You too, Jan. Good luck with the story."

"Thank you. Good luck with the peace and quiet." Jan's smile broadened. As he pulled away in the car, the rear wheel let out a gentle squeak as it rounded the corner.

Cliff stood alone on the edge of the road, looking back at Jan, still wondering what exactly he'd meant by his comment, before turning back to see the large hands of Hans waving him over. The movements of the man were hardly subtle to anyone at the funeral. They all stared back at Cliff expectantly.

With a heavy sigh, Cliff walked across the manicured lawn between towering headstones with various names and memories. At one point, Cliff would have found the walk depressing, but possibly it was getting older that enabled him to reconcile his emotions to the idea that, one day, he would find himself in the ground, same as everyone else.

For whatever reason, that seemed to make the grass under his feet a little easier to walk on as he approached and caught the tail end of one of the prayers by the minister, who stood next to the hole and a wooden stand with a vase on it.

"You made it," Hans said, and whether it was his age, his deep voice, or his particularly heavy Dutch accent despite over sixty-odd years of being in Canada, his attempt at whispering was very ineffective. Luckily, the formal service had ended, and people around the grave started mingling, as, one by one, they stepped up to say a few words to the vase on the stand.

"Barely," Cliff said, sticking his hand out for the large man. "It's good to see you."

Hans looked at the hand, then embraced Cliff in a burly hug. His massive arms and hands encased Cliff, making him feel almost like a child in his arms.

"It's good to see you too, old friend," Hans said giving Cliff's shoulders a tight squeeze. "You look old."

"I am old," Cliff said.

"Aren't we all. Some of us older than others." Hans sent a glance towards the vase.

"Cremation?"

"Flo was never one for taking up too much space." Hans laughed, which caught a few glances from, Cliff presumed, Flo's family.

"I went to the Limestone Manor," Cliff said, tilting his head. "You know it's a yellow brick house, right?"

"Ya, but Limestone Manor sounded much more regal, than Yellow Brick House." Hans laughed. "We thought it would be funny." This last bit caught Cliff's attention.

"We?" he said, looking at his friend.

"Ya. You didn't think I could afford that place on my own, did you?"

"I thought you said it was a B&B?"

"No, I said I had a room open up." Hans glanced over at Flo's urn again.

"You mean to tell me I'm taking Flo's room?"

"Well, she hardly needs it anymore." Hans laughed and leaned in close. "Besides, we all agreed to pay a year in advance, which means you have six free months," he added with a wink. "But you will need to pay the next six upfront. In case of…" He pointed to the urn again. "Think of it as paying it forward." He laughed again, which caught a round of jeers from Flo's family.

Cliff felt more confused than ever, as another sinking feeling landed in the pit of his stomach. "I'm sorry, I thought you said *we*."

"Ya, the gang." He gestured towards the small group of people behind him. "Everyone, this is Cliff. He'll be staying with us."

The group of five elderly people mingling in a circle off to the side all turned to give him a wave.

"Cliff, meet the gang."

"You never told me I would be living with *people*."

"You never asked."

"Why would I ask you that?"

"Why would I tell you?"

"Because I wouldn't have come."

"Exactly! Come on, you did the *live on your own* thing for so long. Why not try the living with others thing. Who knows? Maybe you'll like it."

"I liked the living on my own thing," Cliff hissed.

"Please, you're a grump. Even your letters were grumpy," Hans said, his brows shooting up, just under his impressively thick head of blond hair. "At least here you can be grumpy with people."

"But I'm grumpy *because* of people," Cliff said.

"Don't be absurd. You're grumpy because you lived in that gloomy city for so long, surrounded by cold people and crimes." Hans shrugged. "Here, we are laid back and grumpy because our knees and our back hurt, and we get to complain about it to one another." Hans quickly eyed him up. "Speaking of which, how are your knees and back…you still have all your original parts?"

"Yes! Still have all my original parts," Cliff said, shaking his head.

"Umm." Hans put a finger to his lips. "How are you with stairs?"

"What?"

"Like, can you walk up stairs?"

"Of course, I can. I lived in a three-story apartment building for over thirty years…on my own!"

"Good. So, you don't mind stairs then." He turned and pointed to a small Asian woman who stood on the edge of the circle, a cane tucked behind her back, arms wrapped around it, which appeared to be keeping her upright. "Mrs. Chen, good news! You can have Flo's old room."

"I was going to take the room regardless," she said, shaking her head.

"Well then, I guess it's good you're okay with stairs, Cliff. And this room is only up two flights, so you'll be an expert." Hans laughed and slapped Cliff on the arm.

"What if I don't want the room?" Cliff said.

Hans looked nervous, as he put a massive finger up to Cliff's face. "Shhh! You know how many people in town want this room? The Limestone Manor is one of the most coveted buildings in town, I had to practically bribe people to let you in."

"Right, well, thank you, but I think I was led here under false pretenses."

"No, you just read the message the way you wanted to hear it," Hans retorted. "I told you I lived in the Limestone Manor, which I do. I told you I had a room for let, which I have. You're a detective. Why did you not detect?" Hans shrugged.

Cliff sucked in a deep breath, as if to say something, but Hans was quicker.

"I think you wanted to come back here. I think you missed it here."

"I think you're an idiot," Cliff retorted.

"Thank you."

"What?"

"Idiots keep life exciting." Hans laughed and clapped his hands together. "Look, you're already here. What do you have to lose? If you hate it at the end of the year, then you can leave. If you don't, you can stay," Hans said with a shrug. "Besides it's cheap."

Cliff stood for a long while, debating whether he should grab his bag and leave. "How cheap?"

"Five hundred dollars a month." Hans grinned. "That includes groceries."

Cliff paused while he considered the fact that he'd been paying three times that much in Toronto for rent. He had to admit, it was a good value. That, along with the fact that he had nowhere to go back to, given that he'd already left his apartment, and what few belongings he had would be arriving here in the next few days.

"You didn't leave me with any options."

"Options are for the young! You are old. Come have fun and be old with us. It will be better than sitting alone and waiting to die," Hans pointed out.

Cliff let out a reluctant sigh. "Fine. I'll give it a chance, but I want you to know that I think calling a yellow brick house the Limestone Manor is stupid."

"And I think leaving your apartment and moving here without even doing a Google search is stupid, Mr. Detective."

"Fair point," Cliff said reluctantly.

"Come on, why don't we go get some lunch and you can meet the gang." Hans put a hand on Cliff's back and led him over to the rest of the small group.

"Do I have to?" Cliff asked, and Hans let out another big laugh.

"This is going to be fun."

As it turned out, Trillium Diner wasn't too far away. Well, it was across town, but that hardly seemed a massive distance. And that distance was made all the more convenient when Hans led Cliff into a retrofitted Sprinter van nicknamed The Hearse, which Cliff learned was the house vehicle. It appeared "the gang" shared Hans's morbid perspective on life.

Cliff also learned that, although driving duties were shared amongst them all, Hans often volunteered to drive on most people's behalf, as he was the only one with eyes that were capable of seeing a stop sign more than fifteen feet before him. Cliff made a mental note to not comment on his eyesight capabilities, so as to not get roped into driving duties.

The group walked in, led by a pair Cliff hadn't met yet. He suspected they were a couple, as they seemed practically inseparable, even as they argued over everything except where they sat in the Hearse and what table they ate at, as the slow-moving group plopped down in their chairs.

"Right! Everyone, this is Cliff," Hans said once everyone was seated.

"Speak up, Hans," said a short, rotund man at the end of the table.

"Cliff!" shouted Mrs. Chen. "The detective," she added before giving Hans a thin smile as she hooked her cane on the back of her chair.

"We told you to sit in the middle, Gerald!" the woman across from him said, her long slender body somehow looking both erratic and precise in its movements. Her milky white skin and reddish curly hair kept Cliff guessing at how old she actually was.

"I'm left-handed, Kitty!" Gerald said, as if to end the point, though Kitty seemed less interested in letting it go.

"You say that as if the rest of us should care. We've all seen you eat, Gerald, save for Cliff over here, and not one of us believes you couldn't survive with either hand." Kitty gestured for him to sit in the middle seat.

"What?" Gerald tugged at his ear, as if the action might somehow dislodge whatever might be stuck in there that prevented him from hearing.

"Sol, will you do something about this?" Kitty said, turning to look at her partner, who Cliff now assumed must be Sol. He was a tall with dark skin and a grey stubble on his face and surrounding the crown of his head.

"Kitty said she'd buy you breakfast if you move to the middle," Sol said to Gerald, not bothering to look up from his menu. This received a look of surprise and shock from Kitty.

"Well then, why didn't you say so?" Gerald got up and moved over to sit beside Mrs. Chen.

"You heard *that*," Kitty said, her brows lifting in protest, which received a slight grin from Gerald.

"As I was saying," Hans said, taking a seat at the end of the table between Mrs. Chen and the only woman Cliff hadn't caught the name of. She sat quietly in the corner, examining her menu, as if none of the events had even happened.

Cliff took the seat Gerald had just left.

"Cliff, you might have guessed this is Gerald. He's not as senile as he might lead you to believe."

"I'm as senile as the rest of them," Gerald said, licking his lips as he read over the menu, pausing briefly to give Cliff a nod.

"And Mrs. Chen. Don't let her fool you. She speaks better English than she cares to admit."

"I only don't speak idiot. You're no idiot, are you, Cliff?" Mrs. Chen said, her eyes narrowing in on Cliff, who had trouble understanding if she was joking or not. Though her face seemed to say she most certainly was not.

"Time will make idiots of us all," Cliff said with a shrug, which raised a half smile from Mrs. Chen.

"And then we have Sol and Kitty," Hans said, gesturing to the pair across from Cliff. "They're...lively," Hans added with a smile.

"We enjoy a good debate," Kitty said irritably.

"*You* enjoy a good debate," Sol said, still examining the menu, though he did look up to give Cliff a warm smile.

"It takes two to tango, my dear," Kitty said, placing her own menu back on the table.

"You're right, my love, as always." Sol put a hand on Kitty's hand, which was resting on the table. "However, only one of us gets to dip." Sol winked, and Kitty pulled her hand back, though Cliff thought he caught her trying to hide a smile.

"Finally, this is Bunty," Hans said, gesturing to the quiet woman at the end of the table.

She had long greyish hair wrapped up in a bun. Her thick, round glasses with black frames sat neatly atop her nose as she placed the menu down politely in front of her.

"We've actually met before, Clifford Shaw," Bunty said in a soft nasally voice.

"I'm sorry, but you have me at a disadvantage," Cliff said, trying to wrap his head around where he might have seen this woman.

"Elizabeth Price. I believe you might know my sister. Annabel." She looked away as she said the name.

Cliff felt his stomach drop at the mention of the name.

"You know Annie, Cliff?" Kitty asked excitedly. "Wonderful woman that Annie. Ouch!" She looked quickly down and then glared at Sol.

"I did know her. A very long time ago," Cliff said, trying to regain himself at the sudden shock of hearing that name from his past. The image of a tall woman swirled around in his brain, her deep blue eyes and long fingers clear as he replayed the image of her tucking the strands of her auburn hair back behind her ears as she cried.

Looking across the table at Bunty, Cliff could see vestiges of the only woman he had ever truly loved. Bunty had the same long fingers, though her eyes were green instead of blue, and her hair was grey now. Yet, under all of that, Cliff could see it now. *Annie.*

"What can I get you lovelies today?" A waitress said with an enthusiasm big enough to pull Cliff back from where his mind had taken him.

He was grateful for the respite of the cold memories. The waitress, whose name tag read Zoey, was a tall woman, who Cliff wagered was in her early twenties, although she had the confidence of someone who'd worked in a diner for years, tossing out words like "dear" and "darling" in the casual way diner staff always had. Her long dark hair was pulled back in a high ponytail, and she still wrote on a classic ticket, unlike all the modern restaurants today.

"I was sorry to hear about Flo," Zoey said, taking in the group in front of her as she shook her head. "Such a shame to lose such an amazing woman."

"Indeed," Gerald added sombrely. "She still owed me five bucks." He shook his head.

"Last I heard, you owed her ten," Kitty pointed out, her eyes narrowing in on Gerald.

"She will, indeed, be missed," Gerald said wiggling his fingers before lifting up the menu.

Zoey, who looked as confused as Cliff by the remarks, looked as though she didn't know if she should laugh or be insulted on Flo's behalf.

"I'm sorry, Zoey. When you get to our age, it's best not to dwell on deaths too much. Flo will be deeply missed, but she had a good run." Hans put a hand on his chest.

"Well, the coffees are on the house today, for Flo," Zoey said with a wink.

"Thank you, Zoey," the group said around the table, though Cliff thought Gerald mouthed the words and didn't actually say them.

"Zoey, my dear, meet the newest addition to the Limestone Manor. Cliff Shaw," Hans said graciously.

"He's a retired detective!" Kitty added with a nod, making his old position sound more prestigious than it had been.

"Aww, looks like you came just in time. Likely need people like you these days," Zoey said with a wink. Though it seemed only Cliff understood what she was saying, based on the confusion now going around the table.

"What do you mean by that?" Kitty spoke up first.

"I'll have a coffee and the breakfast, over easy, peameal bacon, and… tots, please," Gerald said, ignoring the rest of the table as he twiddled his fingers eagerly before dropping the menu and looking around at the many eyes now staring at him. "What?" he said innocently. "I'm hungry. Oh!!" He lifted a finger. "And a side of sausages, please." His order placed, he leaned back in his chair looking patiently at everyone else.

Zoey, who'd managed to take down the order with smooth efficiency looked up at the rest of the table, ready and eager to spill the gossip she clearly been hearing all morning to some fresh ears. "They found a body this morning in Trout Creek under the bridge. Poor kid fell off the tracks last night, they say."

"Oh my! Was it someone from town?" Kitty asked, her hand over her mouth.

The rest of the table, other than Cliff, was equally shocked by the news.

"Don't think so. Young, though. In his twenties. Clint Davis found him while he was out walking his dog through Kin Park. Had a bit of a shock when he was going over the steel bridge there. They said his dog was going wild," Zoey said in a conspiratorial fashion.

"I bet!" Kitty said, her hand still resting over her mouth in a much more controlled shock.

"Are we not eating here?" Gerald asked, uninterested in the news.

"A man died, Gerald!" Kitty chastised.

"And so might another, if I don't eat soon."

"You're insatiable, Gerald, you really are," Kitty said.

"Any other news?" Sol said, getting a "harrumph" from Gerald.

"Lisa was in earlier and said that the OPP think it's an accident. She overheard Officer Thomas at the Tim Hortons. He was saying it was likely some drunk college kid visiting friends or something." Zoey winced at the words.

"Wait, the train station?" Hans said, glancing over at Cliff. "Why didn't you mention any of this? You must have seen it when you arrived."

"Sure," Cliff said, pretending to read over the menu, having decided a while ago what he was getting but wanting desperately to avoid this particular conversation.

"So? Why didn't you say anything?" Hans asked, and now everyone was looking at him, except Gerald, who was tapping his chubby fingers on the table irritably.

"Not really my place, is it? Besides, I don't think they even know what's going on down there," Cliff said casually. When he looked up, he realized he'd made a terrible mistake, as everyone was now leaning in a little closer.

"Go on then," Kitty jumped in.

"What?" Cliff asked.

"Why don't you think they know what's going on?" Sol said.

"Nothing really. I just have a hunch."

"A hunch?" Hans asked.

"What aren't you telling us?" Mrs. Chen narrowed her eyes at Cliff.

"I'm *not* not telling you anything. I'm just commenting on what I saw, and a lot of it doesn't add up, that's all."

"Are you always so cryptic?" Sol said with a sigh.

"Sorry, it's just years of being a detective doesn't really lend itself to opening up to share with people who…"

"Who what?" Kitty asked.

"Gossip like bored children?" Mrs. Chen laughed.

"Give it time, Cliff. You'll find there is little else to do other than gossip." Kitty smiled.

"We could always try eating?" Gerald said, rolling his eyes. "I do enjoy that, as well. In fact, I may even enjoy it more."

"You've made your point, Gerald. Zoey, I'll have the French toast with a coffee and a water, please," Kitty said politely before glaring back over at Gerald, who didn't seem to notice, or care. He just sat there and rubbed his stomach affectionately.

It didn't take long for everyone else to order. As it happened, Zoey was well versed in each order, other than Cliff's breakfast of a coffee and water, two eggs over medium, with sausage and—despite the overwhelming love at the table for something called tots—the shredded hashbrowns with onions.

"I'll be right back with your coffees, my dears," Zoey said, as she jotted down the last of the orders and ran off to the large display window, where a couple of cooks could be seen in the back, running around in greased-up white aprons.

Zoey's departure was followed by a series of little stories around the table about different memories each of them had regarding their recently departed roommate, Flo. Cliff sat and listened as they rattled off story after story of Flo and their various adventures around town. At least they had called them adventures, though Cliff wondered what kind of adventures one could really have in such a small town.

One particular tale, which seemed to crack everyone up, was the one about the time they'd decided to drive through the Safari Trails just outside of Cambridge, which had dragged on slowly until the end, where the monkeys began climbing over the roof of the Hearse. As a pair of the monkeys began tugging the windshield wipers off the car, Flo leaned out of the driver's side window and started whacking them away with the extension of her walking stick. Which might have been a success if the moneys were not much younger and stronger than the ninety-two-year-old Flo. They had no difficulty snatching the cane from her hand and tossing it back and forth between them, until one of the little demons decided to smash it to pieces against a tree.

The upside to the story was they seemed to ignore the wiper blades after that.

"How long have you all lived together?" Cliff asked, finding a nice lull in the conversation between fits of laughter.

"We bought the Limestone Manor some eight years back," Sol said, looking up to some nowhere place in the sky while he thought. "Yeah, about that."

"Wait, you *bought* the house?" Cliff asked, looking around the table as Zoey returned with coffees and waters for everyone.

"Of course. Who else would just let seven octogenarians live together without a nurse?" Sol mused.

Cliff, who couldn't hide his disbelief, got up from the table.

"Excuse me," he said, going out towards the back patio. He pushed through the little door and closed it behind him as he struggled to understand what that all meant, when Hans came out behind him.

"You never told me you owned the house," Cliff said, tapping Hans in the chest. "Apparently, there are lots of things you didn't tell me before I packed up my life and moved back here." Cliff glanced in towards the wrapped-up bun of Bunty, who'd gotten up to let Hans out.

"I didn't realize any of this would be a problem," he replied, in earnest.

"You did too. You just didn't care. What is going on here, Hans?" Cliff asked, as Hans waved a finger in front of him.

"I admit not telling you everything might have been a tad selfish. But I knew if I did, you wouldn't have come. And I think that would have been a mistake," Hans added quickly.

"You're right, I wouldn't have come."

"And that would've been a mistake."

"Okay, so what exactly is going on here? And be straight with me."

"Think of the house like a kind of co-op for old people. There's quite a bit of legal mumbo-jumbo, so I'll just give you the Coles Notes, yeah?"

"Sure, Hans, give me the Coles Notes of this little commune you sucked me into."

"Firstly, we're not a commune, although we do share some similarities." Hans laughed, which Cliff did not find funny. "Okay, think about it like this, rather than paying to be in a home, we wanted to find a place where we could still live on our terms but have some help when we need it. So, a group of us bought this house. Each of us owns a room in the house, and each room is about the same value, save for the large master, which currently is held by Sol and Kitty. When one of us dies, the room is paid upfront to include a trial period of six months, which you're currently in."

"I thought you said I agreed to a year?"

"You do, you just have to pay six months. And then you get a full year."

"Wait, you lost me."

"Okay, this is the catch, so to speak."

"I really want to hurt you right now."

"Hear me out." Hans put up a hand. "You get six months for free, under the assumption that you buy out the room at the end of the year."

"What? Buy a room in this godforsaken town. You told me I could have a place to live, not a place to curl up in while I wait to die."

"Easy now. Do I look like someone waiting to die? I don't think you're seeing the full potential here, Cliff. We have freedom and company. It's like a little family."

"I've lived alone for nearly fifty years, Hans. Do I seem like the kind of man who wants people around?"

"Yes, you lived alone for fifty years, yet when I told you I had a room, you came anyways."

"You lied to me."

"I avoided giving you all the details. But I never told you you'd be alone." Hans grinned, and Cliff, frustrated, pulled away from him and paced out towards the parking lot.

"I told myself I would never come back here."

"Because of Annie. And you didn't. You came because of me." Hans smiled broadly.

"Yes, a decision I'm regretting immensely," Cliff said, wiping a hand over his face. "Okay, say I stay." Cliff turned back towards his friend, trying hard not to slap off the stupidly happy grin he had on his face. "What happens? What am I agreeing to?"

"You'll sign a document that states you'll pay five hundred dollars a month, which covers your rent and food, etc., for the next six months. Then, at six months, you can either leave, and we find a replacement, or you can sign a letter of intent, which says that, at the end of the following six months, you buy out Flo's room at cost plus 7%. That money is transferred to her estate, and you own the room."

"How much is the room?" Cliff asked.

Hans thought for a moment. "About $110,000."

Cliff sucked in a breath.

"If you need help covering…" Hans began.

"It's not the money," Cliff said, shaking his head as he began to pace again. "When were you going to tell me all of this?"

"This week sometime. The first papers don't need to be signed until next week. I wanted to get you into the house first."

"Why?" Cliff asked. "You know I'm not going to like it. It's why you didn't tell me before I uprooted my life."

"I didn't tell you, because you are a stubborn old fool," Hans said with a laugh. "You did fifty years on your own. Why not try six months with other people? Who knows? You may even surprise yourself," Hans said with a shrug.

"I'll do the week."

"One week more than if you didn't come." Hans smiled, as he moved in to embrace Cliff.

"You know I'm not going to enjoy this, right?" Cliff said, reluctantly tapping Hans's back as he was buried in his massive chest.

"We'll see." Hans turned to look in through the window, catching Zoey walking by with their food. "Let's eat." He slapped Cliff on the shoulder before slinging his arm around him and walking in. "I should have known I couldn't keep this from you for a week. You've always been such a good detect—"

"Don't do that," Cliff said, putting up a hand.

But his big friend only laughed, which sent vibrations through Cliff, who, despite his current anger at being lied to, couldn't stop himself from smiling.

5

The Hearse pulled into the driveway and the gang of retirees gingerly stepped out of the van, partially from various ailments of age and partially due to the large meal they'd all just enjoyed. Cliff, who'd told himself he wasn't going to enjoy one moment of it, had found it difficult not to be entertained by at least some of the conversation.

As it happened, the group seemed relatively content allowing Kitty and Sol to carry the conversation forward, with the occasional interjection from Hans and Mrs. Chen, who Cliff found appealingly forward and blunt. One comment had stood out and started a rather lengthy debate about "the imbeciles at the grocery store who seem content to wander without purpose."

Kitty was all for wandering, claiming that it gave her a chance to find things she may not have been looking for. This received a groan from Mrs. Chen, who felt that inefficiency was the equivalent to a slow and painful death.

Cliff managed to avoid all conversations, though, if he had opted to join in, he would have admitted he was in complete agreeance with Mrs. Chen.

He hadn't been the only one who kept to themselves. Bunty, who seemed to fade into the background, appeared content to nibble away quietly at her food, her eyes occasionally perking up at various topics, though she was never inclined to jump in. Cliff had trouble believing this was the sister of the wildly spirited woman he'd spent his youth with. Occasionally, a gesture here and there would trigger a deeply buried memory. Cliff began to dread the day her sister turned up.

Gerald, on the other hand, waited patiently through all the various conversations for what he referred to as "delightful after-meal nibbles." The man had an appetite like no one Cliff had ever met, save for Hans, who seemed to also eat like he was a teenager, managing to scarf down something called the Belly Buster. Cliff wagered, between the giant and the pudgy man, they'd cleared out the table, leaving Zoey with nothing but empty plates to carry back to the kitchen.

As Cliff stepped back into the poorly named Limestone Manor, this time without the duress of a potential crime occurring, he still managed to feel wildly uncomfortable. At least before he'd had practice entering homes with potentially violent criminals. It was more than he could say about entering with a band of chatty people, and that caused him a little trouble.

Unlike him, the house and its occupants came alive. The moment they walked in the door, Gerald waddled into the kitchen, though Cliff couldn't understand how in the world he could possibly eat anything else.

"Hans, you have to tell that boy of yours our house is not his snack hut!" Gerald shouted from the kitchen as Cliff heard dishes being tucked away into the dishwasher and the sink tap turn on.

"Jan is a growing boy. What am I supposed to do? Deny him entrance to the house?" Hans slipped his outdoor shoes off, and slid his feet into a ridiculously large, well-used pair of slippers.

"Yes. That would do it," Gerald said, poking his head out from the kitchen to glare at the larger man before popping back in.

"Gerald just gets upset when other people are in his kitchen," Hans said, nudging Cliff and giving him a wink.

"I met Jan. I thought he'd broken in," Cliff said, his head still on a swivel as he watched the people move about around him.

Mrs. Chen had replaced her nice shoes with a pair of small, rubber-soled shoes that were caked in dirt. She grabbed a pair of gardening gloves and pruning scissors from a wicker basket beside the door. Lastly, she pulled a very large-brimmed hat, the size of a small umbrella, off the hook before heading back outside.

"I saw he dropped you off. I was wondering about that," Hans said stepping into the house and giving Cliff a little wave to follow.

"I thought he broke in," Cliff repeated as he watched Sol and Kitty move through one of the side doors into a room with some rather comfortable-looking leather chairs. The sitting room was ornately decorated, although it seemed to clash from the styles of all the various residents of the house.

Cliff poked his head in quickly and caught sight of a stuffed peacock, a wall of miniature blue and white Dutch figurines—which Cliff guessed belonged to Hans—along with various needlepoints of flora. In addition to all of this, there was an abundance of intricately designed quilts that were either draped over the furniture or hung on a rack beside a beautiful turn-of-the-century fireplace with a dark wooden mantelpiece, which housed various framed pictures. From across the room, Cliff couldn't make out any of their details. A nice sized piano tucked up to one of the side walls and Cliff wondered if it was tuned still or simply another table for pictures. The final oddity in the room was an assortment of old wooden bowls that, even at a quick glance, appeared to be on top of every table surface, each one carefully handcrafted to various depths.

Cliff reached for one of the bowls and examined the bottom, which had the neatly written initials of HJV and the word "cherry" burned into it.

"You've been busy," Cliff said looking at Hans, whose face flushed red as he rubbed his hands together awkwardly.

"I've had many hours to practice since leaving the farm," he said shyly. "How did you know?"

"HJV. Hans Jacob VanDosen. It doesn't take a great detective to figure that one out. Plus, if I recall, you had quite the skills in the woodshop at school," Cliff said.

"I have my own shop now in the basement. If you decide to stick around, I can teach you," Hans added with a devilish grin.

Cliff ignored his friend and set the bowl back down on the table. Sol and Kitty took seats at a set of well-used swivel chairs with a flower pattern on them, their cards having already been dealt, as they picked up a game of cribbage as if they'd never left.

"Ya, Jan has a key, and he helps us all out around the house if we need it. So, I don't mind if he sneaks in every now and then and takes a couple pieces of bread," Hans said casually, but loud enough for Gerald to hear in the kitchen.

Cliff wondered if the rotund man heard or cared.

"So, you've already been in the house?"

"Just the entranceway and the kitchen," Cliff said with a shrug.

"Well, then, you'll need a tour." Hans slapped the back of Cliff's shoulder. "This is the den." He gestured around the room they were currently in. "It often gets turned into the card room, as you can see." He added, nodding toward Kitty and Sol.

"Fifteen, two, fifteen, four, and two for the pair is six," Kitty said with mild disappointment as she pegged the board. "Do you play, Cliff?" she asked, still moving her pieces.

"I've played before, though I can't imagine I'd be a great opponent," Cliff replied.

"I wouldn't worry. It's primarily based on the luck of the cards," Sol said, staring miserably at his own hand.

"He only says that because he loses." Kitty grinned.

"We also have bridge nights twice a week if you're into that sort of thing," Sol said, ignoring Kitty's dig.

"I would be interested in that," Cliff said, sounding a little more enthused than he would have liked. He'd always enjoyed the card game and had played it quite a bit. He and a few of the other detectives had had a longstanding game every Wednesday over the years, though it had begun to dwindle down as players died or moved to new locations. There didn't seem to be a lot of young people who were interested in learning bridge, which Cliff had always thought was a shame.

"Good to hear!" Kitty exclaimed. "I was worried we'd be short one after Flo."

Cliff felt a hand pull him back into the hallway as Hans led him across the room into another large room. This one had two sets of different wingback chairs in front of a large window. Across from them was a rather nice leather couch with a dark oval table between them.

"This is the library," Hans said in a tone that said *I hope this is obvious to you*, as the remaining three walls of the room were blanketed from floor to ceiling with a fully stocked walnut bookshelf.

"Who organized this?" Cliff said as he perused the shelves, finding someone had meticulously organized them by author and genre and... *was that the Dewey Decimal System?*

"I did," replied a soft voice behind him.

Cliff turned to see Bunty sitting in one of the dark, bluish green wingback chairs with a diamond stitch pattern across it.

She looked up at him, though her hands continued the delicate needlework for what looked to be a rather large sweater.

"That's incredible," Cliff said, examining more of the shelves.

Bunty shrugged. "Like everything else worth doing, it took time." Bunty smiled faintly.

"Bunty was the librarian here in town for nearly sixty years," Hans said with a smile.

"Fifty-five years," Bunty corrected.

"Like I said, nearly sixty." Hans laughed.

"Nearly. I suppose." Bunty's hands still moved with the smooth efficiency someone only gets from years of practice.

Cliff heard a faint rustling behind him, followed by the meow of a cat, which made him jump.

"Cliff, this is Skittles the house cat." Hans pointed to a rather large, grey tabby cat, who had hopped up on one of the extra chairs and started purring as he nuzzled into the old seat cushion. "You're not allergic, are you?"

Cliff was not allergic to cats, but that did not mean he—in any way, shape, or form—enjoyed cats. Truthfully, he'd never enjoyed many pets. Dogs he liked, though he'd never actually had one. He'd likely say that he tolerated dogs. But cats he'd never been able to trust. There was something about the way they seemed to stalk behind him that left him a little on edge.

As if sensing Cliff's apprehension, Skittles stopped his nuzzling and began to stare directly into Cliff's eyes. Cliff stared back at the large creature for a long moment before turning away from the furry demon.

"No, I'm not allergic. But I also wouldn't say I like them," Cliff added nervously, just as Skittles jumped off the chair and marched up to Cliff's feet and sat watching him with his large black eyes.

"Skittles seems to like you." Hans laughed.

"Well, that's nice for Skittles." Cliff used his foot to politely nudge the cat away from him. But it didn't seem to work, as Skittles closed in and wrapped his body around Cliff's leg.

"Let's maybe let Cliff warm up to you, little guy." Hans bent over and pulled the grey tabby up into his arms and began stroking his coat, saving Cliff from the inevitable punt he was about to deliver to the large feline.

"What's next?" Cliff asked, eager to get away from his newly obtained best friend.

"Well, you've already seen the kitchen, so let's try the sunroom." Hans set Skittles on the chair opposite Bunty, who Cliff now noticed was smiling at him, presumably amused by his discomfort with the grey cat. Her smile disappeared when she caught him looking back at her.

"Sunroom it is." Cliff followed Hans out of the library, passing though the kitchen area, where Gerald appeared to be rummaging through the cupboards.

"What are you looking for?" Hans asked the man, who seemed confused by the question.

"Pasta sauce. I could have sworn we picked some up," he said, his tongue sticking out the side of his mouth as he stood in deep concentration.

Without a word, Hans walked into the pantry and came out holding a glass jar of red pasta sauce.

"I told you I would build you a ladder."

"I told you to stop using the top shelf," Gerald retorted, snatching the jar from out of Hans's hand.

Hans only laughed and continued on into the dining room, which housed a massive table that looked like something from a Viking story. The enormous wooden table was certainly large enough to seat all of the occupants of the house…and then some.

"Gerald is a tough little man, but he means well. He's also a wonderful cook," Hans said, unprompted, though Cliff had begun to wonder about the man.

"How do you know him?" Cliff asked.

Hans thought for a long moment before giving a shrug. "I'm not sure really. One day, he arrived in town. He doesn't talk much about his life before coming here, and mostly we all stopped asking. All we managed to get was that he was from out west."

"Vague," Cliff said suspiciously.

"Don't worry about him. He's harmless. Plus, you'll want to hold off judgement until you've tried his food." Hans tapped his belly.

Hans led them into another large room filled with white wicker furniture. Unlike the rest of the house, which seemed to have hardwood floors, this section had a greyish blue carpet. The afternoon sun peeked in through the glass windows, despite the large pine trees standing tall in the garden. In comparison with the rest of the rooms, it was relatively simple. It didn't have the knickknacks the others held. Instead, it looked as if someone was trying to grow a forest inside, with an abundance of plants and indoor trees scattered around and hanging throughout the room. The only thing Cliff spotted, besides the furniture and plants, was a crokinole board resting on the centre table.

"I like this room," Cliff said with a smile.

"It's got great views of the garden." Hans pointed out the window.

"It is a garden," Cliff said, as he ran his finger along one of the hanging plants beside him.

"True enough." Hans laughed.

Mrs. Chen walked past carrying a water can. She began drenching the plants outside at the base of the sunroom. She looked up and spotted the two men, but other than a stiff nod, she barely acknowledged their presence.

"Mrs. Chen is the house garden specialist, though if you are ever interested in learning, she is always happy for the help," Hans told him.

"I've never had much of garden in the city."

"Well, if you live here, maybe you can." Hans winked.

Cliff had always wondered what it would be like to have a place that could house more plants. He'd lied to Hans, if only a little bit, as he had, in fact, kept *some* plants in his home, along with some vegetables out on his back deck. As a boy, he'd spent some time on his uncle's farm, helping out. He's always loved the idea of farming and, had he made a few different decisions in his life, maybe he would have been a farmer like Hans.

But he hadn't made those decisions, and thus, all he had was a small contingency of house plants. But this room was something else. Although he certainly wasn't sure if having a place to keep plants would outweigh everything that came along with it. The people, the cat, the conversations. *How much privacy will I have in a place like this?*

"Maybe it's time you see your room?" Hans asked, as if he'd been reading Cliff's mind.

The large man left to head back through the dining room towards the main entrance and the stairs, which led to the second landing.

Hans had not been lying when he asked about Cliff's ability to walk up stairs, as there was a serious staircase leading to the second-floor landing. However, not nearly as many as Cliff's apartment building had had, and at least here, they didn't advertise an elevator which had broken at some point in the nineties.

Hans pointed out the various rooms, which made up four in total, before showing Cliff a second flight of stairs, which led to the third-floor landing, where the remaining two bedrooms shared a bathroom.

"It's just you and me up here, my friend. We have our own private bathroom, which is handy, so you don't have to walk up and down the stairs at night. Saves the knees, if only a little." Hans gave Cliff a little wink, along with a tender rub of his left knee. "I'm here on the left, and this is you on the right." He pushed open a large wooden door into a very spacious lofted room.

Cliff took a tentative step into the massive room before giving it a good look around. It had lots of light, with three windows, two small ones at the end of the room and one larger one towards the middle of the room, looking out over the corner of the property and the United Church, which stood kitty-corner to the house.

A queen-sized bed was tucked under the largest window, with fresh bed sheets folded neatly at the foot. On each side of the bed were a matching set of dark wooden side tables.

Towards what Cliff would have called the back of the room, nearest the window which looked out over the back gardens of the house, was a handsome-looking reading chair with matching footrest, which also came with a tall lamp that hooked itself over the back of the chair.

Towards the front of the room, with the windows overlooking Peel Street and the Anglican Church, sat a large, dark wood dresser that would have taken more than a few young men to carry up the double flights of stairs. Cliff counted six large storage units in it. Beside that was a more modern-looking Ikea stand, with fifteen or so hangers hooked on top. Altogether, the room was plenty big enough for Cliff on his own, and to his surprise, was pleasantly self-contained.

"Mrs. Chen has lived up here for years, but she recently ran into a little hip trouble, and we thought it would be easier for her to be closer to the main floor," Hans relayed. "I hope you don't mind."

Cliff, who had been busy admiring the room, couldn't help but feel that, although it might have been only half the size of his previous apartment, it was perfect, especially considering the tiny reading area in the corner.

Hans must have noticed him staring at the chair, because he added, "We can have anything you want moved out of here. Jan and some of his friends are happy to help. But I'll admit it is nice to have a place to sit on your own. Plus, you get some amazing morning sun through the window."

"I can work with this," Cliff said, trying not give too much of his feelings away. He was still relatively upset with his friend about his less-than-forthcoming details of coming to live with him. So, he wasn't prepared to give him the satisfaction of being taken aback by the room. Looking around once more, Cliff didn't imagine he had enough stuff to fill the space provided.

Cliff had never been a guy who'd collected things. His apartment was simple, and when he made the decision to move out, he'd opted to donate most of what he had. For the most part, the delivery truck would only be dropping of four larger tubs, which was all he'd allowed himself to move with. Only one and a half of those contained the clothes he thought he would need, which hadn't been much. The rest was mostly an assortment of books and memorabilia of his time with the police and various assignments he'd been proud of over the years…along with some he wasn't.

"Well, I'll leave you to get settled," Hans said, tapping the edge of the doorway with his knuckles.

Cliff looked back at his friend, who looked as though he might say something else, but then apparently decided against it, giving Cliff a tight nod and turning back around to head into his room across the hall.

Cliff closed the door and spun around to take in the space once again. He might have hated the town he was in, but he had to admit, if only to himself, that he was satisfied with the room. He wasn't quite sure he was ready to say the same for the house's occupants.

The diner earlier had been overwhelming. It was much more stimulus than Cliff got from his corner seat at his local diner back in Toronto. Over the many years on his own, he'd grown used to the silence. It was in stark contrast to the cacophony of conversation around the table that morning.

His only solace was the fact that at least everyone, now that they were back at home, was content to be on their own. This suited Cliff just fine, given that, even after a restful night's sleep, he still wasn't confident he wanted to live here at all. The same miserable thought crossed his mind like a CBC news bulletin: *Has this entire move been a horrible mistake?*

Cliff half expected to walk out after lunch that day and book the next ticket back to the city, his stuff be damned, and yet here he was. He had to keep reminding himself that he had nowhere else to go. He'd told Hans that he'd chosen to leave his apartment in the city, but the truth was, his apartment had been bought for "redevelopment." Just a fancy way of kicking out the old happy tenants to make room for a seventy-floor mega building that would be five times more expensive to live in, despite the fact its rooms would be a fraction of the size.

He'd been in his apartment since 1981, and hadn't needed to search for another one since. He hadn't realized just how much the cost of new places had gone up. He wasn't exactly strapped for cash—committing oneself to work for forty-seven odd years allows one to build up a rather generous nest egg. But there was something about the principal of spending that money on a much smaller "modern apartment" that tore away at his soul.

He'd even shopped around at a few of these apartments, and as far as he could tell, "modern" did not mean better. The white-walled, marble-embellished monstrosity he'd been shown in Riverside, an area of the city that he wouldn't have ever imagined considering living in twenty-five years ago, was now being occupied by young families, squeezing themselves into tiny apartments at $2600 a month plus condo fees, or worse, a whopping one million dollars a pop.

Cliff went over and pushed a palm against the mattress. It was firm, which he liked, and he was happy for it, because it would have been difficult to get a new one all the way up here. He took the clean linens and slowly made up his new bed.

He'd planned on unpacking what few things he had brought with him once he'd finished making the bed, but he made the mistake of lying down, and between the afternoon brunch and travel, it didn't take long before he dozed off.

6

The next morning, Cliff woke early, feeling very well rested. Between his nap the previous afternoon and the wonderful night's sleep, he felt right as rain. Hans had woken him from the nap for the house's nightly dinner, which he'd found to be bittersweet. He knew sleeping longer would've meant he'd have trouble that night, but he also wasn't ready to gather for another "family" meal with his housemates. He was still feeling exhausted from the conversation that morning.

But between that and his stomach growling, he'd forced himself to get up. In the end, he was grateful he had. As it turned out, Gerald *was* an excellent cook, making a particularly delicious spaghetti and meatballs in a thick herb-and-garlic red sauce. When Cliff commented on the food, Gerald gave him a shrug, complaining about the spice level, as he added additional red pepper flakes to the top of his dish before glaring over towards Bunty, who'd had a very modest bowl of the delicious meal. When Cliff pressed him on where he'd learned to cook so well, Gerald seemed to either not hear the remark, or be too distracted by his meal to respond. Either way, Cliff got the impression Gerald wasn't one of those men who enjoyed talking about themselves much.

Once again, Kitty and Sol debated whether skills were associated with cribbage or if it was simply a matter of luck of the cards. Kitty, of course, having won three of their most recent matches, was firmly on the side of skill. But the true skill had been on the part of Mrs. Chen, who seemed wonderfully adept at manipulating the flow of conversation into the areas of the garden that needed to be focused on, unless the house wished to be viewed as simply a second-rate retirement home.

Cliff had managed to sneak in slight praise for the work she'd put into not just her outdoor but indoor plants as well, receiving a rare upward crease of the lips from Mrs. Chen, which had even turned to a full grin when Hans brought up Cliff's love of plants.

This spiralled into a much-unwanted discussion, where Cliff ended up not only receiving a *proper* tour of the gardens, but also a part-time assistant gig, managing the entire enterprise.

After the meal, Cliff offered to help Bunty clean up the dishes and was not surprised to learn the woman was equally as quiet on her own as she seemed in the group. Cliff was happy with the rare silence in the house, and by the time they finished, he'd become very content with his plan to head up to his room to read.

His room had been quiet. So quiet that he wondered if he could even fall asleep. He'd been living in the city for so long, he'd almost forgotten what it was like to hear nothing. Cliff tried opening one of the windows, which was difficult, because it was old and wooden and needed to be propped up with a small piece of wood to prevent it from sliding closed again. But even then, all he heard were crickets...actual crickets. Not one siren, or loud neighbour, not even a car seemed to drive past, and if they did, it was too quiet for Cliff to hear. For the first time, Cliff felt like he was alone, and he wasn't sure he enjoyed the feeling.

But the feeling of loneliness was gone the moment he walked downstairs the next morning and caught sight of Bunty, who looked like she hadn't moved all night from her chair, as she worked her way through the sweater she was knitting.

"Good morning. There's tea or coffee in the kitchen," Bunty said, giving Cliff a warm smile.

"Thank you," Cliff said, continuing around the corner into the kitchen. Sure, enough there was a large pot of coffee and a teapot tucked under a yellow-and-white knitted tea cozy with the words "Bee-Hive" stitched on the side.

Cliff found the collection of mugs in the cabinet above the pots. He grabbed a large blue one in the shape of a honey pot and filled it up with coffee. Years of shift work had given him an acquired taste for crappy black coffee, so he skipped the milk and sugar and made his way into the living room. He'd expected it to be empty, but he found Kitty and Sol in their usual chairs, swapping articles in the *London Free Press*.

It was too late for Cliff to leave and not feel like he was doing it because they were there, which would have been true, so he reluctantly took a seat on the couch.

"Do you read the paper?" Kitty asked, her eyes not leaving the paper in front of her. "If you do, feel free to use ours. The arts section has a particularly interesting review on the festival in there. They're doing *As You Like It*. I'd like to check it out," she added absently.

"We plan a few visits each year, if you like shows," Sol added.

Cliff had never been much of an artist, and the idea of sitting in a show for three hours in dim lighting made him sleepy, so he surprised himself when his next word was "Sure."

Cliff reached for the folded paper on the table, which had the title in bold letters *The Town Gazette* on its front. Cliff guessed this would be the local paper, as the front cover was splashed with a picture of the train tracks and a headline that read, "Body Found in Trout Creek." The author was Jan VanDosen. Cliff grabbed the paper and took a sip of his coffee and was pleasantly surprised.

"This coffee is really good," he commented, taking another quick sip of the hot liquid.

"Don't sound too surprised, city boy," Kitty said with a playful grin. "We do have good coffee here."

"This one's fire-roasted, from a café downtown," Sol jumped in.

"Sorry, I didn't mean…"

"I think you'll be surprised at how much this town as changed in fifty years." Kitty lowered her paper as her brows arched at Cliff.

"Apparently. Good coffee and murders," Cliff joked, but Kitty dropped her paper into her lap.

"It was an accident, Cliff. Not every dead body is a murder."

"If you say so." Cliff smirked.

"What do you know that you're not telling us?" Kitty asked, her eyes narrowing suspiciously.

"Nothing. Like I said…"

"A hunch. You said that yesterday, yet I don't believe you."

"Give the man a break, Kitty. It's not even seven in the morning," Sol chimed in.

"Well, I'm curious is all. I heard rumours."

"You always hear rumours."

"Don't be jealous because people tell me things, Sol."

"Who tells you things?"

"Betty Parkinson was in the salon getting her hair done."

"The rumour mill," Sol joked to Cliff, leaning back and crossing his legs, as if preparing for the tale of the century.

"Mock all you want, but those ladies hear it all before anyone else."

"They hear some, at best." Sol chuckled.

"And what did they hear?" Cliff asked, genuinely curious. He'd found over his years working as a private detective that rumour mills could actually be a great resource, as long as you could sift out the muck from the gold.

"Well, Betty said that Dick, over at the train yard, overheard a couple of the OPP officers going off about who the kid was and why he was there," she said giving a conspiratorial nod.

"And?" Sol asked. "Why was he there?"

"That's the thing. They have no idea. He's some sort of student from Western, but they can't explain why he was here. Ahh!" Kitty gasped. "That's why you think it's murder. You sly little devil." She grinned as she leaned toward Cliff, no longer caring about whichever article she'd been reading.

"It would be my train of thought." Cliff shrugged, taking another sip of coffee.

"Well, if this is a murder, then this town really is going to the wolves," Kitty scoffed.

"How so?" Cliff asked curiously.

"It's far less exciting than a murder."

"Try me."

"Please don't encourage her," Sol said, receiving a whack in the arm with Kitty's paper.

"Shh! Well, Sol used to drive cars for the Ford dealership. He was a mechanic there for years. When he retired, he started driving on the side. It was a good way for him to get out of the house and not distract me from all the things I'd got used to doing on my own."

"The man doesn't need our life story, Kitty." Sol jested.

"I'm providing context." Kitty rolled her eyes. "Anyway, Sol had to stop a few years ago on account of his eyes. They're not very good."

"He's a detective, Kitty, not an idiot," Sol chimed in.

"Anyway." Kitty exhaled. "Sol still meets with some of the guys from the shop every Wednesday down at the creamery for a beer. I don't love it, but what can I say."

"Apparently, a lot," Sol mused, ducking his head back into the paper.

"Sol's friend Pete still drives for the dealership and, apparently, the owner discovered a couple of the young kids who work there taking the cars out for joyrides a couple nights a week." Her brows lifted to almost meet her hairline. "They'd take them out, for the night, only some nights they don't bring them back until the early morning. Can you believe that?"

"It's just a couple kids being kids, that's all. No one was hurt."

"So, what happened?" Cliff asked. He wasn't sure why, but there was something off about this story, and he couldn't quiet place it.

"That's the thing. Nothing," Kitty said with a shrug.

"Nothing?" Cliff asked.

"I guess, the owner agrees with Sol that it's simply kids being kids."

"That and they don't know for sure which kids were doing it," Sol said. "So, he couldn't very well fire them all. And I'm sure they'll have a much stricter policy about who has access to the keys on the lot." Sol laughed.

"How can you laugh at such a violation of trust? It's disrespectful," Kitty said, relaxing back in her chair. "And don't give me that nonsense about them not knowing. They know exactly which boys were doing it. It's more likely, none of the other kids will turn them in because they're afraid."

"Who's that?"

"Randy Gillis and his best friend, Marcus. The two make for odd friends, and they're always causing trouble in this town," Kitty said shaking her head. "Not to mention. Randy's father owns the dealership, and he's less than likely going to turn his own son in." Kitty tilted her head, looking at Cliff to agree to her point.

Cliff didn't know many people in town anymore, and the ones he did, likely wouldn't remember him anyways. Not that it would matter, because it was obvious that, despite his time away, one thing was still clear, problems in small towns were more commonly dealt with by the community, not the police.

"Like I said, no one was hurt," Sol said with a shrug.

"How is anyone supposed to learn from their mistakes if they never even get in trouble for them?"

Cliff mulled this information over in his mind while he pretended to read the paper catching only a few headlines like "Youth Soccer Finds a New Home" and "New Bid for Town Maintenance Appears to be Serious Contender" and something called the "Boo of the Week," which appeared to be someone complaining about increased truck traffic in town.

He wasn't sure why the information felt important, and maybe it wasn't. Maybe Cliff had just spent so long trying to find the problems in stories and places that that was all he could see now. Kitty's story could just be about a couple of kids, who got caught joyriding, and that was that. Yet it seemed to remind him of something he couldn't quite put his finger on.

"Hey, Sol, you think I could join you for a beer sometime?" Cliff asked before his mind could reject the idea outright.

Sol looked up from his own paper and studied Cliff, as if he was trying to sort out for himself if he wanted to introduce this relative stranger to his friends.

"Sure," he said after a moment, "We're meeting up at the creamery, tomorrow night at five, if you want to join," he added with a nod of approval.

"Five?" Cliff said, thinking about it. Then seeing a frown beginning to form on Sol's mouth, he added, "Is perfect. Thank you. Might be nice to meet some people," Cliff lied.

The truth was something was eating away at his insides about the kids joyriding. He knew Sol and his friends were probably right about them just being nitwit kids out for fun, but he had a hunch it was something more. "What is the creamery?" he asked after thinking for a moment.

"It's the old creamery, across from the Water Street Bridge," Sol said.

Cliff vaguely remembered an actual creamery just off Water Street, but he had trouble picturing the old building now as a place one would go get a beer.

"They never changed the name?"

"It changes every decade, but everyone just calls it the same thing. Keeps it easy." Sol laughed.

"I suppose so," Cliff replied, wondering how much of this town had actually changed since he'd been gone. If it was anything like himself, he'd have to assume it had changed a lot.

Growing up, he'd always wanted to leave. It had never been the place he'd seen himself living. It was too quiet and altogether underwhelming. Maybe when he was a boy it hadn't been so bad. Sure, it was hard, but growing up anywhere in those days had been hard. He also had Annabel then. At least, he thought he did.

"I'll see you later," Cliff said with a smile, before setting his paper down and picking up his coffee to head outside. He tried his best not to look in at Bunty in the other room but failed. Cliff had managed to avoid thinking about Annie for over forty years, and now she seemed to swim around in his mind as various memories crawled their way in.

Cliff took his coffee cup to the kitchen, doing his best to avoid the back room, where he heard Mrs. Chen whistling while she presumably tended to her many plants. Cliff might have shown a little interest in the plants, but he wasn't ready to be sucked into any type of morning routines in this place.

He placed his cup in the dishwasher and walked as lightly as he could out of the kitchen, tiptoeing out the front door and making his way toward downtown. At least there he could be alone.

Cliff had forgotten just how many hills there were in St. Marys, and as he stepped to the edge of each one and peered down, he knew he would eventually have to walk back up. He took a deep breath, and his nose was suddenly assaulted by the smell of farmland, more specifically, manure. There was a slight breeze today, and that meant that, somewhere out there in the vast fields of land around the tiny town, an animal had pooped. At least that's what it smelled like to Cliff.

The earthy smell was not the most appealing thing Cliff had ever smelled, but something about it reminded him, if only for a moment, of his childhood. This brought an uncharacteristically warm smile to his lips. He brushed the memory out of his mind. He didn't need the nostalgia to distort the truth he knew, which was that he did not belong here.

It had become clear to Cliff after dinner the night before that he was not cut out for life living with other people. It was too crowded. Crowded might not even be the right word for it. It was, or at least *seemed* to be, crowded. But it was more about people. Cliff had become so used to being on his own for so long that this level of commitment to generic conversations and gathered meals, even if it was only for a short while, wasn't what he wanted.

Cliff was brought out from his silent thinking as he was bumped by a man passing him from behind. The man's balding head was fixed down at the sidewalk in front of him as he walked briskly down the road, letting out deep huffs of air as he did.

"Gerald?" Cliff said, watching the short, portly man waddle down the sidewalk. Cliff wouldn't have guessed he'd see him up this early.

"Sorry?" Gerald said, tilting his head only briefly as he continued his route down Eglin Street, the two towering churches looming over the pair of them as they walked.

"It's me…Cliff," Cliff said, trying not to sound too offended.

"Aww, yes, the new fellow. Good morning," Gerald said, not bothering to break his stride.

Cliff, who was a fair bit taller than Gerald, had been a bit more causal in his morning walking, but only had to up his pace a touch, and no more than a couple of strides later, he was fully caught up to the shorter man.

"Where are you off to?" Cliff asked.

"I'm late for my match this morning. I should have left five minutes ago," Gerald said, not bothering to stop, even as he rounded the corner right for Church Street.

"What match?" Cliff asked, no longer finding it hard to match the shorter man's pace, though Gerald himself was breathing rather hard. Despite that, he kept his feet and arms swinging hard, which appeared to be driving him forward.

"Lawn bowling." Gerald turned to look up at Cliff before glancing over his body as if assessing him.

"Is that near downtown?" Cliff asked, and Gerald let out a "aye-hum" of approval.

Cliff got the impression Gerald wasn't much of a talker. He seemed more preoccupied with getting the next foot in front of the other. This made for a quiet walk. Cliff, more than once, wondered if he should simply step back and follow behind the heavyset man. After all, it didn't appear either really wanted to be walking together, and it was Gerald who was in a hurry, not Cliff. But each time Cliff made a move to back away, he caught a sudden glance from Gerald, which made him unsure if he should leave or not.

"I need to make a stop," Gerald said quietly, as he turned down Queen Street. Cliff wasn't sure, but there was something in the way he said it that made Cliff wonder if he was supposed to follow.

But Cliff didn't have time to think about the meaning of it, as Gerald seemed to pick up the pace a little before he crossed the street and made his way down Wellington Steet. Finally, he stopped outside of one of the storefronts that didn't have a name. In fact, it had no signage at all.

Gerald put up a finger to catch his breath. "One minute," he said.

Cliff was suddenly even more confused as to at what point he'd unwittingly become this man's travel partner. He supposed he could just turn and leave now, but Cliff had no idea where Gerald was going, and he lived with the man. What was he supposed to do, run off?

Cliff followed Gerald into the store. But once inside, Cliff realized it wasn't a storefront at all—it looked like an office— giving Cliff pause as he only poked his head in the first door.

"I told you, Gerald, we don't sell anything in here. We're not an actual store," said a young, irritated man sitting behind a small black desk.

The office had a few desks set up, with only some of them currently being occupied. Off to the sides were a couple of office cubicles with glass walls separating them from the main office space. Behind them were a few people in chairs on the phone, checking briefly to see what the commotion was about, but when they saw it was Gerald, they ignored him, and carried on with whatever work it was they were doing.

"Fascinating. Mind if I—" Gerald started, his pudgy fingers twiddling together at the sight of a small table of candy and food.

"Go ahead," the young man said with a wave.

Gerald licked his lips as he took a couple of treats from the table. Some candies and a small pack of beef jerky. Then, with a thin smile, he turned to leave.

"Thank you," he said, catching Cliff's eye and giving him a shake of the head, as if to say *get out of here.*

"What was that about?" Cliff asked as Gerald left the building and tore open a bag of beef jerky.

"Morning snack." He held the bag out for Cliff, though not long enough to actually let him take anything.

"You went in there for a morning snack?" Cliff asked, confused, but Gerald only nodded. "I don't understand, what do they do?" Cliff looked back at the unmarked building.

"I'm not sure. But they always have snacks," Gerald said, placing large piece of the jerky in his mouth.

Cliff looked around, realizing now he was heading away from downtown.

"Wait a minute. Isn't downtown back that way?" Cliff pointed towards Queen Street. They were now crossing the Wellington Street Bridge and going in the opposite direction. Cliff could see in the distance the area the OPP had blocked off with tape.

"Yes. I'm not going downtown," Gerald said after he finally finished chewing his jerky.

They'd already crossed the bridge and taken a left. Cliff could now see a sign for the liquor store, along with a large warehouse, which Cliff presumed was the creamery, given the sign painted across the top of the building. Cliff took a look at the old building. It hadn't seemed to have change one bit since the last time he'd seen it, except for the picnic table patio and beers signs, which covered the outside of its walls. *At least I know where I'm meeting Sol.*

"I'm going downtown," Cliff said, looking back over the water towards town.

"Then why are you following me?"

"I'm not following you," Cliff said, which caught a curious gaze from Gerald. "Okay, I am following you, but I didn't realize I was following you."

"You should get that checked out." Gerald put another piece of jerky in his mouth before pointing to Cliff's head.

"Easy now," Cliff said, but he was still following the pudgy man down the street towards the flats, a low-lying park that Cliff recalled as having a tendency to flood every year, which made it partially useless for anything other than a park ground.

Getting a little closer, he noticed the flats was now a set of mirroring ball diamonds that shared an outfield. It had been renamed Milt Dunnell Field. Cliff, of course, knew who Milt Dunnell was. He had written for the Stratford newspaper when Cliff was a boy, and he continued to follow his writing when he'd started working for the *Toronto Star*.

Cliff had even met him briefly in 1962, when he'd been invited to watch the Grey Cup at Exhibition Stadium. The city of Toronto had offered their police services for the event, specifically to help assist with Prime Minister Diefenbaker, and Cliff had volunteered. After all, he'd voted for the man and was an Argos fan, having played a little in high school, as well as with the Toronto Police pick-up league. Not that the game was all that pleasing to watch, of course. Cliff could barely see the prime minister, let alone the actual game.

It had been the only Grey Cup final in history to be postponed till the following day because the fog had been so brutal. Milt had written about the entire thing in the Monday paper. Cliff had lucked out on his assignment handling the prime minister as everyone else in the Toronto Police Department was on full alert handling the renegade hooligans who'd decided the fog was good cover for all their shenanigans. Or as other members of law enforcement would call it, rioting.

"So, you think it's a murder," Gerald said gnawing on a piece of jerky.

"What's that?" Cliff asked.

"The body they found. You think it's a murder," Gerald repeated with all the ease of a child asking for a second scoop of ice cream.

"I'm not really thinking about it," Cliff lied. His mind had never really been able to shut off, and when a juicy little case landed in his lap, he wasn't about to completely ignore it.

Gerald seemed to be reading his mind, as he shot him a remarkably annoying smile.

"Okay, I'm interested in it. But who in town isn't?" Cliff said, now walking down the one-way path around the flats still on the heels of Gerald.

Cliff wasn't entirely sure why he was still following his not-so-chatty new roommate, then cringed at the idea of the word *roommate*. But if he was being honest with himself, he knew exactly why he was following Gerald. He had nothing else to do. His only plan had been to leave the house and get a coffee downtown. He didn't need a coffee though, and for whatever reason, he found Gerald to be fascinating. He was the only one in the house he still knew nothing about. Other than that, he was a decent cook.

"Not everyone in town was a cop," Gerald said, his brows lifting high up his forehead as he pulled out another bag of jerky Cliff hadn't even noticed he'd taken.

"I used to be a detective," Cliff said. "I'm not anymore."

"In my experience, people don't stop being police." Gerald stuck a thick finger into the tiny bag of beef jerky. "Jerky?" he asked Cliff, holding out the bag again, this time long enough for Cliff to take some if he'd wanted to.

Cliff shook his head. "Spent a lot of time with police?" Cliff asked narrowing his eyes on this relative stranger.

But Gerald didn't seem at all concerned, as he shrugged off the question.

They'd nearly reached the end of the road. Off to the left was a large, covered building with picnic tables under it. Behind which was the Thames River. Cars were lined up along the other side of the one-way road, lining the river. Some seemed to have people waiting in them—for what, Cliff couldn't be sure. Others were off on the side casting lines. On the river, a young couple shared a double kayak as they crossed under the old Grand Trunk Railway.

Up ahead to the right was a children's playground and a small building with neatly manicured lawns out front. Cliff didn't have to be a detective to guess that this was where the lawn bowling was.

"Why would you suspect foul play? This isn't the city," Gerald said, slowing his pace. He was starting to breathe a little heavily, having kept up a relatively impressive pace for his size.

"I don't want it to be, but I've seen enough of the signs to know when something's not right," Cliff added vaguely.

Gerald stuck his lower lip out and furrowed his brows in thought.

"Do you think it was an accident?" Cliff asked.

"Have you ever bowled before, Brian?" Gerald said, ignoring the question and giving Cliff an appraising look.

"It's Cliff and no. I've played bocce ball before."

"That will have to do," Gerald said as he marched over to two gentlemen sitting on the bench outside of the gated lawn area.

"Gerald," said a tall, thin man with a beige Tilley hat, who promptly stood to meet the shorter man. "You're late."

"I was otherwise disposed," Gerald said sticking another piece of jerky in his mouth.

"I bet you were. Where is Hans?"

"He told me he was off getting wood for his shop and that he would meet me here. Obviously, he's not here, but it's okay. I've got a spare," he said, shooting a thumb out towards a now very confused Cliff. "Steve, Leonard," he said, by way of introduction. "Meet Cliff."

Cliff nodded at Steve, the tall man, and Leonard. Leonard was bald and wore a Hawaiian shirt and a navy-blue bucket hat.

"Cliff Shaw?" Steve said, taking a closer look a Cliff.

Cliff did the same, trying to run the image of the man in front of him over in his mind. He guessed the man was within a year or two of the same age as himself, and his name was Steve.

Somewhere from deep in the recesses of Cliff's mind, he pulled up the image of a scrawny, acne-faced teen from his mind.

"Steve Murray?" Cliff said, sticking out his hand to greet his old acquaintance.

"Hell, I haven't seen you in…what…?" Steve shook Cliff's hand.

"Fifty years or so?" Cliff said, though saying the words out loud almost made him feel bad about the passed time.

"Wow. How have you been?"

"What do you say we get this game started?" Gerald said impatiently.

Cliff turned to look at Gerald. "What game?"

"The bowls match. You're my new partner."

"But I told you, I've never played."

"All the better for us." Leonard laughed as he stood up from his bench.

Cliff went to protest again, but Gerald was already gone, leaving him with Steve and Leonard.

"He's an odd guy," Cliff said, finding his feet moving towards the field with Steve and Leonard.

"You have no idea," Steve said, giving Cliff a pat on the back.

As it turned out, lawn bowling was nothing like bocce ball. It might look the same, if you consider throwing one larger ball across a playing field towards another smaller ball that Cliff learned was called the jack. However, unlike bocce ball, this was much, much harder. The bowl— the name for the larger ball—had a rounded perimeter, but then, rather than being a complete sphere, it had two convex sides which caused the bowl to bend as it rolled. They were playing something called crown green, not that it mattered what it was called. The first time Cliff tried to toss one of the bowls it rolled heavily to one edge and spiralled out less than halfway down the green.

Needless to say, Cliff did little in the way of getting or preventing points in the first match, as they lost twenty-one to five, all five points obviously coming from Gerald, who, despite being told Cliff had never played before, still appeared mildly upset.

Luckily, Cliff had been partnered with Steve, who seemed to take a little pity on him and instructed Cliff on how to at least get the bowl down the green and in the general area of the jack. By the end of the first round, Cliff was at least able to prevent one or two scores from Steve.

During the second game, Cliff wouldn't go so far as to say he was good, but he had certainly made some vast improvements on his initial game. He even managed a lucky two points.

Gerald had a remarkably soft touch as he rolled the bowls neatly down the green each time. This was certainly not his first time playing, and thanks to his additional nineteen points, they were able to take the second round of play.

"I may have taught you too well," Steve said, as he and Cliff switched ends of the green once again, as they now faced the tiny clubhouse attached to the green.

"Beginners luck," Cliff said as he picked up the jack. As Cliff and Gerald won the previous match, it was on him to toss it.

"Just needs to go at least twenty-three metres," Steve said. But, catching the confused look on Cliff's face, he added, "Roughly two-thirds of the green."

"Got it." Cliff rolled the small white ball, which, luckily, had no convex sides, down the field, watching it come to a stop near the back of the green. The one that Gerald tossed sat a good six feet in front of Cliff and Steve.

"So, Hans tricked you into moving into the Limestone Manor," Steve said, picking up from where their previous conversation had ended.

Cliff had found it surprisingly easy to catch up with his old high school acquaintance. As it turned out, he wasn't as boring as Cliff would have suspected. He lived in London, Ontario, for a few years, getting a teacher's degree before moving out to Halifax, Nova Scotia, where he taught high school biology for fifteen years. He managed to convince his wife, who was from St. Johns, Newfoundland, to move back to St. Marys after his parents passed away. They had taken over his family home. He taught at the high school in town after that, which Cliff recalled a new school being built a few years before he left while his old school, St. Marys Collegiate Institute, had changed names a few times over the years before finally shutting its doors for good, two years back in 2010. Cliff shouldn't be too surprised by all the changes. It had been over sixty years since he'd been to high school.

"I suppose 'tricked' might be the operative word." Cliff laughed as he rolled one of the bowls down the green, where it stopped five feet short and to the left of the jack. "I like to think he simply withheld some vital information."

"Sounds like Hans." Steve laughed, his own bowl spinning out just inside the three-foot area.

Just as Cliff was about to release another bowl, a loud burst, like a gunshot, came from up the hill on Queen Street. Cliff and the others on the green all turned to see what the commotion was.

A second later, a group of bikers came rolling down the hill, filling the valley with a cacophony of sound that seemed to rattle off the surrounding hills.

"Not again," Steve said, his hand tightening nervously around one of the bowls.

"Who's that? Cliff watched as the gang of motorcyclists rumbled their way across the Green Bridge before making a left, heading around the road surrounding the flats. Cliff counted roughly twenty or so bikers, with a handful of them carrying passengers on the back.

"Some bike gang from London. They've been causing noise around town for the past couple of months. And I'm not sure I'm referring to their bikes," Steve said as a couple of the bikes let out a deafening crack as they passed.

Cliff noticed the patch on the backs of their jackets, a red and black snake with a pair of fiery wings coming out its back. *The Crimson*

Serpents?

It had been a long time since Cliff had heard much about them. They'd gone quiet in Toronto a decade or so ago. *But that doesn't mean they aren't still active.*

They'd been the largest biker gang in Ontario ever since they'd invited every other club in Ontario to swap patches. Almost overnight, they went from a minor presence in Ontario to the largest concentration of chapters in the world. Needless to say, it caused at least a couple of conversations around the police departments.

But Cliff couldn't guess why they would have any reason to be in St. Marys. Cliff assumed a town like this would be too small to be worth the hassle. *So why were they here?*

The group of bikers wrapped around the flats, parking their bikes on the far side of the ball diamonds, each bike lining up, forming neat columns of two down a narrow patch of gravel along the side of the road.

"You say they've been coming for a couple months?" Cliff asked Steve absently before tossing another bowl down the green.

They hadn't been the only people watching the bikers roll past. Everyone seemed to have at least one eye on them as they now all dismounted their bikes and stood grouped together around them. Cliff watched a couple of them leaning heavily on what he assumed were Harley-Davidsons—the bike of choice for the gang—while they lit a smoke. Cliff also guessed they weren't cigarettes.

"Yeah, they come into town, make a lot of noise, go to the creamery, and repeat." Steve shook his head. "And no one does anything about it."

"Where are the police?" Cliff asked, his last bowl nestling itself in, less than a foot away from the jack, his best shot yet.

Steve must have been distracted, as his shot came up short again. "Nice shot!" he said graciously. "The OPP in town are pulled pretty thin.

They cover too much area to ever really have anyone 'around.' Plus, now with all this business up at the train tracks, they're preoccupied. It's the highest number of police we've had in town in years. Save for the occasional ride program." Steve chuckled.

Cliff tried to ignore the gang, who, even now, stood confidently around in their group, looking as though they didn't have a care in the world.

"It is interesting how St. Marys suddenly became such a hot spot. Although not the hot spot I think we were all hoping for," Steve added darkly.

"Yeah, it's certainly quite the coincidence," Cliff muttered under his breath as he turned back to steal another glance at the group.

The third game finished up quickly after that, and Cliff managed to hold Steve off from scoring too many points, which left the surprisingly soft-handed and very talented Gerald open to bring in the win.

Despite this, they'd lost two to three in their match. But considering Cliff had never played before, he thought that was the best possible outcome. Gerald didn't seem as happy with it as Cliff.

"You could have done better," Gerald mumbled.

As if on cue, Hans pulled up to the green in an old red Ford pickup truck.

"You're late," Gerald said, folding his arms and looking in at the big man now leaning out the driver's window.

"I told you I would be late." Hans shrugged. "I needed to drive to Elmira to pick up this wood." He jerked a thumb back to show the thick slabs of hardwood jetting out the back of the truck, tied down with some straps. "It's amazing what kind of deals you can find on Kijiji," he added with a chuckle.

"You missed our entire game. I was stuck playing with him," Gerald said, cranking his neck in Cliff's direction.

"You're welcome, by the way," Cliff said.

"He played well," Steve jumped in.

"We lost." Gerald pouted, then walked around the truck and hopped in the passenger seat.

"You want a ride home, Cliff?" Hans asked, though the single bench seat did not look like the most appealing place to squeeze in, especially beside Gerald, whose body still appeared to glisten with sweat.

"I think I'll pass. I wanted to head downtown anyway." Cliff gave the red truck a pat on the side as Hans shrugged.

"Sounds good to me," Hans said, as he began to slowly pull away. "Thanks for filling in," he added, leaving before Cliff had a chance to reply.

"Thanks for the game," Steve said.

Cliff resisted the urge to remind everyone that he'd not intended to come down and play the game at all. Instead, he gave a nod to both Steve and Leonard, who'd taken up their seats once again on the little bench outside of the green.

"It was fun," Cliff said, and he was more surprised than anyone when he decided that the statement was true. Despite not intending to play, he had to admit there was something pleasant about being outside, and lawn bowling hadn't been as boring as he'd originally thought it would be.

"You're welcome back anytime. There's always someone in need of a partner," Leonard said gesturing back towards a group of seven trying to figure out how the match was going to work.

"It appears so," Cliff said, laughing at the bickering group on the edge of the green.

"Maybe we'll see you around town," Steve added.

"Maybe." Cliff waved and turned to walk back down the road of the flats towards the Green Bridge.

He spotted Hans's truck continuing around the edge of the flats, slowing down considerably when he reached the large mass of motorcycles and their riders, gathered around the edge of the road, making it challenging for anyone to drive through.

Cliff shook his head at the disrespect of it all. Had he not been in his eighties and alone, he thought he might have had some choice words for them. As it was, he was both these things and was forced to watch his friend creep along the edge of the hill, working hard to not roll off the side or hit any of them.

Cliff had nearly made it all the way back to the Milt Dunnell entrance sign by the time Hans's truck finally reached the end of the road. Han's spotted Cliff, giving him a wave as he turned to head across the bridge.

As his truck passed, Cliff caught sight of something interesting. Standing, talking to the man Cliff had spotted leading the procession of bikes around the flats, were a couple of kids who couldn't have been older than sixteen.

One of the boys had shaggy dark hair, wore a pair of long, dark green shorts and an unbuttoned striped shirt over a white t-shirt. He also seemed to be sporting a new pair of sneakers and a fresh tattoo with some odd-looking patch over it. Cliff had never got a tattoo and seeing this one made him understand why. The little patch made the entire area look red and puffy, leaving the unknown image on the kid's forearm looking like a disgusting black blob.

It was an interesting contrast to the fully tattooed forty-something-year-old man who sported black jeans, a leather jacket with a Metallica t-shirt underneath it. *How could anyone where a leather jacket in this heat?*

The pair seemed to be talking discreetly, though Cliff noticed two of the bikers stood nearby, watching the conversation intensely. The boy doing most of the talking kept turning to glance back at the other, who looked far less comfortable standing with the bikers than his counterpart. Unlike his tattooed, baggy-clothed friend, the second boy sported blond hair, a blue polo shirt, and shorts that seemed too tight and too short to be at all comfortable.

But maybe that was the trend. Not that Cliff had ever understood the various ins and outs of fashion trends. He was well aware of the fact that part of the appeal was that the older generation didn't understand it, which had been a simple truth throughout time.

Cliff didn't need to be a detective for it to be clear from all of their faces that none of them were happy to be having the conversation.

Cliff contemplated taking a completely different route towards downtown. This was none of his business and surely no good would come from him paying any attention to it.

And yet, even as he thought these things, his feet were already cutting back along the grass towards the opposite road, which would bring him nearly parallel to the uncomfortable exchange taking place. By the time his mind had caught up to his feet, it was too late for him to turn back. He silently cursed his feet for their years of walking him into trouble, even as he began to open his ears to the various conversations happening around him, for anything that he might pick up on the pass. There was only one he was interested in though.

"I'm sorry, Hurley," the shaggy-haired kid said to the man Cliff assumed must be Hurley.

"I told you what would happen, Marcus." Hurley rubbed his hand over his face and through his long salt and pepper beard. "What do you plan on doing?"

"I can't do anything, I told you," Marcus said trying and failing to hide the look of terror in his eyes.

Hurley smacked a fist against his bike seat. "Not good enough. I told you this week. You said you could do it," Hurley hissed.

Marcus looked like he wanted to expel something from various orifices of his body.

"What are you looking at, old man?" said a particularly burly looking biker standing off to the side of Hurley.

Cliff hadn't noticed just how close he'd gotten, and realized too late his ears weren't what they used to be. This little interruption had ended any chance of him hearing any more of Marcus and Hurley's conversation, as both of them were staring directly at him now.

"What?" Cliff said, blinking a few times in confusion.

"I said, what are you looking at, old man?" the giant said, a little more aggressively.

Cliff was unsure what he should do, when he was surrounded by a gang of terrifyingly large men and some equally frightening women. So he did the only thing he could think of.

"What?" he said, holding a hand up to his ear politely.

"Dammit, Rocco, leave the old man alone. He's obviously deaf," Hurley said, clearly annoyed.

"What?" Cliff said, getting a final wave of the hand from Rocco, who turned back to the group.

Cliff mentally thanked Gerald for reminding him of one of the few things that was great about getting old. It wasn't the fact that your body aches all the time and you slowly lose all of the attributes you took for granted while you were young. No, that sucked. The one positive thing was that everyone around you so often underestimates you.

Cliff smiled, even though he was now too far away to hear anything else between Hurley and Marcus. What he had heard was enough to convince him that there was certainly something going on, and with what he knew about the Serpents, it wasn't something legal.

Cliff turned back to glance at the blond-haired boy, who'd taken the interruption as a chance to pace over towards the water, where he now stood, looking like all the colour had drained from his face. Given the large bags under his eyes, Cliff guessed it had been a couple days since he'd had a good night's sleep. All in all, he seemed much less put together than Cliff had initially thought. Cliff noticed he was sporting a decent-looking Omega watch, which would have set him back a couple grand, and a new set of keys, which he was now white-knuckling. Cliff guessed they were for the large pickup truck parked across the road. *What kind of trouble have you kids got yourselves into?*

7

It didn't take long for Cliff to track down the coffee shop Kitty and Sol had talked about. There were only three blocks to meander through, and Cliff enjoyed looking around at the buildings downtown to see just how much the town had changed in some ways, and how much it hadn't in others.

Pacing up the main street, Cliff wasn't surprised to see that, more than anything, it was the business names that had changed, not so much the buildings.

Each time he passed a store, he couldn't help but be reminded of the world in which he'd grown up. A time before everything in the town reminded him of her. He saw Woody's Butcher, where his parents would send him and his brother to pick up fresh sausages for dinner. His father would always leave them with enough to treat themselves to a Cherry Coke at the Grill, which, like everything else on the corner, had been converted into a bank.

He remembered rounding the corner on Church Street, past the town hall, heading over to the Lyric with friends to check out whichever movie of the week was playing.

Amidst the happy memories, he also found the difficult ones, like seeing Andrews Jewellers, which sadly remained a jewellers, but by another name. It reminded him of the ring he'd purchased just days before he left the town for good. *Well, not for good, I suppose.*

Cliff still hadn't found the café as he carried on down the opposite side of the street, taking in the façade of the old Grand Hotel, now a travel agency, a real estate office, and what he guessed were apartments. Then he spotted a sign up ahead for a sandwich shop and heard his stomach begin to rumble.

Cliff waited patiently for the light to turn to green and crossed the road, until he reached his target, a small deli, conveniently named the Sandwich Shop. Cliff went inside and was immediately hit by the smell of cold meats and fresh bread. There was a small line gathered up by the meat counter, though Cliff couldn't tell exactly how it was formed. He made his best guess, tucking into the back of the group on the right.

He stood waiting in line patiently while, one by one, the customers were served. The cold fridge at the back of the store housed a collection of cold meats and side dishes, all of which looked appealing to the decidedly starving Cliff.

Reading the sign behind the checkout, he saw the list of options, and halfway down, Cliff saw what he was looking for.

A moment later a woman, with short dark hair, somewhere in her forties, called out to him.

"What can I get you?" she said, greeting Cliff with a smile, despite having clearly been running around all morning.

"Reuben sandwich, please," Cliff said, rubbing his hands together eagerly.

"What type of bread?" she asked, and she must have caught a confused look on Cliff's face, as she added, "We have white, brown, and rye."

"Rye, please."

"Mustard and sauerkraut okay?"

"Of course." Cliff smiled, wondering what kind of person would get a Reuben without.

"Chips or veggies?" she added, as she wrote down the order on a small notepad. She looked up and pointed towards the bags of chips behind the counter. "Or vegetable sticks."

"Chips?" Cliff said, not sounding as confident as he should have at such a simple question. Behind the counter, he saw multiple options, and not wanting the woman to have to further explain his simple choices, he quickly added, "Salt and vinegar, please." That had been one of the options he'd seen.

"Coming right up." She hurried off to start slicing up some of the cold meats.

Cliff stood off to the side, waiting patiently, when he felt a presence behind him.

"You were right."

The voice startled Cliff, and he turned around to see who it was. It took a moment to recognize very casual-looking Lou standing in plain clothes, appearing very nervous behind him.

Looking around the room, he realized it was more or less empty now, except for the two of them, and someone wandering around near the frozen pies.

"You scared the heck out of me, Lou," Cliff said, putting a steadying hand over his chest. He wasn't sure why her appearance had startled him so much. Maybe it was the fact that he barely knew anyone in town, so why would anyone speak to him? "What are you on about?"

"Your prediction, about you know what," Lou said, trying and failing not to look so conspiratorial.

"I'm an old man, Lou. I'm going to need a little more." Cliff turned back to see the woman buttering a nice thick piece of rye bread.

"The boy, wasn't in an accident. He had no alcohol in his system." Lou was practically whispering in his ear as her eyes darted around the shop. The bell rang from the front door, and Lou jerked back as a new patron walked in and stood looking at the collection of cheeses.

"That's a shame," Cliff said, sounding not all that pleased that he'd been right. "Wait, why are you telling me this? Shouldn't it be confidential?"

"They'll be making an announcement later this afternoon."

"Reuben on rye," said the woman as she walked over and placed a white waxed bag on the counter. "Chips are inside," she added politely. "Your total is $8.26." She punched it in on her register.

Cliff pulled a ten-dollar bill out of his wallet, which he'd been carrying in his back pocket, and handed it to the woman. She handed him some change, and he dropped it all in the tip cup at the front of the counter.

"Thank you," he added before turning to leave the store.

Lou, who must have ordered at some point without Cliff noticing, was scrambling to pay her own bill. Cliff could tell she was keeping one eye at the task at hand and another on him leaving.

Cliff had only made it partway down the block when Lou caught up to him.

"Wait, I want to talk to you."

"No, you don't."

"Yes. I do," Lou insisted. "I know a great place to eat." She smiled.

Cliff was annoyed at the interruption to his plan to be alone, but he also didn't know where he was going.

"Fine. But you need to get me a coffee from a fire-roasted coffee place," Cliff said sticking a finger up between them.

"It's called The Beanery, and yes, I can do that."

"Great. But I'm telling you now, I won't be any help."

"We'll see." Lou continued down the road and crossed Water Street.

Cliff recognized where Freddie's Poolhall used to be, and it was now a craft store. She crossed the street again towards a new building Cliff had never seen. It had a little corner store attached to it, but Cliff remembered the less pretty-looking mill that had been there before. This new limestone building was attached to the much older and prettier opera house.

"Did you know that Sir John A. MacDonald spoke here?" Cliff asked. "And he spoke in that building there." Cliff pointed to the Gothic-looking opera house up ahead.

"I didn't. Did you see him speak or something?" Lou asked, and Cliff laughed.

"How old do you think I am?" Cliff scoffed. "John A. died in 1891."

Lou looked at the building and shrugged. "History's not really my thing."

"Clearly."

Lou continued up the road towards the opera house. As it turned out, the café Cliff now knew to be The Beanery was in one of the tiny storefronts on the main level of the old building.

Lou disappeared inside, and Cliff, who was happy to wait out in the warm sun, sat on a chair out front while she got him a much-needed coffee. A few minutes later, Lou reappeared and handed him a large cup.

"Thanks," Cliff said, taking a sip. "So where is this spot?" He looked up and down Water Street.

"Right this way." Lou led him back down towards Queen Street, made a left towards Victoria Bridge, and Cliff noticed some minor differences to it as well.

"What the hell did they do to the bridge?" Cliff asked, eyeing up the limestone arched bridge.

"What are you talking about?"

"It used to be so beautiful."

"I'd say it's still beautiful." Lou shrugged.

"It's changed. Back in my day, you used to have to walk along the side of the bridge and the cars would whiz past you. It was exciting."

"Are you complaining about the fact that they added in sidewalks?"

"And it's bigger."

"To accommodate the sidewalks?"

"You don't understand, Lou."

"I don't understand how a town could possibly put in sidewalks to make it safer for the people of the town to walk along it without getting hit by a car? Or a truck?" Lou asked.

"Yes," Cliff said, as Lou shook her head and walked along a concrete pathway, marked by a little sign with the words "The Loop" written on it.

"This used to be the flour mill," Cliff said, mostly to himself, as he looked over the edge and caught the remnants of the old mill, which had been turned into some sort of monument. He looked around him as if he could still see the shaky old building that once stood here. "All of this was a building."

"You know, for a man who claims to not like this town, you certainly have a lot of things to say about the ways it's changed," Lou said.

Cliff shot her an irritated look. "Tell me, what exactly are you doing here on your day off? I thought you would have been set up somewhere else."

"Nope, I just live out in Hillcrest," Lou said casually.

"What the heck is Hillcrest?"

"It's a new subdivision out past the arena."

"St. Marys has a subdivision?"

"Yes, a few of them, actually." Lou laughed. "You really don't know much about your old home, do you?"

"I never thought I would be coming back here," Cliff said, looking passively down at the river.

"Why did you?"

"A conveniently told combination of half-truths," Cliff mused.

"Funny."

"What's that?" Cliff said, and Lou eyed him up carefully before giving another one of her patented shrugs. "Lou, use your words."

"Well, you don't seem like the kind of person who falls for any sort of half-truths," she said.

"What? You think I *want* to be back in this place? I spent my entire life avoiding it."

"I'm not sure. I just think it's interesting. You, of all people, don't seem like you would do anything you didn't want to do." Lou took a seat on one of the shaded park benches that overlooked the river.

"I disagree. I don't want to be here talking with you, and yet here I am," Cliff said, which seemed hit Lou harder than he intended. "What do you want to ask me, Lou?" Cliff sighed as he sat down next to her.

"Well, you seemed to know before anyone else that what happened on the bridge wasn't an accident. I thought you might have some other insights."

"First of all, I didn't 'know' before anyone. I made a different analysis of the information I had."

"You had less information than we did, and you were still right."

"Luck," Cliff said, unwrapping his Reuben sandwich on his lap.

"I don't believe that for a minute." Lou opened up her own wrap.

"Someone does," Cliff said with a grin.

"What's that supposed to mean?"

"Well, the fact that you're here now, in plain clothes, says a lot."

"I don't know what you're talking about." Lou bit into what appeared to be a chicken Caesar wrap, though her face couldn't hide the sudden redness in her cheeks.

"Okay, let me see. You mentioned to your captain that I had this same theory. No doubt he was thrilled to hear you'd talked about the investigation to someone outside the department. He was probably even less thrilled when you suggested he talk to me." Cliff opened his bag of salt and vinegar chips, pulling one out. "Am I close?"

"He had a few other choice words, but yeah, more or less accurate."

"Yet, here you are, breaking the rules again. Why?"

"Some people just don't know how to ask for help," Lou said, wiping her mouth with a napkin.

"I know the type," Cliff said, smiling, feeling wistful. He'd been a member of the Toronto Police Department for over forty years. He'd met his fair share of men who thought their authority was God. Cliff had seen many changes in the department over the years, but for whatever reason, a majority of those ranking officers often had that fault in common. It led to Cliff's lasting belief that those who should lead don't want it, and those that do, tend to want it too much.

One particular captain stood out in Cliff's mind. He was a young man at the time, and it was his first big case as a new detective. There had been a series of bank robberies at multiple location around the city. The team had also been recorded hitting stops across the country. The case was big news, and no one wanted to be attached to it, in case the whole thing went south. And since they'd supposedly hit over forty-seven locations so far, people were starting to doubt if they ever would catch them.

The gang was meticulous and organized, in and out in less than two minutes. But what no one could wrap their heads around was how they'd been managing to get away without any trace of them being there. It was as if they simply disappeared.

The captain at the time had asked the public for any assistance they could provide to help identify the gang. The phones were, of course, going crazy with "tips" from people around the city. Anything from "my neighbour has been acting suspiciously lately" to the simple, yet elegant, guess of "ghosts."

Cliff had been tasked with sorting through the information. He'd told his team that he wanted every piece of information on his desk to look through. Over the next weeks, thousands of tips had come in, and although most of them were worthless, a few things had come across his desk which appeared helpful. One, in particular, was interesting. A parking lot attendant in the east end had reported a couple of licence plates has been taken from his lot the day before the last heist.

That, in itself, wouldn't have been enough to follow up if it hadn't been for another, completely separate lot, that had reported the same thing the day before another heist.

Cliff had brought the coincidence up with his captain at the time, suggesting that they reach out to all the lots in the city and have them contact a direct line if any of them had any missing plates in the next couple weeks. Cliff and his team figured, at the rate at which they were moving, the next heist would likely happen in under two weeks. That was, if they hadn't decided to move on to another city already.

But Captain Rutherford thought the entire thing would be a waste of time, that there was no way they could reach out to every car park in the city just on a whim, and "politely" suggested Cliff find "another angle." Cliff had pointed out the fact that they wouldn't need to reach out to *every* car park, only the ones located within a few blocks of a bank. This had been the case up until now, and Cliff had no reason to believe they would change their routine. People were creatures of habit, after all.

Captain Rutherford, however, was nothing if not stubborn, and was hell bent on refusing to listen to reason. So, Cliff did the only thing he could think of. He called as many lots as he could, identifying only the ones he thought might be targeted due to their proximity to potential bank targets. Then he gave them each a direct line to him.

However, two weeks later, another bank was hit in the city. As with all the other banks, they were in and out in under two minutes, moving with great efficiency before disappearing without a trace. Not one of the places Cliff had earmarked for a licence plate theft had been targeted, and he assumed his assumptions had been wrong. He'd even reached out to a couple of the lots near the targeted bank. So, if he was right, he should have heard something.

Then again, he hadn't reached out to *all* of the lots. There were two within his targeted range he'd missed, each smaller than the lots he thought to contact, believing that the larger lots had *more options* and were *less conspicuous.*

Cliff decided to reach out to them. The first one was unsuccessful. The second, however, turned up a hit. Two plates had been recorded missing the day before the heist. Thinking he had a breakthrough, he told Captain Rutherford what he'd found, but rather than getting praise like he imagined, he was chastised for not following a direct order and was taken off the case.

As it happened, the robbers went on to rob nearly eighty more banks in Canada and the US before they were eventually captured. When they finally caught them, it was determined they were taking licence plates and swapping them out on two separate vehicles. One to leave the bank with, and another always less than four minutes away to swap out. The three men would strip the plates and toss them in a river before finally getting into a legally registered vehicle.

They had been meticulous in their preparation and moved so quickly that no one knew when or where they were going to strike next. Being told to leave the case was the worst moment of Cliff's career. Even when it turned out his assumptions were right, it had felt like a hollow victory. But he'd learned two things from the experience—never underestimate the value of a coincidence, and never believe that those in charge are smarter than you.

"So, you're asking me for help?" Cliff said as he took another bite of his Reuben. It was really good, and he was ashamed to admit just how surprised he was by that.

"Unofficially I'm asking if maybe you have any idea what might be happening here. 'Cause as far as I can tell, once the autopsy came up negative for alcohol, people seemed to be scrambling with what to do,"

Lou said, finishing off half of her wrap.

"Without details, I could just be running you around in circles," Cliff said. Of course, he had been thinking about the case. It was a murder, after all, and whether or not he was retired, some things never stop being interesting. Sad, of course, but interesting.

"What do you want to know?" Lou said without hesitation.

"You know how many rules you're breaking talking to me?"

"Should rules matter when it's a kid's life?" Lou said with a hint of anger in her voice.

Cliff didn't know much about Lou. After all, he'd only met her for the first time the day before, and it hadn't been by choice. But he could tell, even in that short amount of time, that she was determined, and with this last statement, he could tell she had integrity, something he could say wasn't always there in people of authority.

"No," Cliff said, with a shake of his head. "So, what's going on?"

Lou hadn't been exaggerating when she said the OPP was lost in the investigation. They'd had all their money on it being an accident, and now that it was not an accident, they would have to make an announcement to the public that they had no real idea why on earth this kid was killed or by whom. The one thing the public was not keen on was murder without explanation. It tended to lead to panic, and no one wanted that.

"Like I said, not much," Lou said providing a rather short brief on the investigation, which wasn't much, though they had learned the boy's name was really Sam Benoit and like the rumours going around town, he had in fact, attended Western University. "You have any thoughts on where we can start?"

"Well…it's not much to go on," Cliff said reluctantly. He continued, however, before Lou could interject. "But you need to figure out why the kid was here in the first place. Out of everywhere he could have died, it was in St. Marys. So, what was he doing here? If you're going to get rid of a body, you wouldn't do it in a town with a few thousand people. But they did. So, they are either stupid, or sending a message to other people. Let's assume they aren't stupid. What are they trying to say?"

Lou remained quiet, but looked like she was ready to burst with questions.

"Say it," Cliff insisted.

"You're making this sound like it was some sort of hit," Lou said, her brows furrowed.

"You don't think it is?"

"What would anyone possibly want to kill over in St. Marys?"

"That's the million-dollar question. How does a PhD student from Western end up dead here? What was he studying?" Cliff asked.

Lou pulled out a little black book and flipped through the pages. "Civil engineering. He was apparently in the middle of his thesis, 'Sustainable growth practices in rural communities,'" Lou added, still reading off the page. "According to his professor, he was looking at various new green and sustainable practices for small communities to optimize their smaller budgets."

Cliff thought about that for a moment. "So, a PhD student, who is trying to understand how to build better practices, ends up in a small town that is currently in the process of bidding on a public service contract. That feels like it shouldn't be a coincidence."

"Wait, what? How do you know that?" Lou asked.

"I saw something about it in the paper this morning. It was something about a new bid...I didn't really get a chance to read it," Cliff admitted.

"What's this about the paper?" said a voice from behind them.

Both Cliff and Lou turned sharply to see Jan standing there holding a brown paper bag and a coffee.

"Nothing," Lou said sharply. "What are you doing here?" She

sounded more aggressive than Cliff thought necessary.

"Even lowly journalists need to eat," Jan said, waving the brown bag. "What were you saying about the paper?" he asked again.

Lou looked as if she was going to make another snappy comment, but Cliff jumped in.

"The article about the new bid for the town works. Did you write that?" Cliff asked, and Jan shot him a shy smile.

"It's not my best work, but it's what they tasked me with."

"What's it about?"

"You didn't read it?" Jan looked disappointed.

"Just skimmed it, but I'm interested about it."

"Why?"

"If you don't want to tell us, I can always just go get a paper and read it for myself," Lou said, making to stand up.

"Wait, no," Jan protested "What do you want to know?"

"What's going on?" Cliff asked.

"Well, not much. Typically, the entire thing is boring. Every five years, the town puts out offers for bids on all town construction. You know, maintenance on roads, parks, new town buildings, all of it. It always goes to Wilder and Sons. They're local, and they put in a great deal every time. But this year, a new group out of London have put a bid in. They're competitive, and they're offering to save the town money with new green practices."

Cliff and Lou shared a look. Obviously, Lou had been thinking the same thing as Cliff. A boy with a PhD thesis in sustainability practices ends up dead in a town where a new contractor with similar values is bidding on the town's service contract.

"Why are you two looking at each other like that? Why are you two even talking?"

"Why don't you mind your own business," Lou suggested, standing up to leave. "Thank you for the chat, Cliff. I appreciate it. You've given me a lot to think about," she said before walking away.

"Bye," Jan said sheepishly, but Lou just kept walking without saying a word.

"She doesn't like you," Cliff said, taking a bite of his sandwich.

Jan seemed to take this as an invitation to come and sit beside him, and Cliff immediately regretted saying anything at all.

"I may or may not have used a quote of hers in an article about women in the police force," Jan said, unpacking his own lunch from his bag, which looked to be three tightly wrapped sandwiches, likely peanut butter and jelly, if Cliff had to guess.

"You're a journalist. Seems like that should have been expected." Cliff shrugged.

Jan let out a heavy sigh and continued sullenly, "I got the quote while we were out for wings at the Stag's Head."

"You were on a date?" Cliff said, nearly choking on his most recent bite of Reuben, which, sadly, was almost gone.

Jan gave a sad smile and an almost imperceptible nod.

"Wow, that was stupid" was all Cliff could think of saying.

"So, you going to tell me why you were talking?"

"She wanted to know what it was like working in the city," Cliff lied.

"Come on," Jan said, taking a big bite of his sandwich and chewing loudly as he continued speaking. "You have to give me more than that."

"There is nothing to give." Cliff took the last bite of his sandwich, trying to savour it.

"I'm supposed to believe you two are just a couple of close friends talking about the weather?"

"I'm not here to tell you what you believe." Cliff shrugged.

"Fine. Then what's all this talk about my article? Why would anyone care about who bids on the town maintenance contract? I wrote it, and I barely care. Unless..." Jan paused to either think or just take another bite of his sandwich. Cliff hoped it was the latter. "This also has something to do with the kid's body that was found." He looked at Cliff expectantly, but Cliff was a veteran at playing these games and remained stone-faced, while Jan continued to talk around him. "A kid from the university," Jan continued thoughtfully, before chewing another bite of his sandwich, which was already nearly gone. "A student…PhD in…civil engineering…perhaps with links to the new firm out of London, bidding on the town service contract!" Jan finished excitedly.

Cliff didn't flinch, though he had to admit he was impressed with how quickly this kid, who was currently fingering a glob of peanut butter and jelly off his shirt into his mouth, had got to that conclusion. *Don't judge a book by its cover, I suppose.*

"I'm just an old man who wanted a place to eat his lunch."

"Ohhhh, wow, that is some big news," Jan said rubbing the now-stained shirt as if that would magically make it disappear.

"That's not news, Jan. It's speculation. If you write speculation in your newspaper, then you're no better than someone with an opinion on The Facebook," Cliff said calmly.

"It's just Facebook."

"I don't care," Cliff said "If you think there is something really there, then I suggest you do a little investigating of your own, and I would also suggest you keep me and Lou out of it. Can't imagine that would go over well."

Just then, Cliff caught sight of the two kids he'd seen talking to the bikers at the park, neither of whom looked to be in a good mood. They were having a quietly fierce conversation as they walked through the parking lot behind the opera house.

"Who is that?" Cliff said, pointing to the two boys who'd stopped out in front of a brand new, matte black Ford F-150.

"Who?" Jan looked around before finally landing on the boys Cliff was staring at. "Ummm, looks like Randy Gillis and Marcus Scott.

Randy's dad owns the Ford dealership, obviously." He gestured to the truck. "But I think both boys work up at the dealership detailing cars. Why?"

"No reason. I just saw them earlier and thought I recognized them."

"You haven't lived here for fifty-odd years, and you thought you recognized two seventeen-year-old boys?" Jan asked suspiciously.

"Yes." Cliff made a mental note of the fact that they were seventeen, in case that became important.

"Why won't you share with me?" Jan asked, sounding like a petulant child.

"Hard to trust a guy who takes what he heard on a date and writes about it," Cliff said coolly, causing Jan's cheeks to blush once again.

"I didn't like the way they were treating her. She's a good cop and they have her running around like an errand b— person," Jan said. Cliff's words were obviously painful. "I thought if I let the public know what was happening, it would help. Obviously, I was wrong." His shoulders hunched over.

Cliff put a hand on his back, turning briefly to catch the truck, with oversized tires, rip out of the parking lot.

"You want to try and make it up to her?" Cliff asked, and Jan looked somewhat hopeful. "If you do find any connections in this case, take it to her first, before you print it. If you ever want a chance of having some sort of relationship again with the police, you're going to have to start working *with* them, not against them."

"Are we still talking about Lou?" Jan asked, and Cliff let out a big sigh.

"Yes."

"So does that mean I was right about the connection?" Jan said, shoving at least half a sandwich in his mouth.

"Find out for yourself," Cliff said, getting up from the bench.

"Where are you going?" Jan asked.

"For a walk," Cliff said, turning to press a hand to Jan's shoulder as he was about to stand up. "Alone," he added, giving Jan a comforting pat. "I've had enough bonding for one day."

Cliff turned to walk down the path. He didn't know where he was going, but he knew he needed to get away and think. *What in the world was going on in this town?*

8

If Cliff thought the rest of his afternoon would go by without any further interruptions, he was sadly mistaken. He'd found himself on a rather turned-around loop, wandering back up the path from the tennis courts, and back to where he'd begun his journey downtown.

He was attempting to find his way back to the Grand Trunk Trail, which he'd overheard from some passersby was now a "nice little walking trail." He strolled that way and passed the craft shop, which he now knew to be Carol's Crafts. As he approached the front door, he caught a glimpse of Bunty stepping outside, her arms filled with bags of yarn and various other craft supplies.

"Bunty," Cliff called out, then discovered she wasn't alone. Behind her was the one person Cliff had wished he'd never see again, the one face in town that had pushed him away in the first place.

Annie Price walked out behind her younger sister, smiling, her own bags draped over her arms. They were both laughing. That was until Bunty, and then Annie, noticed Cliff mere feet away from them.

"Cliff?" Annie said, her face awash with confusion and another emotion Cliff couldn't make out, but he hoped was *slight joy*.

"Annie… Hi," Cliff said, unable to stop himself from fidgeting with his shirt.

"What are you doing here?" she said.

She regained her composure quicker than Cliff ever could. He was still bobbling around as if unable to decide what foot he should be standing on. *What am I supposed to do with my hands? Do I go in for a hug? How much time has passed?*

"Cliff is the newest resident at the Limestone Manor," Bunty said, coming in for the rescue.

"Really?" Annie said half curious, half surprised.

"Silly name, the Limestone Manor," Cliff said. The words seemed to bulldoze out of his mouth.

"Because it's yellow brick," Annie said with a chuckle. "I agree. Then again, Hans was always a joker."

"Yes."

"I think it's funny," Bunty said almost imperceptibly.

"Of course, you do." Annie said with another chuckle, which caused Bunty to tuck back into herself.

"I'm not sure if I'll be staying or not," Cliff said, as he shoved a sweaty palm in his pocket, suddenly feeling like he was a teenager again, which was a period of his life that he'd hated.

"You're not?" Bunty asked. Cliff thought maybe she looked disappointed.

"Cliff's a big city guy now, Bunty. Probably doesn't have time for us country bumkins," Annie said with a grin.

"No, that's not it. It's just…" Cliff started, but he neither knew how to end the sentence nor continue his train of thought. This exact moment had been one of the reasons he never wanted to return to town. He hated the idea that he might one day find himself in front of Annabelle Price, and as it had been when he was a young man, have no idea what he should say to her.

He wished he could tell her she'd made the biggest mistake of her life the day he left, that their life would have been so different if she'd only shown up. He wanted to ask her what had happened, why she didn't even have the decency to say goodbye.

These were all things he wanted to say to her. Instead, he stood there feeling like a deer in headlights and staring dumbly. And he would have continued that way if it weren't for the thunderous roar of the Crimson Serpents barreling down the street. Even if he could have said anything, the combined noise of twenty-plus, eight-cylinder engines from the Harleys, grouped together, would have made it impossible.

He'd never been so grateful for a gang of bikers in his life. That is until he saw the woman sitting on the back of Hurley's bike. Cliff hadn't really noticed her before. He'd been too preoccupied with Hurley talking to the two kids to really care about anyone else. But now, as Cliff embraced the sudden respite from this now very awkward encounter, he saw her clear as day.

There was nothing particularly unique about the woman. She was in her midforties with thick, curly red hair that poked out from under her helmet. She hid behind a pair of dark sunglasses and wore a black leather jacket. But it was the t-shirt, exposed underneath the jacket that truly caught Cliff's eye. It was a solid black with a logo across the chest that read "Four Points Ltd." *Where have I heard that name before?*

Cliff ran through the possibilities in his mind. It had been recent, but he couldn't be too sure. It had something to do with St. Marys, so whatever it was, had appeared in the past two days. *Only two days! It feels like I've been here a week!*

The bikers rounded the corner on their way up Queen Street across the new "safer" Victoria Bridge, and Cliff still hadn't put the pieces together. He stood silently for a long moment, and it wasn't until Annie jumped back in that Cliff realized the two women were still staring at him.

"It's just…what?" Annie said, with a look of pure confusion across her face. Even Bunty looked a little worried. It's not always a great sign when people over a certain age seem to just cut out like that, and it was clear to Cliff that they were worried.

Cliff was also worried, not because he was possibly going senile, but because he finally linked the name on the t-shirt. He had seen it in the last two days. In fact, he'd seen it twice today. Four Points Ltd. was the competing construction company Cliff had read about in the paper. The group that had put in the counteroffer for the town service contract. *But why?*

"Cliff?" Bunty asked, sounding worried. "Are you okay?"

"Fine." Cliff gave his head a little shake. "I'm sorry, but I have to go." Cliff took a step away in one direction and then stopped.

"Bunty," Cliff said, turning back to the now-surprised woman. Whether it was his change in tone or the fact that he was speaking directly to her, he didn't know.

"Yes?"

"Where does Jan work?"

"Pardon?"

"Jan, Hans's nephew? I wanted to ask him something."

"*The Town Gazette*," she said softly.

"Wonderful! Thank you." He gave her shoulder a friendly squeeze, and he wondered if maybe she blushed at this. But he didn't have time to think about it as he turned and walked away.

"Cliff?" Bunty called, causing Cliff to spin back around and face her.

"Yes?"

"The *Gazette*'s that way." She pointed in the opposite direction.

Cliff looked around, as if suddenly seeing where he was for the first time. "Of course. Thank you," he said, starting back in the other direction. "Oh." Cliff stopped and faced the two women again. "Great to see you, Annie. Bunty, I guess I'll see you at home." He caught the slightest looks of confusion on their faces as he finally left.

He'd be lying if he wasn't at least a little grateful for the distraction. Suffice it to say that he did not handle the interaction with Annie very well. Not that he ever expected it would go well. At the very least, he hoped he would maintain some composure. But he was fairly certain he had, if not completely, at least *nearly*, embarrassed himself instead. *I would have thought fifty-four years was enough to be able to remain calm.*

He'd have to analyse his failed attempt at small talk later. Right now, he didn't have time to worry about that. He'd had some sort of epiphany. At least it felt like an epiphany. He still wasn't sure what on earth he was looking for, but he hoped perhaps Jan might shed some light on it.

As it happened the *Town Gazette* was a tiny news building tucked away in the far end of the opera house. With only a sign painted across its windows, Cliff wasn't surprised he'd managed to pass without noticing it.

Cliff walked inside. A little bell announced his presence in what he guessed was the main room, which was small by any standard, with only a scattering of desks throughout the building, and a small printing press that Cliff couldn't see, but certainly heard, in the back room.

"Out in a minute," a voice Cliff recognized as Jan's called out from the back room.

A moment later Jan appeared, holding a fresh copy of the paper. "Nothing like a fresh paper hot off the press," he said, flipping out the small newspaper.

"I agree," Cliff said.

"Cliff?" Jan looked first confused but then excited. "You found something."

"How could you possibly know that?" Cliff sighed.

"Well, something tells me you're not in here for a tour of the facility. Which means, you're here to talk to me. Since, from what I can tell, you don't love small talk, my guess is you found something." Jan set the paper down on the table eagerly.

"You know you're not a dumb as you seem," Cliff said with a smile.

"I've got that a lot in my life. Play to underwhelm, and they'll always be impressed." He sat on the edge of one of the desks. "So, what did you find?"

"Nothing." Cliff hesitated. "Well, maybe something. I want you to investigate something for me."

"I'm not here to work for you, Cliff. Not without knowing what it is I'm doing."

"Fair enough, but I don't really know what it is I should be telling you."

"If you're afraid I'm going to write about it in the paper without checking to make sure it's true, then you've got another thing coming," Jan said tapping his nose.

Cliff was worried about that, but that had only been one reason he was hesitant to tell Jan what he'd found. About the woman's shirt.

"It could be dangerous," Cliff said trying to remain calm.

Jan looked at him for a moment, seemingly trying to decipher if he was kidding or not. He obviously assumed it must be a joke, as he buckled over with laughter.

"You've been in the city to long, Cliff. This is St. Marys. Nothing dangerous ever happens here." He picked up the most recent print. The headline read "12 Ducklings Cause Standstill."

"And if you're wondering, all twelve ducklings and their mother made it to the river safely." Jan laughed.

"A body just turned up dead in the river. I think it's fair to say ducks might be the least of your worries."

"So, you did find something." Jan leaned in conspiratorially.

"What do you know about Four Points Ltd?" Cliff asked, narrowing his eyes at Jan, who stood there thinking before he knocked himself on the head with his fist and started rummaging through the desk he'd been using as a stool. It must have been his, as he started pulling out little notepads and sticky notes, before setting them on the already cluttered table. He started skimming the pages until he plucked out the one he was looking for.

"I knew I'd heard it before. It's the new construction company making a play on the town's service contract."

"I thought so. You wrote a little piece about them in your article."

"You read my article?" Jan said sounding pleased.

Cliff ignored him. "What did you learn about them?"

"Nothing really. I didn't do much digging. The contract has gone to Wilder and Sons for the last, I don't know, forty years. I don't see why they would change it now."

"I thought you said they were competitive?" Cliff asked.

"They are. But this is still St. Marys. Too many people in town rely on the contract. They employee a lot of people."

"So, you're absolutely sure, one hundred precent, that there is no way that Four Points Ltd. could take the contract in town?"

"Well, nothing is ever one hundred precent, but I think it is highly unlikely. Next to Wilder and Son's pulling out." Jans laughed. "Which would be wild."

Cliff thought about it for a moment, and then he relaxed a little, Jan was, of course, right. If there was any connection, it was probably irrelevant. But Cliff had never heard of the Crimson Serpents doing anything on speculation.

"You don't look so convinced," Jan said, standing to his full height, which was much taller than Cliff.

"Do some digging into Four Points and see what you find."

"Are you going to tell me why?"

"No. Not yet."

"Okay, but if we find anything, I'm the one who gets to write about it!" Jan said excitedly.

Cliff looked around the empty room. "You're not the only person working here, are you?"

"Of course not, we have a high school intern and Rob."

"Who's Rob?"

"Rob runs the paper. He's just up at his cottage for a few days."

"Must be nice to be Rob." Cliff smiled. "But before you write about anything, I want you to talk to me about it first, deal?" Cliff said, his tone more serious now.

"You know it would be easier to find what I'm looking for if you gave me some hints." Jan lifted his brow.

"Something tells me, if there is anything to find, you won't have any trouble finding it." Cliff sighed. He knew what it was like when gangs got involved. Usually, they were less like a scalpel and more like a hammer, simply smashing their way through whatever obstacles were before them.

After leaving the newspaper office, to Cliff's surprise, he only had minor issues finding his way back to the manor. Even though it had been a long time since he'd been in town, it was amazing what the mind could remember. Sure, things were different, but how much different could a couple of one-hundred-and-fifty-year-old churches be on a conveniently marked street? Once he found the church, it was just a matter of walking around it.

It wasn't the most efficient way, by any means, but it did give him the luxury of thinking about everything that had happened that day, which he concluded was a great deal. So much, in fact, that by the time he got home, he was ready for bed.

"Finally come to help with the garden?" Mrs. Chen called out as Cliff walked up the drive. She'd been tucked behind a rather nice rose bush with a pair of pruning shears, a woven basket on her arm.

"Mrs. Chen! I'm so sorry, I got distracted today and completely forgot about my offer to help with the garden," Cliff said with a yawn.

"Garden will still be here when you do come," she said stepping out from behind the bush to walk towards him. He could now see the woven basket was filled with various flowers. "The garden will still be here after we're all gone."

Cliff was too tired to tell if that was some sort of joke or not.

"I suppose you're right," Cliff said, making his way towards the front door, with Mrs. Chen now by his side.

She'd clearly been in the garden most of the day. Her yellow coveralls were now nearly brown, along with her little boots and orange gloves. Only her large, wide-brimmed hat seemed to be clear of any of the day's work.

"What are you doing with those?" Cliff asked, nodding to the basket of flowers.

"Don't be an idiot. I hear you're a great detective. You can't detect what I do with the flowers?" Mrs. Chen said without hint of a sarcasm. "Maybe not so good of a detective." She eyed him up and down, only letting out the slyest of smiles to let Cliff know she might be kidding.

Cliff did kind of feel like a fool. He'd seen numerous vases around the house, all filled with an assortment of flowers, and he never once put those two together.

He gave Mrs. Chen an exaggerated *ahhh* look. "Of course."

"It's important to keep your eyes open. You never know what you are missing," Mrs. Chen said, as she looked over at a particularly robust set of begonias that had bloomed just under the library window.

When he followed her gaze, he saw Bunty sitting in what Cliff assumed must be her regular spot, focused on whatever project she was working on. She looked up briefly and spotted Cliff and Mrs. Chen. She gave them both a warm smile before getting back down to work.

"Do you like living here?" Cliff asked out of the blue. He wasn't sure why, but he got the impression Mrs. Chen was not one to beat about the bush, and he could use the honesty right now.

If she was thrown by the question, it didn't show. She did, however, appear to think about it very deeply. After a few moments, they reached the door, and Cliff began to wonder if she'd even heard the question in the first place. Just as he was about to give up on getting an answer, she spoke, one hand on the doorknob and the other holding the basket of flowers as she turned to look up at him.

"Is it the best? No. But it is the best right now." She turned the knob and stepped inside.

Cliff followed her into the house, and as he let her words sink in, he was bombarded with the pleasant aroma of a spicy dish.

"Is that Thai green curry?" he asked, getting a head tilt from Mrs. Chen. Cliff knew the smell well. He'd lived around the corner from a Thai restaurant in Toronto and had to walk by it twice a day, to and from work, for many years.

"You have quite the nose," she said. "Yes, it's curry night. Though I warn you, Gerald tends to make it spicy."

Of course, it was Gerald cooking. It seemed to be one of the few things he actually enjoyed. Cliff had planned on going up to bed. After all, today had been extremely long. But how could he resist such a brilliant smell? He held onto a little hope that Gerald wouldn't still be angry about losing the bowls match today. Though something in the back of Cliff's mind worried that he wouldn't forget the loss so quickly.

As it turned out, Cliff was wrong. Gerald gave him about as much attention as he had on any other occasion. Gerald was all too happy to sit down and enjoy his meal without any real conversation with anyone.

Cliff, as well, remained quiet, though not for a lack of conversation, as he sat next to Kitty and Sol for the evening. It was because, on more than one occasion, he threatened to faceplant into his curry from sheer exhaustion. So, it was no surprise, when he finally did make it up the stairs shortly after dinner, that he'd barely hit the bed before he fell asleep.

9

Cliff woke early the next day, or at least he thought six thirty was early. But as it had been the day before, everyone in the house appeared to also be early risers. Downstairs, Cliff found Kitty and Sol sitting in the living room, reading the morning paper and sharing a coffee. Bunty was knitting the sleeve of the same rather large-looking sweater, certainly not something he'd expect to fit the petite woman, unless she enjoyed swimming in bulky fabric. He wasn't about to ask her about it, still feeling embarrassed about their encounter the day before.

He knew it was ridiculous to be feeling like that. That scenario had been bound to happen at some point. He just wished he'd handled it a little better. Instead, he quietly ducked into the kitchen.

Pouring himself a cup of coffee, Cliff heard a light buzzing sound coming from a door just off the kitchen. He assumed it was another closet, but when he opened it up the sound increased, and the now-open door revealed a narrow set of stairs leading downward to what Cliff assumed was the basement. His curiosity got the better of him when he saw the light on, so he walked slowly down the steep, curved stairway. At the bottom was a small hall with doors on either side.

Cliff, now closer to the source, could easily make out the sound of a saw cutting through wood. He walked cautiously through a set of hanging, thick plastic strips, which must be used to dampen the sound and prevent dust from travelling out of what Cliff now saw was a well-facilitated workshop.

Hans was lifting a three foot by eight foot plank of hardwood up onto a table.

"Need help?" Cliff asked, though it was clear, despite the man's age, he had no difficulty lifting the wood on his own.

"Cliff!" Hans said loudly. "I hope the saws aren't too loud. Most of the house doesn't mind…" He took out one of his ear plugs and lowered his voice. "On account of them all being deaf." He laughed heartedly.

"No," Cliff said, suppressing a chuckle. "I just had no idea this was down here."

"Ya. It is my own personal workspace. Although anyone can use it, no one does." He shrugged.

"So, you like bowls?" Cliff said reaching for a partially finished wooden bowl sitting on a side table.

"Yes, though I admit I may need to expand my repertoire." Hans laughed again.

"They are really good," Cliff said, coming over to inspect the wood plank as he took a sip of coffee. He quickly covered the top with his hand as he caught sight of all the dust in the air.

"It was for fun. Everyone needs to do something. And when you have no more fields to plant, and you wake up at four…well, you find yourself with lots of time." Hans shrugged.

"Four a.m.? Every morning?" Cliff shouldn't have been surprised by Hans's early mornings, but he was still a little taken aback.

Hans nodded as he manoeuvred the large wood on the table. "You remember how to use all this stuff?" Hans asked, gesturing around the wood shop.

"I'll admit it's been a long time since I made a birdhouse," Cliff mused.

"It's like riding a bike."

"If the bike could cut off your hand." Cliff laughed.

Hans tossed a hand off in Cliff's direction as if to say, "Don't be ridiculous." Though, if Cliff recalled correctly, more than one of his classmates had lost at least a couple of fingers in those days.

"I can teach you, if you want. It would be nice to have someone else use them." Hans patted the table saw affectionately.

"Between you and Mrs. Chen, I'll be a master at hobbies."

"Hobbies keep us young, Cliff," Hans said, running his hand along the face of the wood plank. "Speaking of hobbies, I'm happy to see Gerald invited you out to lawn bowl yesterday."

"I would hardly say he invited me. I had no idea what I was doing."

"He told me that too." Hans laughed. "But you managed to take one from Steve and Leonard, and they're no spring chickens."

"I suppose that's alright, though I can't imagine Gerald inviting me back out to play anytime soon."

"Give him time. He has a difficult time warming up to people."

"I'm not sure how much time we'll have," Cliff said, removing his hand from the top of the cup and taking another sip of coffee.

"Aww, so you're not sure if you want to stay." The big man's shoulders slumped just a little.

"No. I'm not," Cliff said honestly. "I'll admit it has its advantages. The food is a good touch."

"Gerald is brilliant in the kitchen."

"He is. But this town…it's hard to be back."

"I see. Bunty told me you ran into her and Annie at crafts store yesterday. She also told me you seemed…off."

"I was, and I admit, seeing her threw me into somewhat of a spiral. But if I was being weird, it was because of everything I saw."

"Yes, seeing an old fling—"

"No, not that. And she wasn't just a fling," Cliff said, ready to argue, but deciding against it. "There's something weird going on in town."

Hans narrowed his eyes. "How so?"

"The body found in the river, the bikers—"

"Bikers?"

"Yeah, Steve said yesterday they'd been coming to St. Marys for a while now. These guys are not just any old bikers out for a Sunday drive. They're dangerous," Cliff said.

"Dangerous? Cliff, do you think maybe you're just bored here? I mean, this is St. Marys."

"So, everyone keeps saying. But even Jan agrees there's something going on." Cliff watched Hans's face break into a smile.

"Jan thinks everything is a big case. A few years ago, he wrote a piece about how the Journeyman's annual casino night was rigged so no one would be able to beat the house."

"Was he right?"

"No. At least, no more than any other casino." Hans laughed. "He's a smart boy and a great writer, but if you let him get into your head, he will fill it up with nonsense."

"I'm not so sure he's not onto something this time." Cliff turned away from his friend.

"Well, it's not like it matters."

"What's that supposed to mean?"

"Didn't you just say you're going to leave?"

"I did, but not tomorrow."

"Well, you know you need to sign the papers by Sunday, right? The one that agrees to the six-month trial period."

"Yes, then I have to sign to own the house. I remember the deal," Cliff said coolly. "I remember very well how you lied to get me to come stay in this place."

"No lies."

"Just half-truths."

"I am old. I never see you, my friend. Can you blame an old man for trying to get a few final years with one of his oldest friends?" Hans asked.

"You're a real piece of work, you know." Cliff shook his head, and Hans only laughed. "For the record, I think you're wrong about Jan." Cliff turned to head back upstairs.

"That's okay with me. Like I said, everyone needs a hobby, and if thinking there's some mystery for you to solve in town keeps you here, I am thrilled by it. It's boredom that will kill us."

"I'm not bored, Hans. I like retirement."

"So, do I. But it doesn't mean we can't get bored." Hans laughed as Cliff walked back through the plastic curtains and made his way upstairs.

Is all this just because I'm bored?

It was a fair question, but deep down, Cliff knew that wasn't the case. The things he saw yesterday couldn't be a coincidence, but he needed to know more about what was going on. And Cliff knew exactly where to look next.

Unfortunately, Cliff still had to fill the majority of his day, which was relatively uneventful. He spent most of it around the house, trying to avoid Bunty, and trying to get a moment alone with Sol, which was much harder than he imagined. It seemed he and Kitty were pretty inseparable. Luckily, he still had his invite with him to the creamery tonight. For the next part of Cliff's plan to work, he needed to talk to Sol's friends too.

Cliff arrived at the creamery shortly after five to find Sol and two other larger men on stools, sidled up to the bar. The three men sat in a line, with Sol in the middle. At first, none of them noticed Cliff as he took a seat at one of the open stools beside Sol's friend, who was charismatically telling a funny story. At least Cliff surmised it as funny by the way the other two men were laughing.

"Cliff! You made it," Sol said, noticing Cliff between final chuckles. Cliff heard a little surprise in the man's voice. *Maybe he's invited the entire house, and I'm the first to actually come?*

"Of course, thanks for inviting me. Sorry, I'm a little late. Haven't quite figured out the timing of the walk down. Combination of old knowledge with an old body," Cliff joked.

"This is Callum," Sol said, indicating the very tanned-looking man next to Cliff, whose arms were covered with tattoos.

Buried in the middle of the menagerie of Americana tattoos, Cliff recognized the Canadian Armed Forces symbol on his forearm. The oval-shaped tattoo was layered with an eagle and two swords crossed like an X, both atop a large anchor. The outer ring was horseshoed by ten maples leaves and finally topped with the Sovereign's Orb. Cliff had seen many of these in his days in the Toronto Police Department, and like those men, Callum's bald head and thick nose, left no question to Cliff he was tough.

"Nice to meet you," he said, with a thin smile as he put out a hand for Cliff to shake.

"Nice to meet you too," Cliff offered.

"This is Pete," Sol said, gesturing to the other man on his right.

Unlike Callum, Pete, had very gentle eyes and an inviting smile, nearly hidden beneath a massive beard. He was a large, round man, whose portly belly appeared to keep him seated further back from the bar than his companions.

"Nice to meet you, Pete."

"What can I get you?" asked a short, grey-haired man from behind the bar.

Cliff looked down the bar and spotted the three men all drinking the same thing. He caught the top part of what looked like a partially peeled Old Vienna label. Not that it mattered to him.

"I'll have what they're having," Cliff said absently. He'd been in enough situations in his life to know that, when you are already isolated in a group, as the outsider, it's best to fit in. Especially true when you were trying to get information out of someone.

A moment later, the bartender returned with a perspiring OV.

"Here you are." He slid the long-necked bottle across the bar top.

"Cheers!" Cliff said, holding his bottle towards the three men.

Each one returned the gesture with varying enthusiasm, his neighbour Callum being the least interested.

"So, Sol says you were a cop in Toronto?" Pete asked politely, and Cliff nodded as he took a sip from his bottle.

"I've never been a big fan of cops," Callum said, tilting his head towards Cliff, which caused Cliff to pause. Usually, the only people who didn't like cops were people who had had run-ins with bad ones or had been arrested for one reason or another.

"Not all cops deserve to have fans," Cliff said with a shrug. During his career, he'd definitely witnessed cops doing things he found to be less reputable, which certainly did little to paint the career in a good light.

"Fair enough," Callum said with a smirk and an approving nod.

"I was a detective for most of my career. Handled murders, robberies, that sort of stuff." Cliff took another swig of his beer, and when he looked back, he noticed he had more of the men's attention now.

"Lots of murders in Toronto?" Callum asked, which got a punch in the arm from Sol.

"You can't just ask a man about murders," Sol said, though he himself looked eager for a reply.

Cliff laughed. "It's fine. Yes. But, then again, any city in the world with over 2.5 million people is bound to have a couple. Get that many people crammed into such a small place, it's inevitable," Cliff said, in the cavalier way only a man who'd dealt with hundreds of deaths would.

"Whereas we get one, and the whole town seems to quiver." Callum laughed coldly as he took another swig.

"When you don't get them, it's terrifying," Pete said, his brow raised.

"So, you don't get them often?" Cliff asked.

The three men laughed.

"No," Sol said simply.

"Maybe, one every fifteen or so years. *Maybe*," Pete added.

"Round here, it's more deaths from idiot drunks, motorcycle accidents, and bad weather," Callum said. "Not sure if they still do it, but my son told me, when he was at his first day of high school up there at DCVI, the teachers sat them all down and gave them a little speech. It was quick and dirty. They just had them look around at the hundred or so people around them and told them, *statistically one of you will die before you graduate, due to drugs or alcohol.*"

"Where they right?" Cliff asked sombrely.

"Yep. Three of them, poor kids."

"When things happen here, everyone feels it. Which is why everyone is so on edge about this murder." Pete glanced over at Cliff, as if he might shed some light on the situation.

"Doesn't help the police don't know why it happened. Kitty says the talk around town is that people are afraid they'll be next."

"And Kitty certainly knows the talk around town." Callum said, drawing chuckles from Sol and Pete. Callum finished his beer and another appeared in front of him without him even asking.

"Kitty's got her finger on the pulse of this town like no one else," Pete said, finishing his own beer and receiving the same treatment from the bartender.

"She certainly does," Sol said almost reverently.

"So, Cliff, you liking being back in town? Sol told us you used to live here?" Pete asked.

"I did." Cliff took a quick swig of his beer. He hoped he wouldn't need to answer too many questions about his time in town, especially about why he left.

"Which school were you at?" Pete asked. "I was wondering if maybe we went to school together."

Cliff looked at the other men at the bar and wondered how old they were.

"I went to St. Marys Collegiate. But I think I might be a touch older then you three," Cliff said with a smile. "I only came back for a couple years after going to Queen's before I finally headed off to Toronto for good. So, I wouldn't be surprised if we didn't get a chance to cross paths."

"No siblings then?" Sol asked.

Cliff went silent for a moment. It had been some time since he thought about his brother, Davy. He was four years older than Cliff, and he'd been one of those who were unfortunate enough to go to Europe and never make it back.

"Not anymore," Cliff finally said, soberly. "But he worked at the Grill for a while before he got shipped out." This received a general nod of understanding from the men around the table, who each had likely known someone in their own family who'd suffered a similar fate.

Cliff knew that, somewhere in town, there was a memorial statue to all those from town who lost their lives during the war. He'd received an email from someone in the town at some point, letting him know that David "Davy" Shaw would be on the monument. Cliff couldn't bring himself to go to the ceremony, even though he was the only surviving member of his family. He'd tried to tell himself it was because of work, and the fact that he would be busy, since he volunteered every year to help man the Remembrance Day ceremony in Toronto. But the truth was, he was a coward land didn't want to relive those particularly difficult times in his life.

Davy's death had changed his parents. After his death, they'd become cold and distant, and there was a part of Cliff that had never forgiven his brother for lying about his age to enlist the way he had. Like he had somehow abandoned him. He was only seventeen when he died.

"I remember running off to the Grill almost every day for a Cherry Coke," Callum said softly. "You guys remember that place." The other two nodded. Even the bartender, standing across from them wiping down his glass, had an approving smile on his face.

"There may not have been much to do in this town, but it was sure enough that you would find everyone at that place," Sol said with a smile.

"Or up at Gardner's getting a footlong," Pete said with a grin as he patted his belly.

"At least Gardner's is still a diner and not a bank," Cliff said with a laugh, having eaten breakfast there when he first arrived. "It would appear there are a couple of those in town now."

"Banks and pizza places," Callum said, and the four men began to laugh.

For the next hour, the four of them reminisced about all the ways the town had changed. Cliff eagerly brought up the upgrades to the Victoria Bridge and was vindicated by their collective agreement that it was certainly "less fun," as they laughed, telling stories about how they'd each nearly been hit crossing the bridge at some point in their youths.

Cliff enjoyed the banter. When he'd still lived here, the difference of the six years he'd found out was between them would have felt huge. Now, it was almost meaningless. At this point in time, they were simply "less old."

Cliff had started to enjoy himself so much that he nearly forgot the reason he wanted to come in the first place. He had questions for these men, or at least one of them, but he didn't know which one that was. According to Sol, all three of them had worked at the same dealership as mechanics, and either Callum or Pete could still be working as a driver at the dealership.

"Sol tells me one of you is still working?" Cliff asked delicately during a natural lull in the conversation.

It was Pete who raised his glass. "Although I hardly call driving people around work." Pete laughed. "More or less gives me some time to talk with people during the day and keeps me busy."

"Not a bad gig, if you ask me," Sol said with a note of jealousy in his voice.

"You say that now, but lately, it's been a bit of a nightmare. Almost not worth dealing with," Pete said simply.

"Come on! They're not still hung up on all that joyriding nonsense, are they, Pete?" Callum said, shaking his head. "I mean, come on, the things we used to do in the shop after hours weren't much different."

"It was a *little* different," Sol interrupted. "We never let it get that far."

"*Pfft.*" Callum huffed with a wave of his hand.

Cliff kept the fact that he'd heard about the joyriding from Kitty yesterday morning to himself. He assumed Sol, from the expression on his face, likely wasn't supposed to tell anyone about it. Cliff reassured Sol with a subtle nod, which Sol returned in appreciation.

"Care to fill me in, fellas?" Cliff asked hesitantly, and the other three men looked cautiously at each other, as if they had forgotten anyone else was with them.

"This is all fairly hush-hush, Cliff," Pete said, lowering his voice slightly.

"Mum's the word," Cliff replied with a nod. Whatever was happening there wasn't any of his business. Well, actually, nothing happening in this town was any of his business, but since he'd been dragged into it at every turn, he couldn't help but feel like this particular story had something to do with it all. Cliff told himself that, if it did, it might answer some other questions he had, and if it didn't, it would at least be a good story. *Hopefully.*

The three men shared another look before Sol gave Pete a little nod, and Callum simply shrugged as if he didn't care either way. Given what Cliff had found out about the man in the past hour, he'd say that was closer to the case.

"Well, about a week ago, the owner up there at Gillis Auto realized that some of the cars in the lot were building up miles they shouldn't have. I guess one of the sales reps noticed it when they went to sell one of the new F-150s, and the mileage on the truck was off by 400 km."

"That's a lot?" Cliff jumped in.

"It is when the truck was supposed to be sitting on the lot for the past month or so. Typically, a new car might have two or three hundred kilometres on it. Basically, the amount it takes to go from the manufacturing floor, onto the trains, and then to the dealership. It varies, but more or less, there shouldn't be that much distance on it. And the distance definitely shouldn't change when it's parked on the lot. We have test vehicles for that."

"So, you have specific cars you use for testing?" Cliff asked.

"Yes. But those need to be tracked. So, every time one is taken out, whoever takes it has to mark down how far they took it." Pete sipped his beer, and Cliff felt as though he was beginning to piece together the story.

"So, if someone wanted to, say, 'borrow' a car, taking out one of the test cars wouldn't work, because whoever was in the car next would know that the car had been taken, and since it's used every day or two, it would be recognized quickly."

"Correct." Pete finished his beer and gave the bartender a nod for a fresh one.

"So, someone at the dealership has been borrowing a car to go for joyrides?" Cliff said, getting an approving nod from Pete.

"Not bad, Detective."

"This isn't someone's first rodeo." Callum laughed.

Cliff was also relieved that, had he not heard any of this from Kitty, he still would have pieced it together.

"So, a couple of cars get taken out. What's the big deal?" Cliff said with a shrug.

This got a similar shrug from Callum. "That's what I've been saying," he confirmed with a grin.

"Taking a car out for a joyride is one thing," Pete said, his voice lowering a little more so that Cliff had to strain his ears to hear anything. *Damn I hate getting old!*

"But when they went through the lot and checked all the cars, it looks like they racked up close to 2000 kilometres. That's like driving to Halifax for Christ's sake," Pete said with a laugh. "Anyways, a couple of the kids who worked detailing the cars, I guess, had found out how to access the safe where the keys were kept. So, they figured they'd help themselves to some test drives of their own."

"More like test road trips," Sol mused.

"What happened to the kids?" Cliff asked.

"Not sure yet. As far as I can tell, they've changed the codes on the safe, and the kids are still detailing cars. My guess is they're working off the debt they have from taking the cars," Pete said with a grin.

"Doesn't hurt that the kid they think is the mastermind is the owner's son." Callum chuckled. "Can't say the whole ordeal has been too hard on him. He still drives around like a little pissant in that new F-150. Hard to believe his dad's that upset."

That was the information Cliff needed to confirm his pervious suspicions from the bridge.

"What's the kid's name?" Cliff asked, hoping it didn't sound too intrusive.

"Randy Gillis," Sol said casually. "I think he's in his last year up there at DCVI."

"So, what that makes him sixteen, seventeen years old?" Cliff asked, as his mind scrolled through all of the information he was gathering in his head.

He looked up to find the three men looking at him.

"It would explain why they aren't pressing charges or anything. Just some kids being kids, I imagine," he said with a laugh, and the other three men began to laugh as well.

"Reminds me of the time we got that new '68 GTO in, and a couple of the boys in the shop took it out for a little spin out through Lover's Lane. Boy, did that puppy fly," Callum reminisced.

The rest of the night was filled with stories of how different the rules were now compared to back then, and how you couldn't get away with half the things now that they did back in the day.

Cliff threw in a couple of his—equally hilarious, though slightly less illegal—tales of being on the force in Toronto, but his mind continued running through the information he'd learned about the dealership and what it all might mean. The other guys at the bar seemed convinced it was a couple of kids being kids. But the distance they travelled, and the amount of effort they put into not getting caught, gave Cliff pause. *What exactly are you kids doing?*

10

It had been some time since Cliff had woken up with any sort of hangover, but he did after his night out with Sol and his friends. He'd spent the entirety of the next morning trying to feel normal again, only stepping out of his room for necessities, like water, food, and the occasional bathroom break.

Sol, on the other hand, seemed completely normal. Cliff silently cursed the younger man when he saw him up in the morning as always, drinking his coffee and reading the paper with Kitty.

"Well, if it isn't our new famous resident, right here in the flesh." Kitty smiled at him, and Cliff was too tired and had too much of a headache to try and work out what she could be referring to.

"Thank you," Cliff said, wishing he could blink away the pressure in his forehead.

Other than that, and a little giggle, Kitty didn't say anything else. She simply shook her head at him and watched, amused, as Cliff slugged around the room.

Cliff would have happily stayed in bed all day had the guys from the moving company not shown up that afternoon to drop off his things. Cliff was appreciative of the two young men who lugged three large, black and yellow plastic totes up the stairs, along with an old wooden chest, which had been given to him by his parents as a gift when he left town the first time.

One particular box was very unforgiving, even for two massive, rugby players, who were forced to manoeuvre their way up two sets of narrow staircases. Cliff apologized more than once, rubbing his own head, as he tried to relieve the headache, which had started to form again.

But with a couple small curses and a generous tip, the boys were gone, Cliff managing to get one of their business cards before they left. Although he didn't tell them all that work might be for naught, since he was unsure if he would be packing up and leaving again the following week.

"Not a lot of stuff," Bunty said after the boys left and Cliff had collapsed in one of the library chairs across from where Bunty spent her mornings.

"No," Cliff said with a sigh. "I've never been one to collect or hold onto things."

"Did you move often?" she said.

"No. I just never really get attached to things, I guess. Never saw a point in filling the house with stuff I wouldn't use."

"You must have used more than four boxes. I'm not sure my clothes would even fit in what you brought with you." Bunty giggled. It was soft and very brief, then her face returned to the normal gentle smile she usually wore.

"I'm sure you look a lot more beautiful in your clothes then I do," Cliff said, then felt a sudden rush of embarrassment wash over him. He was about to say more, when he caught sight of the redness in Bunty's cheeks. He resisted the urge to fumble through words that would inevitably come out poorly and generally make the whole thing more awkward. Besides, it wasn't an altogether inaccurate comment.

"Books," Cliff said. The word practically tripped out of his mouth, and he received a look of confusion from Bunty, who took a break from her knitting to stare at him. "I've kept the books I find interesting,

I mean."

"What books do you find interesting?" Bunty smiled before continuing working on what appeared to be a sleeve.

"Jeffery Archer, Dickens, some old piano books…" Cliff began to list absently. His brain still not working altogether well. If it had been, he would have never mentioned his piano.

"You play piano?" Bunty asked excitedly.

"No," he said quickly, getting an odd tilt of the head from Bunty. "Well, yes, I suppose, a little. I played when I was a boy."

"But you don't have a piano?" she asked.

"Toronto apartments don't make it easy to keep such luxuries. If I wanted to play, there was a library down the road that would let you use their piano for practice," Cliff said, wringing his hands together nervously. "Needless to say, I don't play the way I used to." Cliff chuckled.

"Nonsense," Bunty said, with more authority than he'd ever heard from her, though it was still marginally more excited than her speaking voice. "You'll have to play sometime." She smiled.

"Tell you what, I'll play, if you'll sing." Cliff grinned. "If I recall, you were quite the singer."

"Deal," Bunty said, her eye never lifting from the knitted hunter green sleeve. "If I sing, you play piano," she added with a devilish nod.

"That seemed too easy."

"Well, I happen to sing every Sunday in the church choir." Bunty laughed, then raised a hand to stop Cliff's protest. "You never said anything about where and when, Mr. Shaw. I'll see you on Sunday. And I expect a piece from you within the week," she said with a curt nod and a thin smile.

"I can't help but feel tricked."

"That's because you were, Mr. Shaw." Bunty glanced up at him. "The piano in the living room is a lovely place to practice." She nodded toward the other room.

"Here I was thinking you were the kind one in the house," Cliff said with a grin as he got up to leave.

Bunty simply smiled as she held up the piece she was working on and gave it a good once-over.

Cliff had opted not to mention that he might, in fact, not be here past Sunday, as that would be the day he would need to decide whether he was staying in the house or not. Which meant, even if he did happen to see Bunty sing in church, there might not be an opportunity for him to play at all. The thought of letting her down like that did sting him a little, though. Maybe he would find time before Sunday to share a piece with her.

Cliff was in such deep thought about this that he barely had time to move as Jan barreled into the house, nearly knocking Cliff over in the process.

"Jan? What on earth?"

"I need to talk to you," he said, out of breath, even though Cliff could see his beat-up old car in the driveway.

"Son, I think you need to work on your stamina."

"Jokes, hahah, funny. I need to talk to you." Jan made his way into the kitchen.

Cliff, on his heels, looked around at some of the other members of the house. Kitty particularly seemed to be very interested in whatever was going on. Her head poked out from around the doorframe, and quickly pulled back when Cliff turned and saw her.

"Firstly," Jan said after Cliff had joined him in the kitchen, "I'm sorry about the article. I am. It wasn't supposed to be printed, but I'd started writing it before we spoke, and Rob must have seen it on my computer and thought he was supposed to edit it. And then, when he finished, it was all a blur, and I'm sorry." Jan's tone suddenly shifted as he appeared to be begging for forgiveness from Cliff.

"You're going to have to slow down and tell me what it is you're talking about, son."

"You're famous, remember!" Kitty called from the other room.

"Yea, that," Jan said, his brows furrowed.

"What in the world is going on here?" Cliff asked.

Jan pulled today's paper out from under his arm. When Cliff opened it up, he saw an image on the front page of him shaking hands with the mayor, the one Jan had taken of him when he stepped off the train. The headline read, "Former Detective Arrives Just in Time to Shed Light on Murder."

"Jan? What is this?" Cliff said pointing at the images.

"It's an article I may or may not have written about you for paper. Which may or may not have been published."

"Well, it was clearly published."

"Correct," Jan said, staring down at the ground. "But I wrote this before you and I had talked. I didn't…"

"It says I arrived just in time, Jan? I was on the train."

"I maybe have taken a few liberties with the facts."

"But it's not true," Cliff said, still reading the article.

"It's not *not* true. Like I said, some of the details might have been embellished." Jan gestured to the paper. "Did I mention I'm sorry, and this was never supposed to be printed? I wrote it on Tuesday after you arrived, and then I forgot to take it out of the edit pile, and Rob ran with it. Did I mention—"

"You're sorry? Yeah, you did." Cliff looked up from the article, shaking his head. "This is not going to go over well, Jan."

"I know, which sucks, because it really ruins the other thing I wanted to tell you." Jan went into the pantry, returning a moment later with some bread and a jar of peanut butter.

"I'm not sure my heart can handle any more surprises."

"Are you sure? 'Cause this one's a doozy!" Jan placed the bread on the counter and started turning the lid of the peanut butter.

"Young man, you better not have the bread on the counter when we have perfectly good plates in this house!" Kitty called from around the corner.

Jan's face went red, and he opened a cupboard and grabbed a plate.

"Wouldn't dream of it, Kitty," Jan said, quickly transferring the bread onto the plate. He took out a knife and began spreading the peanut butter onto the slice of bread. "You know that thing you told me to look into?"

"This might not be the place to talk about this," Cliff cautioned, trying once again to calm the boy, but to no avail.

"You were right. About everything. Well, everything you told me." He pulled a jar of Maple Hill Farm Raspberry Jam out of the fridge and twisted off the top. "At least it looks like you are. Based on what I found since yesterday." He spread jam on the second piece of bread and slapped the two pieces together.

"I don't know what you're talking about," Cliff said, his brows shooting up in a way he hoped screamed *please stop talking, Jan.* He did not.

"You know, the whole bidding stuff," Jan said, his mouth full of food.

Cliff finally gave up and started to drag Jan back out the front door, though the young man seemed very confused by the action. Just as he opened the door to drag Jan out to the driveway, he was stopped suddenly by a uniformed Lou, whose mid-knock nearly slammed right into Cliff's face.

"I'm sorr— You!" she said, looking past Cliff at Jan, his mouth full of peanut butter and jam sandwich.

"'ou!" Jan said. His eyes narrowed in on Lou, though he was unable to make intelligible words.

"What's he doing here?" Lou asked.

"What are *you* doing here?" Cliff asked.

"Ya, what'r you—"

"Shut up, Jan." Cliff dragged him outside and pulled Lou along with them. He moved around to the back garden and took a quick look around to see if Mrs. Chen was up working already, but he couldn't see her.

"Would you care to tell me why you're talking to a journalist?" Lou chided.

"First of all, his grandfather lives here."

Jan looked as though he might say something, but Cliff held up a finger to stop him.

"Second, I am a citizen of this town. I can speak freely with anyone. Besides, he might have information you'll find helpful," Cliff said.

Jan choked down the bite of PB&J he was working through and protested. "Why would I do that?"

"He's an idiot. What could he possibly have found?" asked Lou.

"Oh, really. I'm the idiot?"

"Yes," Lou said, crossing her arms.

"Well, maybe *you* are."

"Really? That's the best you've got?"

"All right, stop!" Cliff snapped. "Right now, I think you're both idiots. This is a murder investigation, not a who-got-pulled-over-at-the-ride program." Referencing the tactic used by local police to catch impaired drivers, as Cliff gestured for them both to sit in the large double-glider swing chair, forcing them to sit side by side, while he took the bench across from them, facing them like a teacher in the schoolyard.

Jan began to absently rock the entire swing with one leg, never once looking at Lou.

"Can we please put this aside for now, and you can both tell me why you're here?" Cliff asked. He had to put both hands up this time to stop them both from jumping in. "Keep in mind, whatever one of you was going to tell me, I planned on telling the other anyway. And I'm old, so this saves me some precious time."

"You know I can't talk about the investigation with him," Lou said, hitching a thumb toward Jan.

"Jan," Cliff said, getting the kid's attention.

"Yeah," he grumbled as he took another bite of his sandwich.

"My God, you are a child," Lou said.

Jan narrowed his eyes and stuck out his tongue in defiance.

"Look, Jan. I'll let you stay here, but you have to promise that you won't write about any of this until we say you can," Cliff said, his tone serious.

"How is that fair?"

"It's not. But you can't print anything until we're sure about what's going on, and we're confident the OPP is ready to act on it. If you do anything before that, you risk ruining the investigation, or worse, getting someone hurt," Cliff said.

"Why would anyone get hurt?" Lou said cautiously, looking now between Cliff and Jan. "Why would anyone get hurt?"

"What did you find out about the victim and other bidder for the town service contract?" Cliff asked Lou hesitantly.

"Nothing," Lou replied. "As far as anyone could tell me, he had no affiliation whatsoever with the company, Four Points Ltd."

"If you could even call it a company," Jan scoffed.

"What do you mean?" Lou said, shooting him an icy glare.

"We *all* think there is more to this than it appears, so let's just take a deep breath and start sharing what we know," Cliff said calmly.

"I don't want to—" both Lou and Jan chimed in at the same time.

"He's a reporter!"

"She's a cop!"

"I'll go first," Cliff said raising his hands. He proceeded to tell Jan about how he and Lou had figured there must be some connection between Sam Benoit and the new bidder for the contract, and that Lou was working on discovering what it was.

Next, he told Lou about the biker gang and how he'd spotted one of the women on the back of the bike wearing a Four Points Ltd shirt and how he'd asked Jan to do some digging into the company.

"Now you're both here, so I have to assume you've found something, or else you've both wasted a particularly good afternoon of my retirement," Cliff said, strategically leaving out the part about him sleeping off a hangover all morning. "Jan, you go first."

"Why me?"

"Because a gentleman always goes first."

"I thought a gentleman always let the lady go first?"

"Just shut up and say what you have to say," Cliff said, leaning back in the still-rocking swing. Jan looked hesitantly between Cliff and Lou before finally shaking his head.

"Fine." He exhaled. "But I'm not going to like it."

"Your reluctance has been noted. Now speak," Cliff said.

"Well, you asked me to look into Four Points, so I did. And they are clean."

"So it's a dead end?" Lou asked.

"Not exactly. They have all their books in order and things look good on the surface. But if you dig a little deeper, which I did," Jan grinned as if expecting some praise and continued when none came, "Right, well if you go deeper, it seems they do actually "work" on the towns. But it's shotty, they cut corners, and never complete all of the things they say they will."

"What?"

"So all those contracts they won in the past," Cliff asked, looking up through the trees and catching a little light coming through.

"They won legitimately. They went through all the proper channels and got contracts. But then, after that, they pretty much disappear. They say they use green tech to update rural communities. But the only thing I've found is that they get these contracts, and then plunder as much money out of these towns as they can before leaving again."

"How can they get away with that?" Cliff asked.

"All they have to do is pick communities far enough apart that they don't talk to each other. I mean, they don't even have the decency to change the name of the company."

"Someone must catch on though, right?" Lou asked.

"Not when you find out who the primary investor in the company is," Jan said nervously.

"The Crimson Serpents," Cliff mumbled, which received a look of surprise from Lou.

"Ding, ding, ding," Jan said, sounding not so cheerily.

"I don't understand. How you could possibly have known any of that, Cliff?"

"I've heard they have been coming to town the last few months. My guess is, they don't just enjoy the view."

"What would the Crimson Serpents want with a construction company?" Lou asked.

"I can think of a few million reasons why it would be helpful to have a 'legal' company."

Jan looked puzzled for a moment before the implication landed on him and he blurted it out in a hoarse whisper "Money laundering?"

"We don't know that."

"Lou's right, it's best if we stick to what we do know for now. Jan, you said they did this to other towns. You didn't happen to speak with any of them?"

"No." Jan shook his head. "Every time I got a hold of someone, they either refused to talk about what had happened, or they just hung up on me."

"So they're scared?" Lou asked.

"Seems that way."

"Okay, so if you had a phony business and needed to look legit, what would you do?" Cliff asked the pair.

"I'd try everything in my power to make me look legit," Jan said with a shrug.

"Which means…?"

"A representative of the company who visits the towns and wins them over, ideally not someone in a leather jacket." Jan tapped his leg rhythmically while he thought. "Then I'd have someone on my team who actually knew what they were talking about."

"Someone like Sam Benoit!" Lou said excitedly.

"I'm sure if we look hard enough, we will find that Sam recently came into some money," Cliff said.

"Why would they kill him though?" Jan asked. "If he was working for them."

"I'm not sure. But I don't think you become a PhD in something you don't care about." Cliff smiled.

"You think he didn't know," Lou stated as she thought, tapping her two index fingers together.

"Maybe he did or maybe he didn't. Perhaps he turned a blind eye and finally had enough? Or maybe he threatened to come clean? All possible, but all just theories."

"Theories are a good place to start." Jan shrugged.

"They can be."

"Fine, let's say Sam finds out what they are really doing and threatens to expose them," Jan said, nearly jumping off the swing in his excitement at making the connection.

"They kill him to keep him silent." Lou and Jan seemed to be mapping out the same story in their heads.

"Why make the death so public? They must have known it would draw attention to them." Jan asked.

"What if Sam's death wasn't just about him?" Lou says quietly.

"You think they have other people in town in on it?" Jan asked.

"I'm thinking that having a body turn up in a small town is a great way to stop anyone involved from talking about it."

"This contract would be worth millions to whoever got it, more if you factor in the idea that someone might cut corners."

"Sounds like a million good reasons to make sure they get it," Lou said, shaking her head.

"A couple of problems," Cliff interrupted, stopping the two youngsters from getting too far ahead of everything.

They both looked at him, their brows furrowed with a small sense of disappointment in their eyes.

"You're on the right track. At least, I would say you are. Right now, you both have a great theory. What you need is proof."

"What about those other towns?" Jan asked.

"None of them have told you what actually happened. It's good to have a theory, but if you want to move forward, both of you, we'll need either a confession, which is unlikely, or we'll need facts. The sooner you can find those, the sooner you can help this town."

"I thought you hated this town," Lou said.

"I do. But I also hate cilantro. It doesn't mean I want to watch someone burn it all down," Cliff said with a smile.

"I should go. This was supposed to be my lunch break." Lou stood and patted down her uniform.

"I can give you a ride if you want?" Jan suggested.

"I think showing up with a reporter to the office would be mildly suspicious," Lou pointed out, stepping off the swing. "But, thank you," she added with a smile. "I'm going to do some digging into Sam's financials see if anything unusual pops up."

"I'll keep trying these towns, to see if any one of them would be willing to talk about what happened," Jan said, getting up behind Lou. "What are you going to do, Cliff?"

"Be retired," he said leaning back in the seat. This got a laugh from both Lou and Jan. "There is one thing bothering me about it all, though."

"What's that?" they both asked.

"This project isn't cheap. So where is the money coming from?"

"The other towns they ripped off?" Jan shrugged.

"Possibly, but all of that money would have been made legally. In my experience people don't use legally obtained money on projects that almost certainly requires... alternative methods of persuasion we will say."

"Are you talking about brides?" Jan asked. "Like bribe, bribes?"

"I'm not saying that it's happening, just that there is the chance of it happening. There is a difference." Cliff insisted.

"Something like that would be... huge." Jan said softly the gravity of the idea seeming to sink in, though Cliff could see a slight eagerness in his eyes.

"Let's not get ahead of ourselves. For all we know I'm wrong and they are using the money they've taken from the other towns. But I don't think it hurts to keep an opened mind while we figure this out. Understand Jan?" Cliff placed a steady hand on the younger man's shoulder and waited till he received a nod of understanding. "Good. If this were happening," Cliff said putting a large emphasis on the word 'if', "then they would need cash and quickly. When's the bid announcement?"

"They've been deliberating for weeks with this new proposal, but I think the vote's on Monday," Jan said, looking at his watch.

"The vote is in four days?" Cliff said, hardly believing how little time they had to do anything.

"Well, it's not like anyone has really been looking into it," Jan said with a shrug.

"But you're a reporter!"

"You know how many people read articles about community maintenance projects?" Jan said, shaking his head. "Most people skip right to the Boos of the Week."

"The hell is that?" Cliff asked.

"It's pretty good, actually. It's usually a passive aggressive neighbour writing in anonymously," Lou said with a laugh.

"Which is redundant because everyone always knows who it is," Jan agreed, joining in the laughter. "This week's was *to the person who let their dog poo on my flower bed and didn't pick it up, I want you to know that I saw you, and I know who you are, and I am not happy.*" Jan shared another laugh with Lou until the two began to stare awkwardly at one another.

"I think I get the idea," Cliff said, breaking the tension.

"What do you think we should do?" Jan said, turning back to look at Cliff. He wasn't sure of the exact moment that he had apparently been put in charge, but the two youngsters were looking at him as if awaiting orders.

"Well, we need to get some of this information out to the public. Specifically, what we know about Four Points. Jan, how quickly can you put up something in the paper?" Cliff asked.

"Umm, next Thursday."

"That's a week from now."

"Yeah, I know. I didn't say it was good. You just asked me how long."

"How else are we supposed to tell people what's going on?"

"I have a blog. I could put it up on that," Jan said with a shrug. "I don't want to brag, but I have over eight hundred followers."

"I have no idea what you're talking about."

"He posts articles online for people to read," Lou said.

"You read my articles?" Jan asked.

"No," Lou said rather unconvincingly.

"Who in the hell would read an article online?"

"At least eight hundred people." Jan grinned. "Eight hundred and one." He winked at Lou.

"I've got to go." Lou turned to leave.

"Wait!" Jan said quickly. "What are you doing?"

"I'm going to find a way to link the Four Points stuff to our young victim. Maybe see if I can start leaning the captain's focus in that direction. God knows he needs one," she said with a laugh, before looking around with a worried look on her face. "I shouldn't have said that," she added, glancing at Jan.

He smiled widely and Cliff could feel the coldness in her stare.

Jan must have felt it, too, as he promptly shut his mouth and mimed locking it up and throwing away the key.

"Good luck, Lou." Cliff gave her a nod as he slowly stepped down from the porch swing.

"You too. And let me know what you find," Lou said as headed down the drive.

"So, the OPP don't have a clue," Jan said with a little laugh. "Guess I shouldn't be surprised."

"Things are always easier on the outside looking in. You don't have the same pressures, kid. Try and remember that." Cliff gave the tall youth a gentle squeeze on the arm.

"Still, it's hard to believe they don't have any leads."

"They have one," Cliff said giving a nod towards Lou as she turned onto the street.

"Yeah, but isn't that because of you?"

"I offered some insights. She did the work. Same as you. Which reminds me." Cliff turned back to face Jan. "I need you to find out everything you can on these kids who were joyriding at the dealership."

"I heard about that. But what does this have to do with anything?"

"Maybe nothing. But it's too much of a coincidence."

"What is?"

"Think about it. What's been happening the past two months ago?"

"Four Points put in their bid."

"And?" Cliff looked at him thoughtfully.

"And the Crimson Serpents started coming to town?"

"Good. What else?"

"I'm not sure. Nothing, really."

"Except for what?

"Except for…I don't know. Stolen plates?" Jan said, clearly unsure of what he was saying.

Cliff gave him a nod.

"You think the plates have something to do with the kids who were joyriding?"

"I don't know. But I don't believe in coincidences either. Too much seemed to happen at that time for it all not to be linked."

"What could possibly be the link between a bike gang, construction contract, and a couple of kids joyriding and stealing plates?"

"That's what I want to figure out."

"Why didn't you say any of this to Lou?" Jan asked.

"There are certain things that people will say to anyone who isn't a cop. You can ask questions without bringing in the attention of the entire town. Think of that like your superpower, kid."

"I feel like there's something you're not telling us."

"I think you should live under the presumption that I'm always not telling you something," Cliff said, as he walked back into the house and suddenly felt very ready for a midday nap.

11

If Cliff thought the rest of his day was going to be easy, he was sorely mistaken. Since Lou and Jan left earlier that day, Cliff felt more and more confident in what he believed was going on in this town.

That was until he heard a knock on his bedroom door.

"Cliff?" Hans called from the other side.

"Yes?"

"You have a visitor." Hans had a slight hesitation in his voice.

"A visitor? How? I don't know anyone." Cliff stood up from his chair and placed the novel he'd been reading on the table beside it. He went to the door and opened it.

Hans stood there with a furrowed brow and an odd smile. "Well, he certainly seemed to know who you are, and I think maybe you'll want to talk with him."

"What's his name?"

"Captain Marks. He's with—"

"The OPP," Cliff said with a sigh.

"So, you do know him?" Hans asked.

"I'd hardly say we *know* each other. But if he has decided to come all the way here, I can't imagine this is a good visit."

"When the OPP shows up at your house, would you ever say it was a good visit? The last time it happened to me, it was to tell me that three acres of my fields had been used for growing marijuana. It wasn't mine," he added quickly, catching the look on Cliff's face. "But there was something like six hundred pounds in there, so someone was going to be upset." Hans laughed.

"That happen a lot?" Cliff asked.

"More than you think." Hans mused. "So why is he here?"

"No idea." Cliff moved past his large friend and made his way down the stairs.

"You know you really aren't that good at retirement."

"So, I've gathered." Cliff rounded the corner to head to the main floor.

He found Captain Marks in full uniform standing at the front door, his face as stern as always. He could only see Kitty, who had her head poking in from the living room, though Cliff imagined most of the house must be listening in from *somewhere.* Except for Gerald, who Cliff could tell was in the kitchen preparing dinner, based on all the pots and pans clanging.

"You're not being arrested are you, Cliff?"

"Kitty, you can't just ask him that?" Sol shouted from what Cliff guessed was his sitting chair.

"Why not? There's a cop at our door!"

"I'm not being arrested Kitty. Am I?" Cliff asked, suddenly concerned. He wasn't entirely sure why Captain Marks *would* be here.

"No. You are not being arrested, Mr. Shaw," Captain Marks said in a very intimidating tone. "At least not right now." He narrowed his eyes at Cliff.

"Well, see, Kitty? Nothing to be worried about."

"This wouldn't have anything to do with why Officer Polaski was here earlier, would it?" Kitty asked, her words catching the attention of Captain Marks. Cliff saw a flash of anger in his face. *Dammit Kitty.*

"It does now, I suspect," Cliff said, shaking his head at Kitty, who didn't seem the least bit worried by it.

"Mr. Shaw, would you please follow me so we can speak in private?" Captain Marks turned and walked away.

Cliff followed, walking, albeit more slowly, behind him.

The two eventually made it to Captain Marks's patrol car, which happened to be an oversized Ford Explorer. He asked Cliff to hop in, and Cliff was more than a little relieved when he gestured to the front seat.

Captain Marks rounded the car and got in the other side. Inside the car were three monitors of all different sizes. One was built into the dash. The other two were attached to adjustable arms so that both the driver and the passenger could see and use them.

Cliff noticed a copy of the *Town Gazette* sitting on the dash, the title of the article in plain view.

"Evening, *Detective* Shaw," a voice said from the back seat, putting emphasis on the word "detective."

Cliff nearly jumped out of his skin and clutched his heart.

"Jesus, son," Cliff said, turning to see Officer Thomas sitting in the back seat. "Another scare like that, and your boss might be questioning a dead man." Cliff shook his head.

"Who said he was questioning anyone? Should he be?" Officer Thomas said, leaning forward to put his fingers through the metal grate that separated them as Captain Marks opened the driver's door and hopped inside.

"Shut the hell up, Thomas. I told you you could come if you kept your mouth zipped," Captain Marks said, and Officer Thomas leaned back in his seat and mimed zipping his lips.

"If this is about the article in the paper, I want you to know I had no idea he was going to write any of that, and I just learned about it this morning." Cliff pointed to the newspaper on the dash.

"I'm not here about the article, Mr. Shaw. Although, I won't pretend I'm not pissed off about it."

"As you should be," Cliff agreed.

There was nothing displayed on the screen in front of Cliff, not until Captain Marks began silently typing on a keyboard. A moment later, a face appeared on the screen facing Cliff.

"Who is this?" Cliff asked, suddenly unsure what exactly he was doing in the car.

"His name is Nigel Harrow. He was a PhD student at Western before he was caught for plagiarism by the university and expelled a little over six months ago. Any guess who accused him?" Captain Marks asked smugly.

"I think I can hedge my bets, Captain."

"Sam Benoit," Captain Marks said, and Cliff pretended that this was the first time he'd heard the name of the victim. "We had some of our team pick up Mr. Harrow this morning. As it so happens, he has no alibi for the night of the murder, is clearly capable of criminal activities since he was caught cheating, and we've confirmed more than one incident of Mr. Harrow threatening to harm, or even kill, Mr. Benoit."

"What?"

"As it turned out, Mr. Harrow, on more than one occasion, stated he could kill Benoit for what he did to him."

"On what? The Facebook?" Cliff asked.

"It's just Facebook, and yes."

"Doesn't matter. Your biggest proof is that this kid got mad and said he would kill him on some message board? Don't you think it's a little odd for someone to post about this kind of thing and then actually do it?"

"I'd hardly say it's out of the realm of possibility," Captain Marks point out.

"Sure, but it's a little light on the evidence, isn't it?"

"Not when you factor in the fact that he can't account for where he was on the night of the murder."

"Sure, but—"

"I'm not here to get your opinion, old man. I'm here to tell you to stop interfering with our investigation."

"Interfering? What investigation? As far as I can tell, you're waiting for something to land in your lap."

"Enough!" Captain Marks said, smacking his hand on the top of the steering wheel. "You know I have every right to arrest you for obstruction of justice right now."

"Good luck getting that to stick."

"You really are a pain in the ass, you know that?"

"A benefit of retirement," Cliff shot back.

"Case and point. You're retired. I can't have you putting nonsense ideas into the heads of my officers and sending them off looking for fantasies."

Cliff wondered if Lou had brought up some of their theories with Captain Marks, not that he was about to admit his involvement, not yet anyway.

"I don't know what you're talking about." Cliff glanced down at the screen displaying the image and history of Nigel Harrow. "But you think a kid with no priors, trying to get a PhD in green energy tech, is capable of murder because he was caught cheating? When you have a group known for organized crime who has, on more than one occasion, *actually* committed murder to get what they want, directly linked to the town—"

"Four Points Ltd? Don't be ridiculous," Captain marks scoffed. "We've looked into it, and they are 100% above board, a completely legal corporation, working entirely within the law."

"I'm not just talking about Four Points, although I'd hardly say they are *entirely* within the law."

"What do you know that I don't?"

"It's my belief that the Crimson Serpents are laundering money through Four Points. Possibly using illegally obtained money to bribe or persuade certain individuals into accepting their bid for small community contracts, like St. Marys. Once they have these contracts, they abuse the system and systematically undermine and undercut their work, forcing these communities to pay for uncompleted work and other shoddy practices," Cliff said.

"That would be dangerous, especially with the bid coming up this Monday. You have proof of this?" Captain Marks said, a little more intrigued now.

"Not exactly—"

"It's a simple yes or no."

"None of the other towns have been willing to talk about what happened to them. They're clearly afraid."

"What about the money, bribes, *anything*, that points to either Four Points or the Crimson Serpents giving money to anyone on council or in town that could sway which way the votes go?"

"No, we—"

"Then you have evidence showing the Crimson Serpents doing illegal activities."

"I've only been in town a few days. I hardly say that's been enough time to collect and gather evidence on any of this."

"Yet you seem to think it's enough to pull OPP resources into your little theory when we have a perfectly rational line of questioning, on evidence gathered by a trusted member of my team," Captain Marks said, glancing up in the mirror.

I guess I know why Officer Thomas is here.

"I'm not implying that your team isn't doing their best—"

"No, you just believe we're waiting for this to fall in our laps."

"Captain, that's not what I—"

"Let me make myself very clear. We do not need your help!" Captain Marks said, his eyes shifting to the paper on the dash, if only briefly.

It was clear he was not impressed with what had been written. Cliff wasn't either, not that he could say any of that right now. "Do me a favour, Mr. Shaw. I suggest you sit back and enjoy your retirement. Before you end up enjoying it from inside of a jail cell." Captain Marks's words seemed to put a nail in the proverbial coffin.

Cliff knew there was little chance he was going to change the man's mind. Not without some new evidence, which Cliff didn't have. And considering it was less than four days until the bid, he was unlikely to get it without the help of the OPP.

He pulled the latch of the door and swung it open. He was about to hop out when he turned back to the captain, whose eyes seemed full of ire.

"Captain Marks. You may very well be right on this matter. But, if you're wrong and you let this company win this bid, the town will suffer."

"You seem to care a lot for a man who arrived on a train, what…? A few days ago?"

"You're right. I may not care about the town. But that doesn't mean the people here deserve to suffer." Cliff stepped out of the car and shut the door behind him.

The sun had already dropped behind the church as Cliff walked back towards the house. The headlights of the captain's vehicle lit his way as it backed out of the drive and pulled away, leaving Cliff alone on the front stoop with only the single light over the door, illuminating the front entrance in the dimming evening light. That and the sliver of light coming from the window where Kitty, Sol, Mrs. Chen, and what seemed to be the rest of the house, were now crowded around looking out at him.

When he finally spotted them, Kitty masterfully swung the curtain shut.

Cliff entered the Limestone Manor, finding all the residents inside, sitting in the living room, a sight Cliff had not seen once since moving in. That is, everyone minus Gerald, who was still clanging away in the kitchen, although Cliff suspected even he had his ears open to the events transpiring in the living room.

"Hello, everyone," Cliff said nervously.

"Would you care to tell us, Mr. Shaw, why our home was visited by the OPP?" Kitty said sitting, legs crossed, in her chair.

Sol looked uncomfortable beside her, as Mrs. Chen and a very upright Bunty sat on the couch, their heads turned to look at Cliff. Only Hans stood off to the side, looking uncomfortable as he pretended to examine one of his wooden bowls.

"He had some questions," Cliff said calmly.

"I think we all have a couple of questions," Kitty said hotly.

"And I can respect that, but I don't think I need to explain myself," Cliff said, a little more rudely than he intended. But he was tired and annoyed by the conversation with Captain Marks. Or maybe he was just annoyed by how right the man had been. Cliff had no evidence to prove anything. *Am I just hunting a ghost? Could I really just be bored?*

"With respect, Cliff, we're looking for someone to join our home here at the Limestone Manor," Mrs. Chen began. "I think the least you could do is give us an explanation."

"That is, if I decide to stay," Cliff said and was surprised to see the look of shock on most of their faces. But it was the hint of disappointment on Bunty's face that really made him pause.

"Is that true?" Bunty asked, her voice a little above a whisper, yet Cliff had no trouble hearing it.

"I'm not sure," he hedged, unable to meet any of their eyes. The room was quiet for a while before Cliff let out a rather large sigh. "I'm sorry, everyone. I'm not used to living with people. I have been on my own for some time and haven't needed to explain my actions for an even longer time. And, as it would seem, tonight, I will have had to do it twice."

"What do you mean?" Hans asked, still holding the wooden bowl in his hands.

"Apparently, Captain Marks is less than happy with me talking to Lou...Officer Polaski."

"Why *are* you talking to her?" Kitty asked.

Cliff took a deep breath and began to tell them all about the events of the last week. How he'd mentioned to Lou his thoughts on what happened with Sam Benoit's murder, how she'd believed him, and how he'd managed to rope in Jan to research Four Points, because he thought it was actually being funded by the Crimson Serpents. How the company appeared to have done more harm than good to the towns whose bids they had won and how no one seemed to want to talk about it.

Since he had no reason to hold back, Cliff filled them in on seeing the young kids talking to the leader of the Crimson Serpents at the park, and how he suspected it all had something to do with the borrowed cars from the lot.

To Cliff's surprise, the entire room sat in silence and listened to him, though he could tell, on more than one occasion, Kitty wanted to ask something, but Sol was quick to put a hand out to stop her.

It wasn't until the end, when Cliff told them about how Captain Marks had insisted he take a step back unless he wished to find himself in jail that Kitty could no longer hold it in.

"How dare that man? You give him this information about our town, and he ignores it? I have half a mind to go see him and give him a couple of choice words."

"I appreciate that, Kitty, though I imagine that may do more harm than good at this point," Cliff said with a smile.

Now exhausted after telling his story once again, Cliff figured he'd skip dinner, despite smelling the rich aroma of lasagna and garlic bread coming from the other room.

"Where are you going" Hans asked as Cliff turned to leave.

"To bed."

"You can't go to bed," Kitty insisted.

"Why not?"

"How else are we supposed to figure out how to stop these people?"

"What do you mean?" Cliff asked.

"Like you said, the police aren't going to look into this. As far as I can tell, that leaves us," Kitty said with a stern nod of her head.

"We can't do anything. Besides, I told you, Captain Marks told me he'd put me in jail if I continued to look into this."

"He didn't say we couldn't," Bunty said quietly.

"You think this is a good idea?" Cliff said, puzzled by the normally quiet woman's boldness.

"This is our home, Cliff. You may not wish to live here, but we do." Bunty's words weren't malicious, yet Cliff felt the sting in them nonetheless.

"I didn't mean to say…it's just…I could be wrong."

"Do you think you are wrong, Mr. Shaw?" Mrs. Chen asked, her hands neatly in her lap.

"I do not."

"Then what choice do we have?" she said matter-of-factly.

"So, as I said, where do we start?" Kitty asked once again.

"I'm not sure," Cliff said. If his housemates wanted to help, who was he to stop them? "Lou was looking into the Crimson Serpents, to see if she could find out how they might be bringing in the funds to finance this little project, and Jan was trying to reach out to the various town councils to get an understanding of what might have happened there. He hadn't managed to get anyone to talk previously, but he's going to try again."

"What other towns did this happen to?" Sol asked.

"I'm not sure—"

"Hunter's Ridge, Port Cassidy, and Berlin." Hans lifted his head up from his phone. "I just messaged Jan," he said when Cliff looked at him, brow raised.

"Isn't Berlin just outside of Cambridge?" Bunty asked.

"It is, and my nephew and his wife live there. They took over my sister's restaurant. I would imagine that, if anything happened there, they would be able to tell us what it was," Mrs. Chen said, tapping her chin thoughtfully.

"We should be careful about asking around," Cliff cautioned, looking around at the room. "These guys are no joke."

"Perhaps, but obviously they've never met the residents of the Limestone Manor," Kitty said, clapping her hands together eagerly.

"Besides, I can't imagine the Crimson Serpents will be paying much attention to a group of octogenarians gossiping around town." Hans laughed.

"I think it's great that you all want to help," Cliff said, pacing the floor. "But it doesn't change the fact that there are lots of things we still don't have answers for. And without those things, we're never going to get Captain Marks to change his mind about any of this."

"Like what?" Kitty asked.

"Like how are they managed to get this bid in without anyone knowing what they've done? I would think the town does some sort of due diligence when it comes to a selection process. If that's the case, then someone must know something."

"Mary Anne," Kitty said conspiratorially.

"Who?" Cliff asked.

"Mary Anne Crawford. She was the town clerk for years. Pretty much ran the place until she retired."

"But if she's retired, what good is she to us?" Cliff asked.

"She's retired, Cliff, not dead. Knowing Mary Anne, she's likely still got her finger on the pulse of that place. She's ferocious."

"You mean she's terrifying." Sol laughed.

"You bite your tongue, Sol Keen. That woman has got more things done for this town than anyone."

"Because she's terrifying," Sol mock whispered over to Cliff.

"She's passionate. And besides, she's our best hope of getting the inside track."

"And you think you can talk to her?" Cliff asked.

"We just so happen to play bridge together on Friday afternoons," Kitty said, leaning triumphantly back into her chair.

"Well, that is good news."

"Dinner's ready," Gerald said, stepping into the living room as he licked some red sauce off his fingers.

"We're plotting, Gerald," Kitty said, turning on the large man.

"I've heard," he said, shrugging, unperturbed by Kitty's comment. "I just don't see why we can't plot over a hot meal."

Kitty shook her head but didn't protest again as everyone else got up from their seats and made their way into the dining room.

"Besides," Gerald said, wiping his now semi-clean fingers on his apron. "I think you're focusing on the wrong thing."

"What are you on about, Gerald?" Hans said with a laugh.

"It seems to me, you have a theory for everything except where the money is coming from."

"Yes, Gerald, but we have to deal with what we know first," Kitty said.

"Yes, but you *know* where the money is coming from."

"What do you mean?" Cliff asked, his ears perking up. He, of course, had his theories about where the money was coming from, but he couldn't help but think he was missing something.

"The kids from the dealership."

"What about them?" Sol asked.

"Well, if I was going to take a car for a joyride, I would take it out to Granton or something and bring it back. No one's going to notice thirty-odd kilometres on a truck. But these kids were traveling far. They're only doing that if there's something in it for them. Say, payment for doing a job?"

"You think the Crimson Serpents were paying teenagers to do some sort of job for them?" Kitty asked.

"Why not? Kids are stupid and they need money." Gerald shrugged.

"How would they even do this? Someone would notice a dealership vehicle on the road." Sol said shaking his head as if trying to wrap his head around the idea.

Cliff's eyes widened at the sudden realization, the one thing that had been staring him in the face the whole time. "The missing licence plates."

"What?" Kitty asked.

"Jan mentioned a string of licence plate thefts that had been happening recently. If the boys needed to hide a vehicle in plain sight, they could steal plates and then toss them when they were finished. It's rather ingenious if it wasn't so illegal."

"But why get kids?" Sol asked his mind still clearly on the well-being of the boys who might have found themselves wrapped up in something terrible.

"I told you, money, stupid, not to mention they can't be tried as adults," Gerald said.

"They could still go to juvenile detention," Sol argued.

"Yeah, but juvi doesn't sound so bad when the people you're working for are willing to kill people to keep them quiet."

"Sam Benoit," Cliff said quietly.

"Who is Sam Benoit?" Kitty asked shaking her head in confusion.

"The boy who died," Cliff said almost absently to Kitty, the wheels still turning in his mind now. "Gerald, you think Sam Benoit was a message to them to keep their mouths shut?"

"Them, and maybe a couple of others as well," Gerald said as everyone sat down around the table. Gerald had obviously been listening the whole time, and had also managed to ready the table with plates, cutlery, and a couple of bottles of red and white wine. One large lasagna sat in the centre of the table, with two large bowls of garlic bread on either side.

"This looks incredible. Thank you, Gerald," Bunty said, taking her seat.

"Yes, Gerald, you've outdone yourself," Hans agreed.

Each of the other housemates complimented the mysterious chef as they got seated.

"It's a good theory," Sol said after everyone was sitting down. "But I know these boys, and I can't imagine them getting caught up in something like this."

"It's easier than you might think. They might not even have known what they were doing was illegal. But by the time they figured it out, it was too late," Cliff said, seeing the worry beginning to form in Sol's face.

"I'm sure they didn't know, Sol," Kitty said, placing a caring hand over his.

"We don't even know what they're doing yet," Hans added.

"There's only a handful of ways to make cash quickly," Cliff said. "And the Crimson Serpents have their preferred method."

"What's that?" Sol asked cautiously.

Cliff looked at him and shook his head before letting out a sympathetic sigh. "Drugs."

12

Needless to say, dinner was not your typical Thursday night chatter, and the table seemed to come alive with discussions about everything they could do to help, despite Cliff making it very clear, more than once, that it was, most likely, a terrible idea. But each time Cliff protested, it was fought back with a defiant *no,* and a smattering of *this is our town.*

By the time dinner was over and the dishes were cleaned, the residents of the Limestone Manor appeared to have the beginnings of a plan. Cliff volunteered to do the dishes as, apart from Gerald, who had offered his single insight then comfortably picked away at his dinner and then the leftovers, he had the least to contribute to the discussion.

Cliff had completely underestimated the vast network of people his housemates had accumulated over the years. Along with Mrs. Chen's niece and nephew—who he'd learned were Kim and Derek—and Mary Anne Crawford at the town council, the table had managed to pick up a half dozen possible leads for them to start narrowing down. A couple of guys Hans used to play fastball with lived in Port Cassidy, and Bunty knew a teacher in Hunters Ridge from her days volunteering with the Kiwanis Music Festival. Then there was Cliff, who still had friends in Toronto, both local PD and the OPP, and thought he could track down the names of the active members of the Crimson Serpents, though, truthfully, he didn't know how helpful that would actually be.

But it was Sol who seemed to have the biggest immediate help. As it turned out, after a few difficult, long messages, Callum, who Cliff had met the night before at the creamery and who apparently hated cell phones, would be working at the dealership because one of the mechanics was sick. One of the guys he would be working with was Randy Gillis, which meant, with some guidance from Sol, he could probe him about what he was really doing with the cars. Whether or not he'd tell the truth was another thing.

In the end, Cliff, who had all but written off this entire thing hours before, went to bed with a new fire in his belly.

By the time he woke up, he'd formulated a plan. Was it his best plan? No. But if everyone played their part, then he had a feeling they could not only save the town but put some bad guys away as well. There was only one problem. Captain Marks.

"Cliff, we're good to go for this afternoon," Kitty said, looking up from her phone and tapping the side of her nose in a conspiratorial way. "I hope you're up to snuff on your bridge game, because these ladies can be ruthless. Convincing them to let a man into the game was no easy feat. So, I would appreciate it if you didn't embarrass me," she added, somehow managing to both look down her nose at him and push up her glasses at the same time.

"I'll be fine, Kitty. I appreciate you getting me in." Cliff smiled, checking off one of the many boxes in his mental checklist. "I'll need a quick refresher on the rules." He was unable to stop himself from laughing at the sudden aghast look he received from Kitty.

"Clifford Shaw, you best know what Stayman means." She let her hands fall dramatically to her lap.

"I'm only kidding. I promise I won't embarrass you." Cliff didn't bother to mention that he'd been a part of two separate bridge leagues while he lived in Toronto for the past forty-something years, and he had no doubt he would be able to keep up with any player.

"Good. We leave at 11:35 sharp," she said, burying her head in her phone as she began slowly typing out a message to someone.

Cliff looked up at one of the clocks in the room. It was only nine a.m., which meant he had ample time to sort out some of the other details of his plan. Timing it all out would be the most important. It was Friday, and everything needed to be in place for two p.m. on Monday. Which didn't leave much time for fiddling around.

"Sol, are you okay for this afternoon?" Cliff said, noting the man seemed relatively relaxed in his chair with his paper and coffee, considering everything they had planned.

"Callum is going to meet up with me later to talk through the details."

"And you're sure on the details yourself?" Cliff asked.

Sol gave a small nod as he looked up at Cliff from his paper.

"And you're sure he can make this happen."

"Of course, I'm not sure, Cliff. But if anyone is going to get it done, it will be Callum."

"You just let him know, it's the only way no one gets—"

"This is important to all of us, Cliff. But you know how stubborn people can be sometimes."

"Unfortunately, I do." Cliff was reminded of all the times he was forced to ask someone to do something difficult when he was on a case. It didn't matter how big or small the risk was. When you're asking anyone to take a risk, you can't help but feel responsible for them.

"You just make sure you can hold up your end of the bargain. You do that, I don't see us having any problems on our end," Sol said, picking up his paper to give it a read, though Cliff could tell Sol's mind was no longer on the articles.

Cliff got up from the couch and moved into the kitchen, where he found Gerald hard at work preparing what he presumed to be eggs Benedict. He was carefully whisking the yolk and cream mixture on the stovetop, making sure the eggs didn't curdle. Hans walked out from the pantry carrying a bag of white bread and a tub of peanut butter. Gerald shook his head at the tall man and his choices.

"You know what I'm making," Gerald asked.

"I do." Hans pulled out a couple slices of bread with one hand as he pulled open a drawer and removed a knife with the other.

"But you're still going to have that?" Gerald asked, nodding at the thick swipe of peanut butter Hans was smothering on the bread.

"I am." He slapped the two pieces of bread together. "But don't worry," Hans said, his mouth full of sandwich. "I'm sure I'll find room." He laughed as he gave his belly an affectionate pat.

After his insights the night before, Gerald had remained steadfast in his desire to not contribute or discuss the events of the weekend, although Cliff reckoned the mysterious foodie was paying more attention than he let on. Unlike the other residents of the house, Gerald had not grown up in town, and therefore didn't share their rich desire to not have the town overrun by people who wished to see it destroyed. Though it would appear that the small town had gripped its little talons into the pudgy old man.

"Have you spoken with Jan?" Cliff asked Hans between bites of his sandwich.

He nodded as he wiped his mouth with his faded blue button-down shirt, which seemed permanently covered in wood chips and sawdust. Looking at his old friend now, biting down on a peanut butter sandwich, Cliff had no doubt the man and the young reporter were related.

"Can he do it?"

"Of course. It's his blog, so he can write anything he wants," Hans said. "He also wanted me to apologize again for the article in the paper yesterday," Hans added.

Cliff raised a hand to stop his friend. "It's fine. What's done is done. Who knows? That might be the push we needed to make sure this whole thing happens."

"Well, he definitely didn't want to see you getting into any trouble."

"Something tells me Captain Marks would have found one reason or another to come and talk to me. He'd been looking into Lou, as well, which means he had his suspicions about me beforehand. All that article did was embarrass him," Cliff said with a shrug.

"Do you think he has anything to do with all of this? I mean, there must be a reason he's choosing not to look into the Crimson Serpents."

"No one *wants* to believe they're involved. It complicates things and that makes his life harder."

"So, you don't think he's being paid?"

"Honestly, at this point I don't know who to trust. As far as I can tell, there are too many people in this town who seem to be avoiding the difficult questions, like is any of this connected or is it simply a coincidence? Perhaps the wool has been pulled over their eyes and they don't even know it."

"Someone like the mayor?"

"Perhaps, but I'm not sure what he has to gain from the deal, unless he's being pressured to push the deal through someway. He seems—"

"A little oblivious?" Hans said, licking a little bit of peanut butter off his thumb as he chuckled as his own joke.

"Yes."

"That doesn't mean he's clueless." Hans shrugged. "And if he isn't, then the people need to know about it."

"I couldn't agree more. So you'll just tell Jan to stick to the plan and everything will be fine."

"You're sure about this, Cliff? There seems to be a lot of things here that could go wrong."

"It wouldn't be a good plan if things couldn't go wrong." Cliff gave his old friend a toothy grin as Hans shook his head.

"I feel like you and I have different ideas of good plans," Hans mused.

"I'll make sure Jan gets the news out."

"By tomorrow ideally. The more time we have to let people know the better."

Hans gave a nod and then disappeared down into the basement. Gerald was still stirring frantically, apparently indifferent to the plan.

"Smells delicious, Gerald."

"That's because it is delicious," he said, taking out a spoon and giving the yellow sauce a little taste. He smiled happily as he pulled the spoon away from his lips. "Hungry?"

"I am now." Cliff reached into the cupboard and grabbed seven plates. He set them beside the stove.

Gerald turned off the heat and set the sauce off to the side as he bent over and opened the oven. A rich aroma of spiced hashbrowns and toasted English muffins wafted out from the oven.

The shorter man directed Cliff on how to plate the meal as he began poaching the eggs, which he managed to do with extreme efficiency, and the two men managed to serve the food in under ten minutes.

"Food's ready," Gerald said unceremoniously as he grabbed his own plate and made his way to the table.

Cliff followed after him as the other members of the house headed in one at a time, each wasting no time getting to their seat and devouring the delicious meal.

***

It was early afternoon when Cliff and Kitty made their way to Kitty's bridge game. It was clear as the pair walked in that not everyone was thrilled about the new guest. There were fifteen women and Cliff sitting in the main hall of a small community centre Kitty passionately referred to as simply "The Clubhouse" which happened to be a smaller red bricked building tucked in down the road from Trillium Diner.

Kitty, who looked more nervous than anyone, waved at each table, greeting each pair as they walked by. The women gave her a polite nod before turning back to shuffle their decks of cards, chatting in semi-hushed tones about Cliff's presence at their weekly game.

"Mary Anne," Cliff heard Kitty say as she approached a very stern-looking woman, who was obviously the most intimidating person in the room.

"Kitty, I see you brought your new friend," Mary Anne said, nodding towards Cliff. She wore a smattering of makeup on her face, highlighted with a red lipstick and black eyeliner, and had remarkably straight posture. When she stood, she reached for a long cane that hung off the back of her chair to help push her up to her full height, which was an inch or so taller than Cliff. Her white blouse and red dress pants seemed to flow off her body.

"Pleasure to meet you, Mary Anne," Cliff said, putting his hand out to greet the woman.

She looked him up and down before putting her hand out to greet him, and Cliff understood immediately that this was a woman who was used to being heard.

"Nice to meet you, as well," she said with a calculated smile. "Kitty tells me you have something you would like to discuss." She gestured for them to have a seat at the two remaining chairs at the table. "This is Delores Pullman, my partner." Mary Anne gestured to the other woman at the table. Unlike Mary Anne, Delores seemed to shrink back into her chair, and her words were barely audible as she greeted Cliff and Kitty. Delores mostly just smiled at them and shuffled the cards.

"Nice to meet you, Delores. As for our chat, I think we'll have plenty of time to talk about that later. It seems it would be best if we got started," he said, gesturing to the rest of the room, where other tables seemed to all be starting their first deal.

"True enough. Draw for deal?" Mary Anne said, as Delores smoothly slid the deck of cards across the table. Each of them flipped over a card.

It was Kitty with the king of hearts who received the first deal. Delores handed her the spare deck and cut it as she did, while Cliff grabbed the other deck and began to shuffle it. Once he'd finished, he set the deck beside Delores on his right, for her to use on the next round.

There was very little small talk while Kitty dealt the first hand, which Cliff thought was a surprise as he'd not seen Kitty quiet for that long since he'd arrived in town.

"You seem awfully quiet today, Kitty," Mary Anne said, as Kitty finished up her deal and everyone began to gather their cards up.

"Do I?" Kitty said, sorting her own cards. "I must just be nervous about my new partner." She gave Cliff a thin smile. "He tells me he knows what he's doing."

"You don't trust him?" Mary Anne asked.

"Of course, I trust him. But what does that have to do with being good at cards?" Kitty laughed, which seemed to relax her a little. "One club," she said, giving her hand a glance over. *Opening points and looking for a major suit.*

"Pass," Delores said quietly.

Cliff had finished sorting his own hand. He counted sixteen points, seventeen with the single diamond, although he wondered if Kitty played that way or not. Either way, he had five hearts, with one of his two aces also being a heart. Knowing all he needed was six to ten points to respond, he was in a great position. The two of them should have a good hand, assuming it lined up well.

"Two hearts," Cliff said. It was aggressive, but he wanted her to know he also had points and some hearts. If they played it right, they could get some good opening points.

"Pass," Mary Anne said, giving Cliff a once-over before she did.

Cliff wondered if this first hand was a test.

Cliff ended up taking the first contract with six hearts, which left

Kitty as the very-willing dummy. It had been a more aggressive first hand than Cliff had expected, but as he played the queen of diamonds to complete the small slam, he managed to catch the nod of approval from Kitty, who'd been watching patiently across from him.

"Well, it would appear as though we have a game on our hands, Delores," Mary Anne said with a smile.

If it was a test, Cliff felt as though he and Kitty had passed with flying colours.

After that, Kitty appeared to be back to her normal chatty self, picking away at the various threads of gossip she'd heard throughout the week.

"Kitty, you always seem to have your finger on the pulse of this little town of ours."

"Well, when one has the time, they have to fill it with something."

"Indeed," Mary Anne said with a smile. "Mr. Shaw—"

"Cliff, please."

"Alright, Cliff. Very interesting article in the paper yesterday. I had no idea St. Marys had such a decorated officer in our little town. No wonder they want your assistance on this mysterious death."

"The article was…misleading."

"So, you didn't work as a detective in Toronto Police Department."

"No, I did."

"You aren't decorated then?"

"I've been awarded some medals over the years."

"Then I don't understand. How was it misleading?"

"I didn't come to town to help with this investigation. I just happened to arrive on the day the body was found. That, and an unfortunate photo with the mayor, seemed to draw the wrong conclusion."

"I see. So, you're not working on the case?" Mary Anne asked, and both Cliff and Kitty shared a look.

"Not exactly. I didn't *come* here to work on the case."

"This does seem confusing." Mary Anne picked the cards up from the table and gave a little giggle.

Cliff and Kitty gave each other a look.

"Well, if you'll indulge me, I would like to make it more confusing," Cliff said, placing down his own hand, as he'd already finished sorting through it.

Mary Anne looked at him for a long moment before turning to Kitty, who looked almost giddy at the idea of being a part of this secret meeting.

"Can I trust your discretion?" Cliff asked when Mary Anne didn't say anything.

She still didn't say anything, but she gave Cliff a long, stiff nod.

Cliff proceeded to tell Mary Anne, and simultaneously Delores, who was content to sit diligently silent on the sidelines, only glancing up at Cliff with confusion a few times as he made his request.

Mary Anne, on the other hand, did not. Cliff could understand why this woman had been a formidable counsellor in her past, as she seemed very well versed in when to ask questions and when to give the space for the explanation to come. Cliff couldn't understand why Mary Anne wasn't the one running the town.

"Let me get this straight. You want me to try and have the council change the meeting. A meeting that is scheduled to take place on Monday and has been in the books for over two months?" Mary Anne asked as she placed a card down on the pile, though the game had seemed to take a back seat to the conversation, especially for Cliff, who sat with his own hand face up on the table in the dummy position.

"I know it's difficult…"

"Difficult?" Mary Anne scoffed. "You do understand. This is a small town. Everyone on this council is either still working or only recently retired. Trying to organize that many people in one place at the best of times takes effort."

"I'm sure it won't be easy…"

"You're right, it won't. Not to mention your other request. I'm choosing not to lie to you here, Mr. Shaw. It's a tough pill to swallow. You'd be asking me to humiliate our councillors."

"I'm not asking you to do anything like that. But we know someone is providing Four Points and therefore the Crimson Serpents with information, and we don't know who it is. With more selective information, we can figure that out." Cliff watched as Kitty hesitantly pulled another card from her hand.

"If you're wrong, this will be a problem," Mary Anne said, looking right at Cliff. "And as much as I want to believe you, I don't know who you are. You've been gone a long time, Mr. Shaw."

"He has," Kitty said, playing a card from her own hand and watching as Delores silently tossed down hers. Kitty trumped it with ten of clubs from the dummy and waited for Mary Anne to toss a card before adding the winning trick to her growing pile. "But you know me, and I'm telling you right now, Mary Anne, that if we're wrong…you may very well be right, it would be embarrassing. But embarrassment is not a problem." She tossed down an ace of clubs.

"Not a problem?" Mary Anne asked as the hand went around, Kitty's ace taking it.

"No, the problem will be if we let these people win the bid in this town. We've heard what they do to the towns where they win, and I'm telling you right now, that would be a problem."

"You seem pretty sure about this."

"I am. I trust Cliff." She gave Cliff a firm nod.

Cliff wondered what he had done to earn this much trust from a relative stranger. He'd been in the house for under a week, yet she was willing to vouch for him on something so obscure. Though he supposed this had less to do with him and more to do with what might happen to the town. But still, it felt good.

Mary Anne glared at Kitty for a long while, and then finally over at Cliff, before she played her card and let out a heavy sigh. "I can't promise you anything, but I will try."

Kitty took her final trick, taking the last hand, along with the three tricks she'd bid. "You certainly are a formidable player, Mr. Shaw."

"Only when I have a good partner," Cliff said, giving a thoughtful smile to Kitty, who looked pleased as she watched Delores tally up the points.

"That's game," Delores said as she placed her pen on top of the score card.

"That was fun. Maybe we can play again sometime." Cliff stood and shook Kitty's hand, and then the hands of the two other women.

"With respect, Mr. Shaw, this is the women's league. I don't imagine your presence will be welcomed twice, Mary Anne pointed out, as the women at the other tables sent sideways glances at him.

"Fair enough." Cliff laughed.

"But there is a coed game every week, Cliff, and if I'm not mistaken, Bunty has been looking for a partner," Kitty said, her eyes lifting playfully toward him.

"Bunty plays?" Cliff asked.

"Very well, in fact," Kitty said. "If you're interested."

"Maybe you should get through this weekend before you both start planning your next bridge game." Mary Anne laughed.

Kitty, Cliff, and even Delores, began to laugh.

"We should get home, Delores, if we plan on getting these calls in today for our new friend here," Mary Anne said.

With a small nod, the pair were off and out the door, leaving Cliff and Kitty standing in the room of green-felted card tables in a sea of women still not entirely happy to have Cliff Shaw in the room.

"That went well," Kitty said, dusting her hands off in the air.

"Thank you, Kitty. I couldn't have done that without you."

"I agree. Some of your bidding was rather aggressive, but I think, in the end, we managed to use it to our advantage."

"That's not what I meant."

"I know." Kitty smiled.

Cliff followed her out of the hall. "You really think I play aggressive?" Cliff laughed.

"Let's talk singletons and doubletons." Kitty dove into a long-winded explanation about the value of not having cards in your hand and when they should count as actual value. Something she'd obviously put a huge amount of thought into.

Cliff, on the other hand, was too busy thinking about what he was going to do next. Now that Kitty had helped get Mary Anne on board, they needed to implement part two of the plan.

13

By the time Kitty and Cliff made it back to the Limestone Manor, only Bunty was around, knitting in her usual spot with a cup of tea beside her.

Kitty decided to go for a walk downtown to meet Sol, in order to inform him about the details of the card game. With any luck, Sol would have already spoken with Callum about what they needed to set up for the Sunday night. Cliff wished he could have been there himself to help, but Sol was adamant that it would be easier if it was just him and Callum. All they needed from Cliff was a little reassurance that everything was going to be okay on his end.

Cliff was reluctant to tell them it would be. He'd been on enough jobs to know that reassurances were nothing but words. In the end, it was the actions people took that determined the outcome. As long as everyone followed the plan, there was no reason for anyone to worry.

"How did it go at the game?" Bunty asked, glancing up briefly to smile at Cliff. "I see you came out relatively unscathed, which I imagine is a victory of its own." She giggled.

"If looks could kill, I'd be mortally wounded. But as it was, we left with two victories." Cliff collapsed in his chair, rubbing his knee absently.

"That's good news."

"Where is everyone?" Cliff asked, looking around the silent house.

"Mrs. Chen was in the garden for most of the day, Hans left a while ago to meet Jan, and Gerald, I believe, went with him. If I had to guess, I would say he went grocery shopping, seeing as it's his third favourite activity behind cooking and eating." She smiled at her own joke as she knit away at what appeared to be another sleeve of a sweater.

Bunty suddenly stopped knitting and looked up at Cliff with a frown on her face. "I shouldn't have said that. It was mean, and Gerald is very kind to make us so many wonderful meals." She looked racked with guilt.

"I don't think you have anything to apologize for. I've only known Gerald a short time, but if I had to wager a bet, he would likely say that those are, in fact, his top three things to do." Cliff said giving Bunty a reassuring smile.

This seemed to be enough to ease Bunty's mind, if only just a little, as she returned to her knitting. Cliff watched as she neatly looped the thread around the needle and cast off one stitch at a time.

"You make that look so easy," Cliff said, his eyes still on her hands.

"That's because it is easy." Bunty laughed.

"I'd hardly say that. I tried when I was a kid and got nowhere."

"Well, you were a boy in the forties. I would hardly say you were ever going to put your best foot forward at the task," Bunty mused.

"Fair enough. Still wish I could have learned," Cliff said.

"Well then, it's a good thing you're not dead, Mr. Shaw."

"You know you can call me Cliff."

"I know."

"So does that mean you'll teach me?" Cliff stood up and grabbed an extra pair of knitting needles from out of the wicker yarn basket Bunty kept beside her chair.

"Does this mean you're going to stay?" Bunty asked, as she peered up at him.

"That's a good question." Cliff hadn't been thinking about this at all today, but he was keenly aware that, at some point, he would need to make a decision about what he was going to do. Every part of him was screaming to leave this godforsaken town. Ever since he'd arrived, he'd been thrown into all of its chaos and drama. A town he never wanted to return to in the first place. Yet, here he was, and with Elizabeth Price of all people.

"You probably don't remember. You were just a kid when I left."

"Oh, I remember." Bunty smiled. "And I was hardly a kid, Mr. Shaw. I was twenty-one, and I remember it all very well. You caused quite the stir in the Price family home."

"I'm sorry, I never meant—"

"You have no reason to apologize. Annie was…*is* a handful and a bit of a drama queen. I always felt like she should have shown up that day. Even if she wasn't going to go, she owed you that much." Bunty gave her head a little disapproving shake.

"Can I ask you a question, Bunty?" Cliff said, trying his best to steer the conversation away from anything to do with the day he left town. He'd always hated thinking about it, and he wasn't about to start doing it now.

"Of course."

"Why did you move to the Limestone Manor? It seems hectic."

"It is. All the time." She laughed. "Which is hardly my cup of tea, so to speak. But I have to admit, I find it fun."

"You find this house fun?"

"Of course. There is always something going on, and it's quite different from the house I grew up in. And the house I grew old in, for that matter."

"Did you marry?" Cliff asked.

"Yes, to a nice enough man, his name was Bill Hutchinson. He died when he was sixty-four."

"I'm sorry to hear that."

"Thank you."

"How did it happen?"

"He was hit by a truck," Bunty said, looking up from her knitting.

"Oh my God, really?" Cliff asked shocked.

"No." Bunty laughed. "It was a heart attack. But your face! It was very much worth it."

"Was it?" Cliff asked, his eyes narrowing playfully.

"Oh yes. One hundred percent." She smiled and then went back to her knitting. "Anyway, it was just the two of us in the house, and when he died, I decided to change my name back to Price, give myself a fresh start, and just be alone for a while. And for a few years, I was okay with that. But then, about eight years ago, Hans began looking around town for people who might be open to this little idea, and I thought, what the heck."

"So, you just moved into this circus on a whim? And you knew what the plan was?"

"Of course. I'm the one who helped organize how it might all work. Though, admittedly, Flo was the first one of us to actually die here, so this whole thing a bit new."

"I'm the first new member of the house?" Cliff asked.

Bunty nodded, not skipping a beat in her knitting.

"So, the letter of intent, the free rent, and the room transfer has never actually been done before."

"Well, we weren't really hoping for anyone to die, Cliff. But it did feel like a contingency we all needed to plan for." Bunty looked up at Cliff before looking around the room conspiratorially. "Between you and me, I had my money on Gerald."

Cliff tried to stop himself from laughing, though the hint of a smile poked through.

"I wouldn't have pegged you for a 'who's going to die next' kinda woman, Bunty."

"You think I sit silently praying for everyone to live?"

"You are in the church choir."

"I like to sing," she said with a shrug. "Music has always been the one thing I find brings people together. Apparently, that and murder." They both began to laugh.

"Murders *always* bring people together," Cliff joked.

"It's my first one, so I'll have to take your word for it," Bunty mused.

"Let's hope it's your last."

"Agreed. I just hope that we get whoever did kill that young man. No one should die that young. It's not fair."

"Sadly, life rarely is."

"What? Fair?"

Cliff nodded absently.

"That's a pretty cynical view."

"It's hard not to be a little cynical when you've seen everything I've seen." Cliff shrugged.

"Well, I can't say I envy your life then, Cliff. But a person who seeks out evil, will find nothing but evil."

"That from the Bible?"

"Everything in one form or another is from the Bible. It's a rather long book, I'm afraid." Bunty's eyes seemed calm, but there was a seriousness in them, that Cliff could just make out.

"I know that not everything always works out. It's naive to think that it will, especially when you've lived as long as we have. But please promise me that you will try and fix this?"

"I'm going to do my best," Cliff said letting out a little sigh.

"Your best is all anyone can hope for." Bunty smiled and tucked her head back into her knitting as the front door burst open.

Kitty and Sol barged in.

"Good you're here," Kitty said frantically. "We may have a bit of a problem."

"What kind of problem?" Cliff asked, trying not to let the sudden tightness in his breath show.

"Sol and Callum went and talked to the boys, like you asked," Kitty started as Sol walked in behind her, putting a hand on her shoulder.

"The boys agreed, once I told them the plan. Not like they had much choice at this point."

"Well, that's good news." Cliff sighed.

"It was, until Randy got a call telling him that someone from the Serpents would be following them this time to and from the pick-up location in Windsor."

"Has that ever happened before?" Cliff asked.

"Not according to Randy. Usually, it's just him and Marcus."

"They must be worried about something."

"I'd say it's this." Sol pulled out his phone. "Hold on," he said, fiddling with it. "I just had it up here. Kitty?" Sol said, showing her the phone. "What's going on here?"

"My God, Sol, what is the point of having one of these if you refuse to learn how to use it?" She snatched the phone away and began typing away, though her own speed was nothing too impressive.

"Not as easy as it looks," Sol mumbled to himself.

"Got it!" Kitty nearly shouted as she gave Sol a victorious smile. "It's Jan's blog." She handed Cliff the phone. On it was an article written by Jan that read "Possible Corruption in Town Bidding Causes Changes to Upcoming Town Council Meeting."

"I thought he was supposed to release this tomorrow?" Kitty asked.

"He was, but obviously, he got a little excited." Cliff read the piece silently. It was a good blog, exactly what Cliff had hoped it would be. Just enough information to cause doubt and confusion.

"That boy's always putting the cart before the horse," Kitty said slumping down on the couch.

"This shouldn't change the plan too much. As long as the boys have agreed, we should still be fine," Cliff said trying to calm the situation down.

But Sol didn't look convinced. "This isn't even the worst part," Sol said as he wrung his hands together nervously.

"It's not?" Cliff and Bunty asked at the same time.

"No," Sol said looking worried again. "They asked them to bump up the pickup to tonight."

"What?" Cliff rubbed his free hand down over his face. "Why didn't you lead with that?"

"I don't know! I'm nervous. This is my first sting operation." Sol shrugged.

"This isn't a sting operation, Sol," Cliff said.

"A sting operation is a deceptive operation designed to catch a person attempting to commit a crime," Bunty said, continuing to knit away at her sweater, her eyes peering up briefly to look at Cliff.

"This sounds like a sting operation," Kitty jumped in.

"Okay, fine." Cliff sighed. "I guess this is somewhat of a sting operation. But we also don't have time to leave out the important bits."

"How am I supposed to know what's important?" Sol shrugged.

"Fair enough. Let's just say, anything that deviates from the plan is important information," Cliff said.

"Like Jan's article being released early?" Sol asked.

"Exactly," Cliff said.

"So, you knew about that?" asked Kitty.

"No," Cliff admitted.

"I'm confused." Sol asked. "You want to know about changes?"

"I would prefer if people *stopped* changing—"

"Operation Stonetown," Kitty jumped in.

"What?" Cliff asked.

"I've named it Operation Stonetown. All good operations have a name."

"We don't need a name. This isn't an operation."

"An operation is a highly organized activity that involves many people doing different things," Bunty said, giving Cliff a little smile.

"Sounds like an operation," Sol said.

"Okay, fine, it's sort of like an operation," Cliff admitted. "But we still don't need to give it a name."

"Names make things less confusing, Cliff." Kitty folded her arms across her chest.

Cliff looked between Sol and Kitty before letting out a heavy sigh. "Fine, I would prefer it if people stopped changing Operation Stonetown on me. There are a lot of moving parts, and we need—"

"What are you going to do about the boys now?" Kitty asked.

"I was getting to that."

"Slowly," Kitty grumbled, eliciting agreeable nods from the others in the room.

Cliff shook his head. "I'll make a few calls. With any luck, we can bump up tomorrow's plans, and make sure these kids are safe."

"What should we do?" Kitty asked.

"Nothing. I think it's best if, at this point, you just let me sort out how to fix this."

"He who walks alone, will find no comfort in the journey," Bunty quipped as she wrapped another thread around her finger.

Cliff looked around at the room. All of their eyes seemed to fall on him, waiting for some sort of guidance. This was one of the reasons Cliff had always preferred to work alone. If he had a plan, he wanted to see it through. At least that way, there was no chance of it being anyone else's fault if it went south.

Yet, here he was, in a house with a bunch of retirees, who all seemed hell bent on working through this problem.

"Who said that?" Cliff asked with a heavy sigh.

"I did. Right now," Bunty said, as she paused for the first time from her knitting to look up at Cliff, a big smile across her face. She let out a little giggle. The honesty in her laugh seemed to be contagious, as first Kitty, and then Sol, began to laugh themselves.

Despite himself, Cliff found himself laughing along with the rest of them, just as Hans, Gerald, and Jan walked in.

"What's so funny?" Hans asked as he stepped into the living room.

Gerald didn't bother to stop, but marched into the kitchen. Cliff could hear his heavy footsteps crossing the floor and then sounds of rummaging through the pantry.

"I'm not really sure," Bunty said as she sucked in a short breath of air.

"Well, I'm sorry I missed it." Hans laughed.

Gerald returned with a bowl of potato chips and slumped down into one of the couches near the sliding door.

"It would appear that isn't all you missed," Kitty said, shooting a glance over towards Jan, who looked confused as he leaned casually against the door frame.

"Me? What did I do?" Jan protested.

"You remember when the plan was to release your blog post tomorrow? On Saturday?"

"Saturday?" Jan said.

"That was my fault," Hans explained. "I thought we would need more time."

"Well, you thought wrong," Kitty insisted.

"What do you mean?" Hans said.

"You all fill Hans and Jan in on what's happening. I need to make some phone calls before we run out of time." Cliff walked out of the room, giving his massive friend a tight squeeze on the shoulder when he saw the worry on his face.

"All will be well, my friend," Cliff whispered as he hurried upstairs to his room to get started on those calls, catching the slightest "oh my God" from Hans as he rounded the last set of stairs to his room.

Cliff wished he could have been the one to tell his friend about the sudden shift in plans with the boys. He knew the big man would blame himself. But that would do no one any good. Cliff had just lost a day and he needed to coordinate with his friends at the OPP to make sure the boys were picked up safely, like he had promised. The new tail would certainly make it more difficult to sell, but they would make it all work out. They had to. He just needed to get his old friend, Captain Cavanaugh, on the phone and hope to God that some remnant of the plan they had set up could be adjusted.

Cliff walked into his room and slumped down in his chair, scrolling through his phone until he found Cavanaugh's number. He clicked on the name and waited a few moments before he finally picked up.

"Hello?" Cavanaugh answered.

"Tom, it's Cliff. We have a bit of a problem."

14

It took a little time to explain everything, but once Cliff caught Tom up on the details of what had happened, things seemed to start moving with a lot more urgency. It didn't help that the team Tom had put together was scattered across the city of Toronto, and they had all been preparing for the big night going down on Saturday.

The first thing Cliff and Tom decided to do was to reach out to his team, get them organized, and ready to head out. This meant that Cliff would be out of the loop for the next couple of hours. That would give him some time to sort out the details with Sol. They needed to know whatever they could about where these boys would be going and who was with them.

Cliff headed down to the living room and found Hans and Jan looking very somber, and sitting in the cushioned window bay. Cliff guessed they'd told Hans about the boys, which meant it was only Gerald who didn't appear worried as he noshed on a bag of chips.

"What's the plan?" Kitty asked when she spotted Cliff walking down the stairs.

"I need to know everything you know about where the boys will be going and when. And if you're able to give me one of their numbers, they might be able to track them, which would be very helpful," Cliff said to Sol.

"I can tell you everything I know. As for the number, I'll have to get

181

that from Callum, but it shouldn't be a problem." He sounded a little more hopeful.

"What can the rest of us do?" Hans asked, rubbing his hands together before adding, "I'm really sorry—"

"No apology needed, Hans. You did what you thought was right. Next time, just give us a heads up before you switch things up on us." Cliff gave his friend a warm smile.

This was not the response Cliff would have likely had when he was in the Toronto PD. In fact, he would have had a few choice words for his friend had it been a different time and a different place. But in the here and now, Cliff resigned himself to the fact that he was no longer a detective or in the police department. He was an old man, living in a house of retirees, whose only desire was to do everything in their power to save their town.

Hans' shoulders dropped a little at Cliff's words, but there was still pain in his eyes. He wasn't the only one. Everyone seemed to be looking up at Cliff now for guidance on what they should be doing.

"I know everyone just wants to help, but there are things we cannot control here," Cliff said to his silent housemates.

"I thought you said it would all be okay?" Kitty asked.

"I hope it is, Kitty. But the reality is, whatever plan they've been building up has been happening for months. We're trying to pull a rabbit out of a hat here without anyone else getting hurt."

"I can understand that you think we can't control everything," Kitty said after a long moment, "but you also have to understand that you've only just met most of us, and I for one, do not enjoy the lack of control, especially when it's our town at stake. No offence to your friends in Toronto," Kitty said, folding her arms across her chest.

"No offence taken. I understand your frustration—"

"Do you? Because it seems like a lot of this is relying heavily on you and your plan, Cliff. And God forbid something happens to you. We would all be screwed. I can't see any harm in casting a wider net." Kitty looked around the room at everyone else.

"Kitty, calm down," Sol said, raising a sympathetic hand.

"Don't you dare tell me to calm down, Sol Keen! And that is not what this is about."

"She's right," Cliff said looking at the faces of everyone in the room. They all seemed to be looking at him expectantly. "But I don't see what else we can do."

"Maybe that's the point," Bunty said quietly as she continued to knit away.

"What do you mean?" Cliff asked.

"Well, maybe that's what Kitty is trying to say. You're looking at the problem from one direction, and it's difficult so see the forest for the trees. But if you were to share your plan with the rest of us, then maybe there's something we can add to the mix that you haven't thought about. After all, if this was a war, I'd say we know the battlefield a little better than you do, with respect, Cliff." Bunty broke her gaze only once as she said this last part to Cliff, who was now standing at the door wringing his hands.

The whole point of not getting people involved was to protect them, but was that being naive? Could he protect them if things went wrong?

Cliff collapsed in a chair and let out a heavy sigh. "You're right. You both are. I was just trying to protect you," he said softly.

"That's very kind, Cliff. But we've managed this long without your help. Besides, only one person in this room has a less than ideal relationship with the local law enforcement, and I'll give you a hint…it's not us," Kitty said gesturing to herself and the other original Limestone Manor residents. That brought a smile to Cliff's lips.

"Again, I'm sorry about that," Hans said quietly.

"It was my post," Jan added. "I should be the one that's sorry."

"There will be enough time later for people to say sorry. But right now, I think we should really be more worried about what we are going to do," Sol said, clapping his hands together eagerly.

Cliff who had suddenly gone quiet, was now deep in thought. "You're right, Kitty. The OPP is not too keen on having me in town, stepping on their toes."

"I know, that's why I said that."

"I agree. But maybe we can use that to our advantage." Cliff looked at all their confused faces looking back towards him.

"I'm not sure I'm following," Kitty said finally.

"Cliff wants to use the OPP's dislike of him against them. Divert their attention so that the rest of us might be able to work under their noses," Bunty said, still looking casually at her knitting. When she glanced up, all eyes were on her. "What? It's called deflection. It's common practice in most strategy games."

"Bunty is absolutely right. I'm just not sure how to do that yet."

"Well, it's obvious, isn't it?" Bunty said setting her knitting needles on her lap.

"Bunty, dear, if it were obvious, we wouldn't all be staring at you. Now would be a most excellent time to share with the group," Kitty said. The rest of the gang now stared eagerly at Bunty, who suddenly began to blush.

"Right, well, I think it's best if Cliff tells us the plan that's already in motion. Then we can add to that." Bunty gestured for Cliff to take over.

As it turned out, Cliff's plan wasn't overly complicated, help protect Randy and Marcus, derail the Serpents drug operations, stall the council, and save the town. It would have been best described as "by the book." He'd crossed his t's and dotted his i's, but there was very little wiggle room for things to go wrong. Seeing as things had already gone wrong from almost every front, the plan left a little to be desired.

In the end, it shouldn't have been as surprising as it was that it was Bunty who seemed the most adept at sorting through the plans and coming up with a more tactical approach to organizing another one. She attributed her skills to years of skimming through the mystery/crime section of the library, but Cliff suspected there was more to Ms. Elizabeth Price than met the eye.

It was the first time Cliff had seen her so energized by any conversation since he'd arrived, and more than once, he caught some genuine smiles, as piece by piece, a more comprehensive plan began to form.

By the time they'd combed through all the information they had, a plan was in place. Cliff had managed to get Tom all the information he needed including both Randy and Marcus's numbers, so they could keep tabs on both boys. He was also told that the team Tom put together was on its way to set up the arrest, though they figured that wouldn't happen for another few hours.

With nothing more for them to do, and everyone's eyes were beginning to droop, save for Gerald's. He'd fallen asleep in his chair some time before, despite multiple attempts to move him to his room, as his snoring was of mild annoyance. Each of them was now confident they had a working plan to go by, so they headed to bed.

15

The thing about all good plans is that that don't ever seem to go to plan. Though interestingly enough for Cliff, he'd never had so many parts of a plan go south so quickly.

He woke early Saturday morning to a message on his phone letting him know that both Marcus and Randy were safe with Tom and that they managed to get all of the product they'd been sent to retrieve.

Neither of the boys seemed to know anything about what they were picking up, deciding early on that it was likely safer not to ask questions. As it turned out, they were offloading cocaine, which was being delivered from across the border in Detroit to Windsor. The boys were picking it up and dropping it off in London before making their way back home again. The only thing they were doing was getting in and out of the car to fill up with gas. The rest was handled by the Crimson Serpents. This, by no means got the boys off the hook, but Tom made note to say they were being very cooperative and that, for their protection, they were being held by Tom and his team.

So as to not raise too much suspicion in town, they'd contacted their parents and told them they caught them joyriding in one of the dealership trucks, and that they should come and pick them up. When their parents arrived, everything would be explained to them, and they would be asked to stay until after the vote on Monday.

The only catch was that the biker tracking the boys had gotten away.

This was less than ideal, and Cliff wasn't sure what that would mean for their now-well-curated plan.

Just as Cliff was trying to sort out what he should be doing next with all this new information, there was a knock at his bedroom door.

He got up from his bed and walked to the door, picking up a navy blue and grey striped housecoat from the hanger behind his door just as another knock occurred.

"Just a minute," he said, slipping the housecoat on as he opened the door to find Hans's large frame a little shrunken as he wrung his hands together nervously. "Hans? What's going on?"

"Well, it's just…well, it's likely nothing…but umm…" He scratched the side of his head, clearly trying to decide if whatever was on his mind was worth coming to get Cliff for.

"It's early, Hans. Just spit it out," Cliff said, stifling a yawn.

"Like I said, it's probably nothing. It's just, there's a man…on a bike…sitting across the road," Hans said shakily.

"What do you mean a man on a bike?"

"Umm, well, I'm not sure how to say it any differently. Like I said, it's probably nothing. But he's been there for hours. At least that's what Kitty's said."

Cliff walked quickly over to one of his bedroom windows…the octagon window that had a clear view of the Anglican Church across the road and thus the road outside.

Sure enough, as he peered out the window, there was a rather large and gruff-looking man leaning against a stylish and well cared for Harley. Cliff didn't need to see the patch on the man's back to know who he was affiliated with, and based on the collection of cigarette butts piled beside him, he'd been standing there for some time.

"There is, indeed, a man standing outside of our place," Cliff confirmed to Hans, who'd followed him gingerly into his room and was now peering out the window over Cliff's shoulder.

"What should we do?" Hans asked.

Cliff stepped back from the window and rubbed his chin thoughtfully. His first thought was that he needed a shave. His second was equally less thrilling.

"Nothing. There's not much we can do, unfortunately. Not unless he directly does anything to any of us. Sitting outside of a church is not actually a crime."

"But he's trying to intimidate us," Hans said.

"Yes, I suspect he is. And if I had to guess, he's the escort that evaded the police last night when they brought in the boys," Cliff said, still pondering what else he could do.

"How would he know to come here?" Hans asked.

Cliff didn't have to say anything for the realization to dawn on his big friend, whose shoulders seemed to slump at the reminder. "Right, the article. Well, if he is actually the man who got away last night, can't we just call your friend and have them pick him up?"

"We have no proof that he's the guy. He could be someone else entirely. I'm simply assuming that's the case." Cliff dropped his hands to his sides and patted his thighs rhythmically. "Who's up?"

"Only Gerald's still sleeping, though I suspect his stomach will start to rumble any time now, and Mrs. Chen is still away visiting her niece and nephew. No one has been able to reach her, but she is notoriously difficult to reach unless she wants to be."

"I thought she was just going to ask them about the Four Points? She was only supposed to be gone for the day," Cliff asked.

"Mrs. Chen never does anything without a reason. If she's gone, I'm sure it's for a good one. Maybe they're afraid to talk? I know my friends from fastball have been less than helpful when I asked them Four Points. People appear to not understand there's a problem at all, or they're too afraid to talk."

"Right. Well. One problem at a time, I suppose. Follow me," Cliff said, walking out the bedroom door and making his way down towards the main living area.

Bunty, who wasn't seated in her regular chair, had joined Sol and Kitty in the living room that morning, and was knitting the cuff of a cable knit sweater. Cliff could see the steam rise from her mug of hot tea on the table in front of her. Sol was in his chair, reading the paper, and Kitty, who was not in her usual spot beside him, was currently tucked indiscreetly behind the curtains peering out at the road.

"He's been here all morning," Kitty whispered.

"Since we've been up," Sol clarified, letting the paper he was reading fall to his lap.

"Like I said, all morning," Kitty whispered back. "What are we going to do?"

"Nothing right now," Cliff said, moving to take the empty seat beside Bunty, with Hans following closely behind him. "I'm afraid we may have drawn too much attention to ourselves with that article. Which isn't a problem," Cliff added quickly before Hans had a chance to feel any worse than he already did. "It's what we wanted to happen. It just speeds up our timeline a little."

"We have a timeline?" Kitty asked.

"Well, we always knew the vote was on Monday, and Mary Anne was able to help us as much as she could, which means we have two days to lock in everything we need to convince the town not to choose Four Points," Cliff said, his hand rubbing his knee subconsciously.

"Are we sure the town is going to choose them?" Sol asked looking up from his paper.

"What do you mean?" Cliff asked.

"Well, as far as I can remember, the contract has always gone local, which has always been Wilder and Sons. Why on earth would they do something different now?"

"Sol's, right," Bunty whispered. "Not every town has a company like them in their backyard."

"It's a very compelling proposal on paper, the town would stand to save a lot of money." Sol put in.

"True," Bunty said her head rocking side to side.

Cliff tapped his chin with a finger for a moment, "Okay, let's say I'm wrong about the bribes, and everyone on the council is in fact just voting on what they think is a good deal for the town."

"That still doesn't explain why they would come here. There must be lots of other communities they could choose, ones without such a formidable local competition." Bunty said.

"You're right," Cliff said, standing up and starting to pace the room. "So, something is different about St. Marys. Something worth the risk of coming."

"Its position," Gerald said, lumbering down the stairs, letting out a massive yawn as he did and causing the rest of the residents to jump.

"What?" Sol said, his gaze turning towards Gerald as he poked his head into the living room.

"Haven't you ever wondered why St. Marys has so many small factories and what nots around it?" he said, stepping into the living room, scratching his stomach. "You have a small town conveniently located in the heart of southern Ontario."

"Surely there must be more convenient places to live." Kitty laughed.

"No, Gerald's right. You'd need a town small enough to hide in, but big enough to go unnoticed by the locals," Cliff said.

"The town has been expanding quite a bit over the last couple years," Hans said.

"New development everywhere. I barely know who lives here half the time," Kitty agreed.

"So, if you wanted to start a new distribution network, you'd have affordable land in a prime location," Cliff said.

"A distribution network?" Kitty asked. "I thought Four Points was just coming in and trying to swindle the town out of money?"

"No," Cliff said then stopped, "Well yes."

Kitty shook her head "I'm confused."

"That makes two of us," Sol confessed.

"Wait I think I understand," Kitty began. "Four Points moves into small towns, lies about the work they do, and demands being paid despite their shotty workmanship. If towns don't pay up, their silent partners, the Crimson Serpents, come in and threaten them. The Crimson Serpents are also selling drugs and using Four Points for their town contracts to launder their drug money. That about right?" Bunty asked.

"Pretty much spot on with my thoughts yes." Cliff smiled.

"And St. Marys is an ideal location?" Sol asked tentatively, receiving a nod from Cliff.

"And no one would bat an eye," Kitty said.

"Well, you might," Sol mused, which got a glare from Kitty.

"Gerald, you might be right," Cliff said, but he was no longer in the room, and Cliff could hear the rustling of pans from the kitchen. "Right," Cliff continued. "But that doesn't explain *why* the town would give them the contract."

"I'm sure there are at least a couple of the councillors whose mouths would water at the chance to take a lower bid," Sol joked.

"Maybe, but that's a big risk to take a chance on," Cliff said.

"Perhaps they are being threatened? I mean someone was just killed." Kitty grimaced.

"Hmm, who would have the most sway in the town? The mayor?" Cliff asked.

"Oh my! He's coming," Kitty exclaimed, causing the entire room to turn and look at her.

"The mayor is coming?" Sol asked.

"Not the mayor! The man...the biker man! From the road." She darted from the window back to the room. "He's walking up the driveway. He's approaching the door. He's staring directly at me!" Kitty voice began to rise as she quickly shut the curtains. "Maybe he'll just leave?"

There was a loud rap on the door.

"Everyone stay calm," Cliff said, though he had to admit his own palms were beginning to sweat. "I'll get it."

"I'll go with you," Hans said, getting up from the chair.

Cliff was about to protest his friend's offer, but having the big man beside him would give him some comfort.

"I know you're in there! I saw you through the window," yelled the man from outside. "Open the door. Now."

The room grew eerily quiet. Cliff walked over to the door, Hans right behind him. He reached the door and took a deep breath before turning the knob and opening it.

"Clifford Shaw?" asked the large, bearded man, wearing a thick, black leather jacket and loose-fitting jeans. The man wreaked of cigarette smoke and leather. He held a phone in his hand and looked at the screen before turning it to show Cliff. It was the article Jan had posted the other day in the paper. The man pointed at the picture then at Cliff. "Yep, you. Come with me." He turned without any more words.

"He's not going with you," Hans said, putting a hand on Cliff's shoulder.

The man slowly turned back to look at Hans, though he seemed unfazed by the obvious height difference. "He is."

"Or what?"

"It's a nice place you have here. It certainly would be a shame to see it in a pile of ashes." he said coldly. "So, what's it going to be?"

Cliff removed his friend's hand from his shoulder giving it a gentle pat as he did.

"Thank you, Hans. But I think this man just wants to chat."

"See, he gets it." The man turned to walk away again.

"Cliff you can't go with him, isn't that incredibly…stupid?" Hans said quietly.

"Maybe, but what choice do I have? Given their history, I think burning down a house isn't an empty threat."

"But—"

"I'll be fine, old friend. Not my first time in this situation," Cliff lied. This was the first time anyone had ever come for him. "But maybe, to be safe, you can send word to Lou. Let her know what's going on." Cliff gave his friend a forced smile, before following his would-be captor out of the driveway, his large red and black fiery winged snake patch now visible as he walked away.

"I will. And Cliff, be careful," Hans said.

As Cliff walked out of the drive, he turned back to see Kitty, Sol, Bunty, and even Gerald, staring out the window at him. He tried to look as confident as possible, though, in truth, it was hard to do when he still looked a little foolish wearing his housecoat. He doubted this man would give him the time to change. Still, he gave his friends a firm nod as if to say *it'll be fine.* Even so, he could see it didn't wash away the fear in their eyes.

"Where are we going?" Cliff asked as he tried to keep up with the big man in front of him.

He didn't say anything, just turned to look Cliff up and down. He remained silent until he reached his bike where, once again, he gave Cliff a menacing grin.

He rummaged in one of the side pouches on his bike and pulled out a small black helmet. "Wear this. We wouldn't want to break any laws now, would we?" He laughed.

Cliff, in all of his years of living, had never been on a motorcycle. He'd avoided them like the plague. He'd been to enough accidents involving them to know the genuine risk there was in riding one. He also knew that the risk was higher depending on the driver. It was Cliff's turn to eye the man in front of him, who began climbing on the bike with unnatural ease for a man his size.

"Get on. Now." He revved the engine.

Cliff put the helmet on and buckled the strap, double-checking it was tight enough that it wouldn't fall off mid-ride. He had no idea how tight it needed to be, so he gave it an extra cautious cinch. Once he was confident the helmet was secure, he attempted to climb on the back of the bike, which he was sure wasn't nearly as graceful or effortless as the large man he was now clinging to.

"I just realized I don't know your name," Cliff said, trying his darndest to distract himself.

"And you likely never will," chuckled the man. "But if you have to call me anything, call me Tug."

"Okay, Tug, where are we—"

But Cliff couldn't finish his sentence, as the bike abruptly lurched forward, causing Cliff to grip his captor even tighter. For a moment, Cliff thought maybe his heart had stopped, but was relieved when it was only his breathing. He promptly sucked in a deep breath to calm his nerves.

They were heading down Peel Street towards Queen, and Cliff felt as though Tug was propping him up in place, the only thing preventing him from falling face first into the ground. What was going to happen when they inevitably travelled uphill, which was a particularly common direction in St. Marys?

To Cliff's chagrin, Tug took a left, heading straight for downtown and what was certain to be the worst hill of them all. Cliff fought to keep his eyes open, though they only managed to see half the town, as his face was pressed firmly to Tug's back, his cheek rubbing against the Crimson Serpents insignia on the back of his leather jacket.

Cliff watched each set of lights they passed in agony. He peered over at the falls as they crossed Victoria Bridge, and Cliff was acutely aware of its increased width as he heard, though was unable to look at, the cars passing beside them.

Knowing what was coming, Cliff clenched his thighs together and managed to squeeze Tug a little tighter as he accelerated up the hill, something Cliff guessed was for his torment and Tug's amusement. Cliff could feel the air sweeping over his helmet, and his housecoat flapped wildly in the wind, although he was relieved that, for the most part, the large man shielded him from the brunt of it.

After what felt like an eternity of gripping, Cliff spotted the stone stairs to nowhere at the top of the hill, and he knew the worst of the ride was over.

Cliff allowed himself to ease up on Tug's waist and look around. He hadn't been aware just how fast his heart was beating, but now that they were cruising, he almost felt comfortable. Well, as comfortable as someone could be, riding on the back of a motorcycle with a mysterious man named Tug, who wouldn't say where they were going.

"Will you tell me where we are going now?" Cliff yelled over the wind.

If Tug heard him, he ignored him, and accelerated forward, causing the massive machine to rumble below him.

Luckily, Cliff didn't have to wait long, as Tug took a right on Thames Road, just before the town limits. Cliff hadn't been out this way in a long time, but he certainly remembered it from his days of cruising around with Hans in a *four-wheeled* vehicle.

The winding road appeared to have a few more houses on it now than it did back in the day when it was just small farms. Tug rounded a particularly tight bend before pulling off the road towards a no trespassing sign, which he ignored. The ground here was much bumpier than the road they'd just been on, and Cliff kept popping off his seat, then slamming back down into it. It was not the most relaxing voyage.

Tug didn't seem to be bothered by it as he drove down a long patch of dirt, until, finally, Cliff made out an old barn and farmhouse in the distance. Cliff guessed they were in the right place by the twenty or so Harleys parked out front.

They must have heard Tug's bike coming down the path as, one by one, various large men, and a few women, in matching leather jackets strolled out of the barn. Cliff watched them funnel out and immediately regretted coming here on his own. At first, he figured he would be fine. His friend knew who'd taken him, and that would be enough to keep him safe. But being here now and spotting more than a few weapons, Cliff quickly sensed how terrible of a decision this was.

Tug's bike rolled to a stop, and he kicked out the stand and waited for Cliff to hop off. This took a little longer than getting on, which received a few chuckles from the gang members standing around watching.

"First time on a bike, fellas," Cliff said, trying to ease his own fear with a joke. If they were amused, Cliff couldn't tell. He was too busy trying to stop his legs from wobbling and taking him down to the ground. He hadn't noticed just out tightly he'd been squeezing.

"How was it, Mr. Shaw?" said a voice from the middle of the pack.

When Cliff finally glanced up to see who it was, he recognized the man immediately as the who'd been talking to the boys in the park. Hurley.

"What?" Cliff said, back to pretending he had trouble hearing if only to keep up appearances and to be mildly frustrating at the same time.

"How was it!" Hurley called out a little louder.

"Oh, other than the feeling I may collapse at any moment, I'd almost say it was fun," Cliff said.

"Tell that to my ribs." Tug slid off the bike with ease. "Thought the old man was going to break 'em when we hit the hill there." Tug laughed as he rubbed his side.

"Like I said, first time," Cliff said. "Now, any chance you'd like to tell me why I was forced onto a bike and brought here?"

"I'd hardly say forced, Mr. Shaw. As far as I can tell, you don't look bruised or broken in any way. In fact, Tug here is actually quite the gentleman. If I wanted to force you here, I would have sent Hatchet over there." Hurley said slightly louder than before as he pointed to a particularly nasty-looking fellow, whose face looked as though it had been beaten down and rebuilt multiple times. Various scars crisscrossed his face, each one looking like it masked an old one.

"Right, well, I guess I'm grateful for that. I didn't catch your name," Cliff lied. Then trying to find some hidden courage from deep inside him, he added, "And I know I probably never will, but what do they call you?"

This gave Hurley a chuckle. "You've got guts, old man. I'll give you that."

"At my age, you tend to lose almost everything else. You might as well keep something," Cliff said with a wink.

"Fair enough. They call me Hurley."

"Hurley on a Harley. Sounds like a kid's book," Cliff joked.

This might have been going a bit far, as some of the men took a step forward, including Hatchet, which caused Cliff to stumble back. Luckily, Hurley raised his hand, and they all seemed to calm down at that.

"Bring him inside," Hurley said, giving Tug a nod.

Before Cliff could protest, Tug grabbed his arm and began pulling him into the barn.

16

Cliff wasn't entirely sure what to expect as he was being dragged into an abandoned-looking barn out in the country. It certainly hadn't been that he would be pushed down on a rather luxurious black leather sofa. It was one of dozens of furniture pieces scattered throughout the space, along with tables and TVs. The whole room looked like a large living room. It smelled, on the other hand, like twenty or so grown men lived in some sort of nineties dive bar, complete with the smell of stale beer, cigarette smoke, and marijuana. Not to mention a little smattering of some other illicit drugs, which appeared to dust the tables.

"Nice place you got here," Cliff said as he tried not to look too ridged on the couch, even as Tug plopped down beside him, causing him to bobble up and down a bit.

"It is a pleasant home away from home," Hurley said taking a seat across from Cliff in his own black leather chair. A couple of the men huddled around watching, but for the most part, the rest of them scattered across the room, giving no care to the fact that there was an ex-detective with them. The room began to feel more and more like a bar. Someone had even set up a speaker playing music nearby. None of this seemed to bother Hurley.

"We would like to keep it that way, Clifford Shaw," Hurley said as someone brought him a beer. "Drink?" He gestured to his own bottle.

"A little early for me," Cliff said, shaking his head.

"Right, I forgot. It's just a little late for us. You see, we were up all night."

"Trouble sleeping?" Cliff asked.

"I guess you could say that." Hurley smiled and took a swig. "You see, we've had a pretty good thing going in this town the last little while, and well, as of late, things seem to have changed."

"I'm sorry to hear that."

"I appreciate that, Cliff, because I'm afraid you may have something to do with that."

"Me? Fellas, look at me. I'm just some old man who lives in a house with a bunch of other old people. What could I have possibly done to you?" Cliff crossed his legs, trying to look as comfortable as he could in a rather uncomfortable predicament.

Hurley leaned back in his chair and stared at Cliff, eyeing him up. He nodded to Tug, who promptly placed the *Gazette*'s Thursday edition on the table with the large picture of Cliff standing with the mayor at the train station.

"You're talking about this?" Cliff laughed. "Funny story this—"

"I'd love to hear it, Mr. Shaw. Because from where I'm sitting, since you've got here, things have changed."

"I imagine Sam Benoit's dead body didn't help," Cliff said, pointing to the page.

"Tragic suicide in a small town. It was a shame," Hurley said.

"It was tragic, though the police don't think it was a suicide."

"Why wouldn't they think that?" Hurley sipped his beer.

"I'm sure they have their reasons, but if you wanted to know what those were, I think you should talk to them," Cliff said.

"But I'm talking to you." Hurley shrugged.

"Then I'm afraid you're not going to get the answers you're looking for. Because, despite what that article says, I have no idea what's going on here. In fact, the only reason I was in that picture in the first place is because I arrived that morning on that train." Cliff pointed to the train parked in the background.

"A rather strange coincidence."

"It is. But that's all it is. A coincidence," Cliff said confidently. He might not be used to riding a motorcycle, but he was no stranger to dealing with intimidation.

"Let me get to the point, Cliff. I'm not sure how or why you've decided to get involved in all of this. But I strongly suggest you *uninvolve* yourself immediately. Maybe enjoy your retirement a little."

"That's all I've been trying to do."

"Well then. Might I suggest you try a little harder before you find yourself *fully* retired," Hurley said. He then hammered back his beer and slammed the empty on the table. "Accidents like that keep happening in this quiet little town after all. If you'll excuse me, I need to get some shut-eye." Hurley got up from his chair and walked away without another word.

Tug stood and pulled Cliff to his feet. Cliff was once again dragged out of the barn by Tug and given the helmet to place on his head. Cliff struggled to get on the bike—his legs were still sore from the initial ride—but at least one thing was clearer to him now. There was no denying why he'd been brought here.

***

"Stop investigating or we will kill you," Cliff said, a warm cup of coffee in his hand and his friends sitting all around, staring at him. Gerald had been kind enough to save him a plate of food, though when Cliff told him he wasn't hungry, the large man began picking away at it slowly. But even he stopped eating at Cliff's statement.

"That's what they said?" Hans asked, clearly trying not to sound scared, but it was obvious he wasn't used to being threatened.

"Well, not in so many words, but yes, that was the intention," Cliff said slowly.

"And you say they took you out of town on Thames Road?" Sol asked.

Cliff gave him a nod.

"How far?"

"Not sure. I haven't been out there in ages." Cliff shrugged.

"Did you pass a golf course?" Sol continued.

Cliff thought a moment and then shook his head. "No."

"So, between town and Chemistry Pines then." Sol nodded.

"Why does any of that matter? The man was threatened to be killed," Kitty said, shaking her head at her husband.

Sol shrugged. "Well, it's good to know where their base camp is, in case we need to raid it, or tell someone about it."

"Raid it? Sol, who do you think we are, the damn army? Most of the people in this house can't make it up to the top floor, for heaven's sake," Kitty protested.

"Well, it doesn't have to be us. It could be the police."

"Right, we tell the police, they raid the barn, then they come and kill us in our sleep." Kitty dusted off her hands. "Simple as that."

"I'm just trying to get all the information, Kitty." Sol picked up his paper and pretended to read it.

"I'm sorry, Sol. I'm just nervous."

"We all are," Hans said quietly.

The room seemed to fall into a heavy silence for a moment until Bunty, who'd been finishing up the arm of a sweater, held it up to examine the length. "I'm not."

"I'm sorry?" Kitty asked, brows furrowed.

"That is to say, I guess I'm a *little* nervous. I'd hardly say I want to die. Who does?" she asked, looking around the room, though no one answered.

"I don't," Cliff said after a moment.

"Neither do I," Hans followed.

"I rather enjoy life," Gerald said "And food. Yes. Mostly food." This prompted a laugh from around the room.

"None of us want to die, Bunty," Kitty said, giving Sol a warm smile, which appeared to have more than enough words behind it to appease her husband, who placed the paper back down on his lap.

"My point is, when we decided to do this, we knew there was a risk involved. A young man was killed. Of course they would be willing to kill a couple old people if they got in their way. But everyone here thought that we were right to take up the case in the first place. Besides, whether we want to admit it or not, we all have one foot in the grave anyways. We even buried someone just this week."

"And may she rest in peace," Hans said, making the sign of the cross. A few others whispered their own prayers.

"My point is, I've rather enjoyed this little mystery. It's like being in one of my books. And now I would certainly like to be one of those characters in those books who comes out the other side, entirely not dead. But should I not be, I would at least like to be the character who died trying to protect their town from hooligans who want to destroy it," Bunty said, giving the room a rather firm nod. She leaned forward, picked up her tea from the table, and blew on it before taking a sip.

"Right then, Bunty," Cliff said looking around the room. "A rather excellent speech."

"I'm not sure I've heard you string together so many words in my life," Kitty said, as she began clapping pleasantly. "I have to say I rather enjoyed it."

"Thank you, Kitty." Bunty smiled.

"I mean, again, I really do not want to die doing this," Sol said, "but you have my vote to continue."

"Hold on a minute, everyone," Cliff said, trying to settle the now rather excited room. "Bunty, that was, indeed, an excellent speech, and

I'm glad that the rest of you seem ready for this. But there is the small matter that we still don't know who is behind any of this. And the vote is in two days."

This seemed to suck the wind out of everyone's sails.

"Maybe that's not entirely true." Bunty said.

"What do you mean?" Cliff asked.

"What *exactly* did they say to you while you were there? Maybe there's something you missed? Something we can help with," Bunty said, receiving more than a few stares as she gathered up her knitting needles and placed them in the wicker basket beside her. She looked back up at Cliff and smiled.

Cliff had already gone over in his head the conversations he'd had with Hurley in the barn—as well as summarized them to his housemates—and still he couldn't think of anything that would be of any help. At the very least, he was more unnerved by the man's completely relaxed attitude at having an ex-detective in his den. However, Bunty was right. Cliff had gotten nowhere on his own, and maybe it was time to get a little more outside help. *Besides Bunty placed down her knitting needles to listen to me, and from the looks of everyone else, this is a rather big deal.*

"Alright, but as far as I can tell, he didn't say much. The entire thing simply felt like a giant warning." Cliff sighed. "But here we go."

Cliff proceeded to tell his friends, in detail, the story of his little abduction, from the moment he left on the bike—leaving out the particularly embarrassing fear that had gripped him as they raced up the hill—until Hurley had said he could leave. Everyone sat patiently listening. Even Gerald sat quietly on the couch beside him, though Cliff suspected that had more to do with the fact that he'd already finished off the plate of food that he'd been "holding" for Cliff.

A couple of moments earned some exasperated breaths from a few of his listeners, but all in all, they listened attentively. By the time Cliff had finished, he still didn't feel like there was much he could have missed in the story, though he admitted, if only to himself, that saying it out loud did seem to offer a different depth to the words than just repeating them over in his mind.

"And then Tug dropped me off here. What do we all think?" Cliff asked, turning to look at each of his friends, who all seemed to be thinking hard about his story. Cliff admired this about them. Though none of them had likely ever been put in this type of dangerous situation, he found it incredible to watch their pure persistence when it came to saving their town.

"All I got was that they seem to be onto the fact that you're working on this investigation and that they want you to stop," Sol said with a shrug. "Though I have to imagine that is not new information for you?"

Cliff nodded in agreeance.

"I wish Mrs. Chen was here. She always has a keen eye for puzzles." Hans patted his hands rhythmically on his knees. "Speaking of, has anyone heard from her? She should have been back by now."

"She sent me a message last night, telling me she was working on something big and that she planned on being back here by Monday before the meeting," Kitty said, tapping her phone resting on the table beside her. "I meant to tell you all this morning, but with everything that was going on, it completely slipped my mind."

"That's fine, Kitty," Cliff said, leaning back on the couch, as a wave of uncertainty washed over him. "I just hope she's having better luck then we are." He sighed.

"What if," Bunty said, slowly as she tapped the side of her mug, "we're looking at this in the wrong way?"

"What do you mean?" Cliff asked, as he and everyone else fixed their eyes on her.

Bunty was about to speak when there was a sudden knock at the front door, followed by a ringing of the doorbell.

"My lord! Who could that possibly be?" Kitty stood and walked over to the window to peer out.

"It's not the damned skull people again, is it?" Sol asked, clearly unimpressed at the interruption.

"They're snakes," Hans said.

"Truer words have never been spoken, Hans." Sol joked.

"I'm afraid not," Kitty said.

"Well then, who is it Kitty?" Sol pressed.

"It's Lou."

"Lou? Then why isn't she just letting herself in?" Hans asked.

"Because, she's not alone." Kitty looked back at everyone.

17

"There's another officer with her," Kitty explained.

"I could use a snack." Gerald got up from the couch. "Any of you need a little nibble?" he asked, but was out of the room before anyone could answer him.

"Should we let her in?" Kitty asked.

"She's the police, my love. I'd hardly say we can refuse her," Sol pointed out.

"Doesn't she need a warrant or something?" Kitty asked Cliff.

"It's probably best if we simply ask what it is she wants first," Cliff said as there was another knock at the door.

"Just a moment!" Kitty yelled. "Why would the police be here?"

"I can see you in the window, Kitty. Can you please open the door?" Lou yelled from outside.

"Rude." Kitty snorted, as Cliff made his way over to the front door.

"I think there is only one way to find out. Bunty, hold your thought," he added.

Bunty nestled back into her chair and picked up her knitting needles, briefly looking up at Cliff with a smile.

"Everyone best just stay in here and let me handle this." Cliff waited a moment to make sure he received an affirmative nod from each present member of the house.

Cliff approached the door, equal parts curious and nervous about what Lou would be doing here, and why she felt the need to bring anyone with her. Taking a deep breath, he opened the door.

Lou looked a little unsettled. When she moved, Cliff finally caught sight of her company and grimaced. Behind her stood the slightly smaller-statured Officer Thomas, the man who'd been with Captain Marks in the back of the SUV the night before. He looked annoyingly stern, his eyes hidden beneath a pair of black sunglasses, despite the morning not being all that sunny.

"Officer Polaski, Officer Thomas. What can I help you with?" Cliff said, trying his best to be as formal as possible.

"Cliff, you know you can call me Lou."

"This feels much less casual to me, Officer Polaski." Cliff nodded to the man behind her.

"Right, and I'm sorry about that. This is Officer Thomas. He insisted on coming with me." Lou did a small eye roll, only noticeable to Cliff.

"We've met." Officer Thomas gave Cliff a curt nod.

"Yes, we have. Is there a reason you stopped by?" Cliff asked.

"Do you have a problem with me being here, Mr. Shaw?" Officer Thomas said, as he gripped the top of his standard-issue police vest.

"Why would I possibly have a problem with you being here, Officer? We were just having coffee."

"Aren't you going to invite us in?"

"I think it's best, for the time being, if we carry on this conversation out here. Not everyone in our house is dressed for company," Cliff said, not leaving his position from the centre of the door.

"Well then, I guess you wouldn't mind answering some questions?" Officer Thomas said. He pulled off his sunglasses, probably just so he could narrow his eyes at Cliff.

"Dammit, Hank, I thought you told me you'd be a fly on the wall here. I told you I could handle this." Lou shook her head.

"Seems to me you're the one getting handled here, Lou," he snapped.

"Go wait in the car, please." Lou turned to face the man, who didn't look at all pleased to be told what to do.

"Fine. I'll give you three minutes to do it," he said ominously as he turned away, glancing into the window and catching sight of Kitty peering out. As their eyes met, she tucked back inside, causing Officer Thomas to smile before he walked to the car.

Once he was far enough away and could no longer hear them, Lou turned back to Cliff.

"I'm sorry. He insisted on coming, and for some stupid reason, Captain Marks seems to like him and made me bring him along." Lou sounded more than a little annoyed.

"Do you want to tell me what is going on?" Cliff asked. He heard footsteps behind him and turned to find Hans, Kitty, Sol, and Bunty stepping into the entrance way. "I told you all to stay inside."

"But it's Lou," Hans said, gesturing over at her, though this only seemed to cause Lou to shrink.

"I'm here to bring you in, Cliff," Lou said, blurting out the words, as if knowing, if she didn't get them out soon, she never would.

"What?!" seemed to be the general reaction of the house. Even Gerald poked his head out from the kitchen, and Cliff guessed he'd been listening in the entire time.

"It's just to ask you a few questions, but Captain Marks has this idea in his head that you're trying something," said Lou.

"Does it have anything to do with why he was here the other night?" Kitty asked.

"What?" It was Lou's turn to look surprised. "What do you mean he was here?"

"Captain Marks came by the other night to talk with me about the investigation. Asked me to stop whatever it is I was doing," Cliff said, though he was more interested in Lou's reaction. "Did he not tell you he came to speak with me?"

Lou shook her head. "What did he ask you?"

"If I was investigating this case."

"What did you say?"

"I told him, of course, I wasn't."

"But you are."

"I like to think of it as being concerned citizens."

"Concerned citizens who helped disrupt a distribution network for some drug dealers."

"I may have called in a favour to help out a couple of kids who got into a little trouble. They will be released Monday, and I have it on good authority that it won't reach the papers." Cliff turned to give Hans a smile.

"Thank God," Lou said.

"He also asked me to stop talking to you about the investigation," Cliff said.

"Wait, what? How did he even know I was talking to you?" Lou asked.

"I'm not sure he did, but I think he had his suspicions. Hence why I imagine you haven't been around the past couple of days."

"No. I mean, yes, but it's just 'cause we've been busy." Lou seemed taken aback.

"Did you ever find a connection to between Sam and Four Points?" Cliff asked getting a couple of gasps from the audience behind him.

"Possibly," Lou said tilting her head side to side. "There was evidence on Sam's computer that had him meeting with a representative at Four Points. But when Captain Marks reached out, they said he didn't have time with his thesis. That was a year and a half ago."

Cliffs brows shot up, "He must have made an impression,"

"Agreed. But nothing ties him directly."

"So, it's another dead end?" Cliff asked.

"Yes, and no, it appears Sam received four rather substantial deposits over the past year, all from the same account. But again, no way of knowing who sent them exactly," Lou said.

"More coincidences and not a lot of facts." Cliff said rubbing his chin.

Lou nodded.

"You have an account number, right?" Gerald said from behind them, as he whisked something in a bowl. "Obviously you just need to see if anyone else from town has received similar payments?"

"What?" Lou asked.

"Gerald, you're a genius," Cliff said with a smile. "We don't need to know *who* paid him to stop this vote from going through, we just need to find out if anyone else is also getting paid and confront them."

"How do you know anyone is being paid?" Lou asked.

"The body. If it was a message, it was a message to anyone else who might have been getting paid." Gerald said.

"Anyone who knows what's really going on," Cliff added.

"We can't just go through people's personal bank information," Lou said. "Not without cause. All we have now is a suspicion that this is going on. Legally, I can't do anything." Lou shook her head.

"But, illegally, I can," Kitty piped up. "Wait no, not illegally. I just mean I might have a way to find out if anyone on council has recently deposited a large sum of money." Kitty smiled.

"That *is* illegal, Kitty," Lou said.

"Are we sure it's not just a community service?" Kitty asked.

"Getting *gossip* about people's personal banking isn't a good idea, Kitty," Sol said.

"And it's most definitely illegal, sharing private banking information," Lou shook her head at Kitty. "No. Best if you just let me handle that. I'll see what I can do." Lou looked back at her squad car. "Look, I'm sorry, but I only have a couple minutes to get you to the truck before Officer Nimrod over there comes back and does something stupid,"

Lou told Cliff.

"But why are you taking him?" Hans asked.

"Because someone thought they saw him this morning on a bike with someone from the Crimson Serpents." Lou narrowed her eyes on him. "Is that true?"

Cliff nodded. "Yes."

"But he was practically forced to go," Kitty explained. "They threatened to burn down our house if he didn't."

"Jesus Christ." Lou ran her palm across her face.

"Not in this house, young lady," Kitty said.

"Sorry, Kitty. Well, I'm sure that, if you explain that to the captain, everything will be fine."

"Maybe. But also, possibly not," Bunty said quietly as she stepped out from behind Hans.

"What do you mean?" Lou asked.

"It was just something that Cliff mentioned happened when he was at the barn."

"Barn?"

"It's the place they took him," Hans said.

"What barn?" Lou asked.

"I think we're missing the point here," Cliff interjected. "What did you hear, Bunty?"

"Well, it's just…" Bunty began but stopped when she spotted Officer Thomas walking over.

"What's going on over here, Lou? You need some back up?" Officer Thomas asked, his hands dropping to his side.

"Everything is fine, Hank. Just get back in the car!" Lou shouted.

"Well, you're certainly taking your sweet time. He's one man, Lou." He stared at the rest of the residents inside. "Unless you think we should bring them all in," he added, tapping his handcuffs.

"Jesu—" Lou began but stopped herself when she caught the death glare from Kitty. "Hank, everything is fine. Cliff was just about to come out." She sent a pleading glare at Cliff to step outside.

He looked back at the house and then at Bunty. He would have loved to hear what it was she was going to say about his conversation, because he was lost. Instead, he forced himself to slip on a pair of comfortable loafers and for the second time that day he followed someone, still in his pajamas and robe, out to the stoop.

"Maybe you can all continue our conversation without me. See if you can't figure something out about our little problem," Cliff said, making sure to get a nod from Bunty before he turned to leave.

"Weird thing to say on your way out, old man." Officer Thomas glared at Cliff. "If it was me, I'd say you were up to something."

"That's some mighty fine police work you've done there, son. Someone should do us all a favour and give you a promotion." Cliff gave Officer Thomas a pat on the shoulder as he walked by.

He swatted Cliff's hand away. "You going to tell me what it is?"

"Unlikely." Cliff smiled. "But I'm sure a brain such as yours will deduce the meaning in no time." Cliff winked. This received a chuckle from Lou.

"Easy, old timer," Officer Thomas shot back.

"You know you make these old references as if it's somehow a negative. But you forget I've lived nearly three of your lives, so whatever you think you've learned during your minute existence on this planet is barely a drop in the bucket. Whereas myself, and the people who live here, have done it all tenfold. Remember, son, it's a gift to be young. But it's a privilege to be old." Cliff walked over to the car, leaving a frustrated Officer Thomas in his wake.

The ride to the police station was at least shorter and more comfortable than the ride to the barn. Cliff thought it was funny they'd even bothered to drive, seeing as the station was two blocks away. *Small towns, I suppose.*

The first thing Cliff noticed when he walked into the station was that it was not at all like the ones he'd been used to in Toronto. They typically had large entryways leading into a compact room filled with desks and temporary cells for anyone they hadn't had the chance to book yet.

He supposed this was kind of similar to the one in Toronto, only a tenth of the size. When they arrived at the holding area, Lou asked Cliff to take a seat while she told Captain Marks that he was there.

"I would have figured this place to be busier, considering the investigation," Cliff said, looking around at the limited desks that didn't appear to be used.

"St. Marys isn't really equipped for housing many police at one time for an investigation, so the Stratford PD have given us some facilities to use while we're working on this. We mainly use St. Marys as a local headquarters to collect and gather evidence before it gets transferred," Lou said as she began to walk away.

"And questioning people, I suppose." Cliff chuckled.

Lou stopped to face him. "I'm sorry about this, Cliff, but as far as I'm aware, you're not being questioned." Lou seemed unable to meet his eyes.

"It's fine, Lou. I'm not worried," Cliff replied.

Lou let out a sad smile and turned to leave to get Captain Marks.

"Maybe you should be," Officer Thomas said, leaning against the wall, staring at Cliff.

"Really? And what is it you think happened here?" Cliff asked, crossing his legs and leaning back in a red plastic chair.

"My money is still on a jumper. All this other stuff feels a bit like patterns. If you look hard enough, you'll find something." Officer Thomas gripped the top of his vest, a position he clearly found comfortable.

"You mean police work," Cliff said with a slow nod.

"What?"

"You said all 'all this other stuff feels like patterns.' I'm assuming that, by 'other stuff,' you mean police work, and when you say, 'patterns' you're referring to evidence?" Cliff asked.

"Not everything is complicated," Thomas retorted.

"No, just the things that are." Cliff laughed.

"What's so funny?"

"One day, I'm sure you'll understand." Cliff chuckled again.

Officer Thomas stepped in closer. "You know, it all seems rather suspicious that all of this stuff started to happen on the day you arrived. Doesn't it?" he asked, eyes narrowing in on Cliff.

"Suspicious might not be the best word. Unfortunate, maybe, considering all anyone seems to think is that I'm investigating this somehow."

"So, you're not investigating?"

"I'm retired."

"Why did you come to town?"

"I was invited."

"By who?"

"An old friend."

"For what reason?"

"To consider living here."

"Only to consider?"

"It wasn't exactly laid out the way he explained it," Cliff said, tilting his head side to side.

"What does that mean?"

"It means I thought he had a room for me in his house."

"But he didn't?"

"No, he does."

"I'm confused."

"So was I, son."

"So, there is a room," Officer Thomas asked.

"Yes."

"Then what was the problem? Did you take it?" Officer Thomas asked, scratching his head.

"It's a room in a house. The house comes with some roommates, as you might have deduced. And the room is only mine if I decide I want to live with all these people. I just have to agree to buy out the room."

"So, you mean to tell me they just happened to have an open room."

"No, the previous owner died."

"Sam Benoit lived in your house!"

"No, Flo did."

"Who's Flo?"

"I never met Flo. She died before I arrived. Then Hans asked me if I wanted to take her room, but he never told me I had to commit to buying it, like it was some sort of elderly commune. Anyways, they've given me this week to decide whether I want to live with them. If I do, I sign commitment papers for one year. After that, I buy out the room," Cliff said, surprised at how long it had been since he'd even thought about the house and the room and the people he was committing to live with. *This is certainly not how I expected to spend my week.*

"So? What are you going to do?" Officer Thomas asked when Cliff seemed a little deeper in thought.

"I'm not sure yet." Cliff shrugged.

"What does this have to do with the murder?"

"You tell me." Cliff leaned back in his chair. "You're the one asking the questions."

"You're not…I'm just… So let me get this straight. You show up to town and there are two deaths, and you're having private meetings with biker gangs. Sounds a bit suspicious, if you ask me."

"Well, to be fair, I'd never met either of the deceased. They both died before I arrived. Also, Flo was ninety-two, so I'd hardly say people were shocked." Cliff chuckled.

"Cold way to talk about someone's life."

"We all have to die, son. Not everyone is lucky enough to do it at ninety-two. Sam Benoit, for example. As for the biker gang—" Cliff held a finger up to prevent Officer Thomas from jumping in, "—when a large man threatens you and your home unless you go for a ride with him, you go."

"So, you were threatened? At least that's the story you're sticking with."

"Yes."

"We'll see about that." Officer Thomas pulled his sunglasses down so he could peer over the top of them at Cliff.

"Mr. Shaw," Captain Marks said as he rounded the corner into the sitting area. Lou was close on his tail. "I appreciate you coming in."

"Well, hard to say no to the town's finest." Cliff said gave a nod to both Lou and Officer Thomas. "Although I have to admit, I'm not entirely sure why your resources are being spent on me."

"I think you know why," Captain Marks said.

"I assure you, I don't. You made it very clear that you didn't want me having any part of this murder investigation, and I have done everything in my power to keep myself out of it," Cliff replied.

"Umm, so you didn't go see anyone at the Crimson Serpents?"

"No. As I told Officer Thomas here, a large man told me to come with him or else. It would appear that, ever since that little article in the paper, people seem to be under the impression I have something to do with this investigation."

"But you don't," Captain Marks said.

"Since you're leading the investigation, and you personally asked me to stay out of it, I have."

"Well, I very much appreciate that, Mr. Shaw." Captain Marks gave Cliff a wry smile. "So, it would appear this whole thing is just a misunderstanding," Captain Marks said, though Cliff got the impression something else was going on.

"It appears so."

"I don't see any reason why we can't send you home then, Mr. Shaw. Put all this nonsense behind us and get back to doing the work that really matters."

"That all sounds good to me," Cliff said, getting up from the chair and brushing himself off despite getting the feeling that the other shoe was about to drop. Even Lou's face looked a little worried, despite the pleasantries. "I'm sorry to have wasted your time." Cliff held out his hand to the captain, who stared at it for a moment before taking it. But when Cliff tried to release it, Captain Marks didn't let go.

"It's just…you're lying to me, Mr. Shaw. You see, I have multiple witnesses who put you on the back of a bike this morning, going somewhere with a known associate of the Crimson Serpents. Not only that, but I have it on good authority that, last night, some local teens were caught in some sort of drug trafficking scandal. I would tell you that they're fine and that, given their age and willingness to cooperate, they have been told they'll be let go." Captain Marks released Cliff's hand and held up a finger to keep him quiet. "Ahh, not yet. You see, I assume you don't need to know any of these little details, considering that the arresting officer, as it turns out, is an old friend of yours, which is quite a coincidence. It also seems strange that all of this came from some anonymous source?"

"Very strange," Cliff said.

"But you're not the only one with friends in the OPP. So, you wouldn't have believed my shock when I learned where the tip came from."

"Well, technically, I told you I would stay out of the murder investigation, and I have." Cliff said, trying to worm his way out of it, though Captain Marks seemed more than a little annoyed at this point.

"Stop it. I warned you, Mr. Shaw. You get in my way, I bring you in."

"Sir, I'm sure he was just trying to hel—"

"As for you, Officer Polaski, it would appear that we have an open threat on our hands. I want you to keep an eye on the residents at the Limestone Manor. Is that clear?" he added when it looked like Lou was about to protest, but she didn't.

"Officer Thomas, please escort Clifford Shaw to one of our holding cells. I'd say a couple of nights here will suffice to warn to our retired friend here not to interfere with the law."

"I would hardly say that what I did was interfering. Someone had to help those boys, and as far as I was aware, you didn't even know what was going on."

"What is that supposed to mean?"

"I'm sorry, was that not clear enough for you?"

"Cliff, I think you should calm down," Lou said, stepping between the two men.

"No. Something odd is going on here, and I'm having a hard time figuring out why you seem so adamant about not having any help on the matter. If I didn't know any better, I would think you have something to hide, Captain Marks." Cliff felt his face flush, though he couldn't help but think it was not nearly as red as Captain Marks's, as his eyes seemed to burrow into Cliff with all the fury one might expect from a starved wolf.

"I'm going to pretend you didn't just imply what I think you did, Mr. Shaw," he said through gritted teeth.

Cliff was no stranger to angry men. He'd been one himself, and he was unafraid of this man's wrath. He was too old and too tired to care, so it was no surprise when he continued.

"Oh, I'm not *implying*, sir. What exactly are you investigating?"

"I want this man out of my sight now! Thomas, get him in a cell."

"Sir, please," Lou started, but she was turned on immediately.

"As for you," Marks snapped, "I suggest you get over to that house and keep an eye on it while I try and figure out exactly where it is you're going to be in a few weeks."

"Why am I watching the house?"

"You heard it from Mr. Shaw himself. He and his home were threatened. As you seem to have such close connection with the house, I figured you could be the one to watch it. Now go." He pointed with such anger, Lou clearly understood it was best not to answer.

As for Cliff, he was promptly guided out of the room by Officer Thomas and into a back room, which seemed to house three fairly small cells with their own toilets and beds. Before he knew it, Cliff was sitting slouched over on the bed, staring at his feet, trying to figure out just how he managed to get himself in this position. *Shoot!*

18

Cliff woke the next morning, his back unsurprisingly stiff from having slept on the unimpressive single mattress. His one saving grace was that one of the guards had offered to bring him an additional pillow to rest on.

This marked the first time in his eighty-two years that he'd spent a night in jail. The only reason he was able to sleep at all was knowing that Lou was watching over the house. Captain Marks might have done it out of spite, but Cliff had little doubt that the house and its occupants were in danger.

The one gift this had provided him was that, for the first time this week, he was able to be on his own, thinking. He'd almost forgotten what it was like to have a nearly silent room around him. His first thought, of course, had been how strange it was for the captain to keep him locked up here when, so clearly, there was something amiss with this whole investigation. *Could he be the one hiding something?*

Cliff was confident that someone in the community had to know what was going on and was potentially being paid to keep it all quiet. Up till now, Cliff's focus had been on the town council, since they had been the ones preparing to vote. But seeing how difficult it had been for this investigation to get started, despite all the information they'd been given, Cliff wondered if maybe someone in the police could be involved. *It would certainly be one way to slow the investigation down.*

"Morning, Mr. Shaw," said Officer Prescott as she entered the little room which housed the three cells. Only Cliff's cell was currently occupied.

Officer Prescott was a touch shorter than Cliff, though, despite the layers of uniform and body armour, Cliff got the impression she was no small potato.

"Morning, Officer Prescott, and might I add a very big thank you for the extra pillow you offered to me last night." Cliff slid his feet over the side of the bed and leaned his back against the wall, using one of the pillows as a small support.

"Not a problem. I think it's criminal that we don't provide appropriate bedding. I understand not everyone thinks they deserve it, but here, in St. Marys? You're mostly getting the same five or six people skipping through, and truthfully, I think they're just happy to have a safe place to sleep sometimes." She shook her head. "Though I guess with you, Mr. Shaw, we can make it seven." She let out a cheerful laugh.

"Well, young lady, I personally hope this does not become a regular occurrence. Eighty-two years staying out of one of these, and I'll spend whatever I have left avoiding them." Cliff rubbed the ache he was beginning to feel in his lower back.

"Fair enough, sir," she said moving over to drop off a tray of food, which consisted of a small bowl of oatmeal with some brown sugar on top, a healthy-looking banana, and a cup of watered-down coffee. "I'm sorry for the coffee." She grimaced as she laid the tray on Cliff's lap.

"This all looks wonderful. Thank you, Officer Prescott. I've seen what we used to serve in the precincts in Toronto, and I'm happy to inform you this looks like the Ritz by comparison." He laughed as he graciously took the tray from her hands.

"Oh and I got a bag of clothes in here for you. It was dropped off this morning by very tall gentleman." She chuckled and disappeared into the other room before returning with a small bag of clothes which Cliff was grateful for.

"That would have been Hans, thank you." He said picking through the tiny selection of fresh clothes.

"Not a problem, she said standing around looking uneasy as Cliff picked away at his food. "I read in your report that you used to be a detective," she finally said after a minute. "I bet you have some pretty interesting stories from back in the day," she said, smiling enthusiastically.

"One or two, I'm sure." Cliff returned her smile. "But nothing like the things you deal with now. I feel like the standards have changed. For instance, I hope you don't mind me saying this, but you look like you could take down any of the men I used to work with. We certainly didn't have the same level of physical discipline," Cliff remarked, trying a sip of the coffee, which was, in fact, both lukewarm and watered down.

Officer Prescott laughed. "I try to stay on top of those sorts of things."

"I'd say you've sufficiently reached the top, young lady."

"Thank you, sir. You may not be surprised to learn that doesn't always get you ahead."

"Just because we've come a long way, doesn't mean we don't have a longer way to go still. I've always assumed that's why they call it a journey," Cliff said with a sad smile.

"I suppose you're right." She sighed.

"Can I offer you some unsolicited advice?" Cliff set down his coffee. Officer Prescott gave him a little nod. "Sometimes, what's right isn't always what's good. Most of our lives are spent trying to sort the two of those things out." Cliff chuckled.

"Thank you." Officer Prescott turned to walk out of the cell. As she shut the cell door, she looked back at Cliff. "Why exactly are you here?"

"I suppose it has something to do with stubbornness. Though, truth be told, I've been asking myself that same question all night." Cliff sighed as he began mixing up his oatmeal.

"I was told you're interrupting the investigation."

"I suppose that's one perspective."

"What's the other perspective?"

"We have marginally different views about what it is you all should be investigating," Cliff joked, though he wasn't entirely sure how much he could trust Officer Prescott. She seemed nice, but at the end of the day, she was with the OPP.

"What should we be investigating?" she asked.

"I guess, in the simplest terms, who has the most to gain from the town signing a new town maintenance contract."

"Interesting." She appeared as though she was thinking about something.

"There is only one problem with your little conspiracy theory, Mr. Shaw." Captain Marks stepped out from around the corner. "It doesn't add up. We haven't found any links to anyone on the town council who might have taken any amount of money that could been seen as a bribe." He moved to the centre of the small room. "Thank you, Officer Prescott, I got what I needed, I'll take it from here. Oh, and I suggest you take the day off. I expect you back in here with your new friend tonight." He gave Cliff a tiny smirk.

Officer Prescott had turned away, only to look back briefly as if to say something, but didn't. She just turned and walked out.

"You know, if you wanted to ask me these things, I would have told you," Cliff said feeling more guilty that the young officer was being used for some reason.

"I doubt you would tell me much, Mr. Shaw. You seem to have a knack for lying to me."

"I've never lied. I've simply answered your questions in a method that suited my own needs, as well as yours. You can hardly fault me for the fact that you didn't ask the right questions." Cliff shrugged, as he put a spoonful of oatmeal in his mouth and began chewing, grateful for the fact that the oatmeal was still hot.

"You see why I can't trust you," Captain Marks said. "You seem to think you're smarter than everyone else here, but you're not. Your theory is wrong."

"So, you checked to see if anyone on the council had possibly accepted a bribe?" Cliff asked. "And they hadn't?"

Captain Marks nodded smugly.

"Well, all that means is you have an honest town council. Not that someone isn't preventing this investigation from gaining any real traction before the meeting tomorrow morning, which decides on who gets a multi-million-dollar contract."

"Why are you so convinced these two things are connected?" Captain Marks asked.

"How can you not see that they are? One of the primary investors in Four Points is a shell company owned by the Crimson Serpents. One of the women I saw on the back of one of their bikes had a Four Points shirt on. Sam Benoit was paid by Four Points to write up a report which outlined how the company could upgrade the town to more sustainable practices. But when he discovered that they didn't plan on making good on any of those promises he threatened to tell the town. Which is likely what had him killed."

"We can't prove who he wrote those reports for. Besides, say I buy your theory, how did he find out about what they were planning?" Captain Marks asked.

"Best guess is looking into the other towns they placed bids on. Every one of them has financial difficulties and has suffered under this contract. But none of them can say anything for fear of the Crimson Serpents coming back and hurting them," Cliff said, setting his tray down beside him on the bed and standing up. "You may not believe me, Captain Marks, but there is something going on here, and the only people who are going to suffer when this all comes to an end are the people living in the town of St. Marys."

Captain Marks stared defiantly at Cliff for a long while, although if he had thoughts on the matter, he didn't voice them out loud. Instead, he turned on his heel and began to walk out.

"I'll see you in the morning, Mr. Shaw," he said as he rounded the corner and disappeared.

The rest of the day was spent pacing back and forth within his cell, thinking over all of the information he had and all the information he wouldn't be able to use, given that he was now trapped inside of a cell. Other than being allowed to pace up and down the street with an armed escort, Cliff was more or less confined to his cell. He found this entire situation to be rather funny, as within the short walk up and down Jones Street East, he reckoned he couldn't have been more than a hundred feet away from the Limestone Manor and, therefore, his friends.

It wasn't until 8:15 in the evening, when Officer Prescott arrived back at the jail, that anything of note really happened. Even then, it wasn't as if they'd let him go. Instead, Officer Prescott—who was unable to meet Cliff's eye, arrived with a note from Lou.

"If anyone asks, you didn't get this from me," Officer Prescott said, reluctantly handing Cliff a folded piece of paper, before turning around to leave.

"Thank you," Cliff said more out of habit than anything.

"For what?" she said walking out of the room.

Cliff chuckled at that, although the entire thing felt a little too cloak-and-dagger for him. However, he was certainly happy to have something other than a blank wall and some bars to look at.

Cliff unfolded the paper with its neat, clean lines, which made Cliff immediately think of Bunty, who he suspected took care in all her little projects, including something so mundane as folding a piece of paper.

Once he had the paper open, he found a small handwritten message.

Cliff, we hope you are holding up well in the slammer. Kitty said she spotted you walking around early today, so we're happy they're giving to some exercise and fresh air. As for our little situation, we believe we have found a solution. Sit tight. We have it covered. Best wishes, the residents of the Limestone Manor. P.S. We will not hold your recent run-in with the law against you in your consideration to join the Limestone Manor. We look forward to hearing your decision when you are released.

Cliff didn't know if he should be scared or grateful for the message. On the one hand, it appeared they discovered something while he was away that could help sort out the problem. On the other, none of them had any real idea of the dangers they might be getting themselves into. Not that Cliff could have changed any of their minds if he'd been there.

He did wonder just what information they might have found. Cliff folded up the letter and placed it in his pocket just as Officer Prescott entered with a plate of food. She stepped into the cell and placed the tray on Cliff's lap. The contents appeared to be a ham sandwich on rye.

"This looks great, thank you," Cliff said.

"Don't thank me. It was delivered with the note." She stepped back towards the doorway. "I was hesitant about giving it to you, but you don't really seem like the type of person who would try and break out of prison and definitely not someone capable to doing it with a sandwich.

"You've clearly never tried Gerald's cooking." Cliff laughed as he opened up the sandwich, which had been wrapped up with care.

"I just wanted to say," Officer Prescott began, unable to lift her eyes from her feet. "Well, it's just…I'm sorry about this morning, he told me if I didn't..." she let out a sigh.

"Don't worry about it. You forget I was in the service for forty years. It's hard when a superior officer tells you to do something you might not want to do. The important thing is that no one was hurt." Cliff tried to give Officer Prescott a sincere smile.

She managed a small smile of her own.

"Thank you for the sandwich," he added before picking up one of the pieces and taking a bite. It was cold but tasty.

"You're welcome." Officer Prescott took a seat at the tiny desk off to the side of the room.

"Any chance you can tell me what the plan is for me tomorrow morning?" Cliff asked between bites. He hadn't known just how hungry he was until he started to eat.

"As far as I'm aware, the plan is to release you in the morning. Captain Marks just wanted to make an example of you, I think."

"I think he might have had other reasons. It's no coincidence he's holding me in here until tomorrow morning. I'll likely not be out in time to make the town meeting." Cliff chuckled at the bitterness of the situation.

"What meeting?" Officer Prescott asked.

"The town council meeting to decide who gets the contract for the town maintenance projects."

"Why would Captain Marks care about that?" she asked.

"I have no idea. But he's been pretty adamant about me not looking into anything with regard to the body of the young boy." Cliff shrugged.

"You can't take any of that to heart. Captain Marks is under a lot of pressure. He's up for a promotion, and it was as good as his until this case popped up out of nowhere. Since then, he's had all this pressure to sort it out."

"That's no excuse to ignore the obvious."

"I agree, he and Officer Thomas figured they would have time to sort it out. Then you show up talking about town conspiracies, the Crimson Serpents, and now, just like that—" she snapped her fingers, "—it's completely out of their hands."

"Wait, what does Officer Thomas have to do with any of this?" Cliff asked, setting down his sandwich.

"Well, he was a shoe-in to take over for Captain Marks once he was promoted. This was as much his show as Captain Marks's, though it was Captain Marks who's been taking the most shots," Officer Prescott said, shaking her head.

"Wait, so you mean to tell me, Officer Thomas has been leading this investigation?" Cliff asked, the wheels of his mind turning.

"Unofficially, yes. I should go through. I have some paperwork to sort out." Officer Prescott turned to leave Cliff alone in the cell.

"Wait, just one more question. Who thought it was a suicide?" Cliff asked.

"We all did, at first." Officer Prescott's brow furrowed in thought.

"Right, but who presented the idea first?" Cliff pressed.

"I'm not sure, sorry."

Cliff was left on his own, his mind racing with all the new information. Officer Thomas had just as much to gain as Captain Marks. Maybe more. He wished desperately that he could talk to his friends about all of this information. Together, they could all come up with a plan, and maybe, just maybe, they could save the town from potential disaster.

Yet here he was, trapped in a jail cell, of no use to anyone. Even the delicious sandwich did little to settle the sinking feeling he had in his stomach.

<h1 style="text-align:center">19</h1>

Cliff wasn't able to get the good night's sleep he would have preferred to get. Instead, he spent a majority of the night trying to get comfortable in the foreign bed and trying to calm his mind from racing around with all the information he'd gathered that day. All he wanted to do was get a message to his friends and let them know what he'd discovered.

It was a little after six in the morning when Cliff decided to get up. Not that it mattered. He had nowhere to go, and he wasn't even sure when they would be letting him out. So, he simply went from a prone position thinking about all the things he should be doing, to a seated one still thinking about things he should be doing.

The vote was this morning, in just under four hours, assuming that all went well and there were no other delays. But considering this was a small town and things rarely went wrong, Cliff assumed he and his friends were quickly running out of time.

"Time to get up, Mr. Shaw." Officer Thomas appeared at the door to Cliff's cell.

Cliff couldn't be sure how long he'd been sitting there, as, at some point, he'd managed to dose off. Apparently, sitting and doing nothing had taken a lot out of him. But now he awoke with a start.

"I'm leaving?" Cliff asked through a yawn.

"Yes, you're free to go. But I've been instructed to take you home," Officer Thomas added as he unlocked the door.

"It's only a few blocks, I'm sure I can manage on my own."

"You know how these things work, sir. I can't just let you go. Orders are orders."

"So, Captain Marks told you to let me go?" Cliff asked.

"Those are the orders I got. So, come with me, and I'll take you home." Officer Thomas gave Cliff a friendly wave.

"Where is Officer Prescott? I'd like to say goodbye."

"She's out. Got sent out on a call this morning." Officer Thomas shrugged. "But you're always welcome to stay here until she gets back?" He made a motion to close the door.

"No, I think I've had enough time in this place. Thank you," Cliff joked, as he stood up from the tiny bed and had a big stretch.

He followed Officer Thomas to the door, turning back briefly to look over his tiny cell, feeling very grateful he was about to get out. And with a couple hours to spare. Maybe there was enough time to tell his friends what he'd found out to see if it could help their own plan.

Officer Thomas led Cliff out of the tiny precinct and into a waiting SUV.

"The house is really close. I don't mind the walk," Cliff said, indicating the large hill leading up to Jones Street, where he knew his friends would be up having coffee.

"It's no trouble." Officer Thomas guided Cliff into the back of the SUV.

Something didn't feel right in Cliff's gut, as he felt the man's hand press into his back. A sudden rush of uneasiness was rattling his old bones. Cliff was about to step inside when he stopped. "I'm sure Captain Marks would understand. I'm sure you have better things to do than to drive an old man a couple blocks." Cliff kept one hand firmly on the door so it couldn't be closed.

"Like I said, orders are orders," Officer Thomas insisted, beginning to sound frustrated.

"It's only a few blo—"

"Get in the car, Mr. Shaw. I won't ask again." Thomas looked around nervously and was now visibly agitated.

"You're not taking me home, are you?" Cliff sighed.

"As long as you play along, you'll be home soon enough."

"What's to stop me from yelling and just leaving on my own right now?" Cliff asked defiantly.

"You could do that. But I don't think that would be in your best interest."

"How do you know what's in my best interest?"

"We have your house under surveillance. If you, or anyone in that house, tries to do anything, well then, you know the track record my friends have," Officer Thomas said, his eyes narrowing in on Cliff. "All they want to do is talk with you."

"They did talk with me."

"Then they want to talk again! So, get in the car now!" He put a hand on Cliff's back and gave him a not-so-light nudge.

Cliff climbed into the back of the car. Once he was in, Officer Thomas slammed the door and walked around to the driver's side and hopped in.

He didn't say anything as he started up the SUV and began to drive, taking a quick right before getting up to Queen Street and turning right at the water tower.

Cliff watched people who had already begun heading into the town hall. Perhaps they wanted to get a good seat. He half expected to see some of the Limestone Manor residents already there, but Cliff didn't see anyone he knew. Not even the trusted Hearse was out and about. *Are they okay?*

Cliff couldn't help but feel guilty. He'd somehow managed to bring a household of people he'd come to enjoy the company of into so much danger in under a week. In spite of their note, it occurred to him that, perhaps, he should prepare himself for the possibility they might not want him to live at their house. After all, since he'd arrived, they'd been dragged into a murder investigation, watched two kids from the community get arrested, and have their home threatened by a group of thugs and murderers. It would be no shock to Cliff if they wanted nothing to do with him. *Heck, they've probably already packed my bags.*

Cliff watched as they passed the high school on his left, and he started to wonder just where in the world they were going.

"Son, you don't have to do this," Cliff said, and to his surprise this resulted in a laugh from Officer Thomas.

"You're right. I don't have to do this. But I want to. You worked as an officer for what? Forty years, you said. All that time putting yourself at risk, and for what? At least in your day, there was a general respect for police. Now it's like we're always in the wrong."

"That's a fairly naive way of looking at it."

"Are you calling me naive?"

"I'm not sure yet. But you have to realize that things are not always black and white. Of course, there has been some mistrust in the police. And rightfully so. Some people have taken the position of power and abused it. Unfortunately, that kind of thing sets us all back. But it doesn't mean you give up on your duty to protect the people of your community."

"But this isn't my community."

"It became your community the moment you committed to the OPP. You took up that mantle, and to turn your back on it now would only prove so many people right." Cliff stared out the window, trying to figure out where on earth they could be heading.

"I think we're a little late for turning around, Mr. Shaw. And after today, we are going to be perfectly positioned to make some money. The only issue I can see right now is you. I mean, you've caused nothing but problems since you arrived."

"So, what? You're going to kill me?"

"I'm not, no. I would be entirely happy to turn a blind eye and have you return to whatever part of Toronto you disappeared to before. Go home, travel the world. Just don't stay here." Officer Thomas turned to give Cliff a smile.

"Such a generous offer."

The SUV turn into a large parking lot.

"Where are we going?"

"The Ice House," Thomas replied, as if Cliff would know exactly what that was. He must have spotted the confusion on Cliff's face. "It's the town hockey arena. But also, the community spaces are not all that busy on Monday morning, and it makes it a rather quiet place to chat."

"Not a bad-looking facility. A step up from what we used to play hockey in."

"How so?"

"Well, for one thing, this place has a roof. We played in an open-air rink down by Trout Creek. Until they built one with a dome down on Water Street. All in all, I'd say this place is better."

"Well, as much as I appreciate your critique of the town and its hockey arena, I think it's time we head inside." Officer Thomas exited the SUV and walked around to open the door for Cliff to get out.

"Thank you, my good man." Cliff stepped out of the car and looked around at the large complex and nearly empty parking lot.

"I'm not your chauffeur."

"Well, you're driving me around to places I've never been before and opening the door for me. What would you call yourself?"

"Your captor."

"Well, I freely came with you, so I would hardly say you're that." Cliff grinned.

"Just move it, old man." Officer Thomas gave Cliff a shove in the back.

"You know, people say that like it's a bad thing. But I get discounted groceries, and no one cares if I take forever in a lineup."

"I'd hardly say no one cares."

"No one cares enough to say anything. And truth be told, I could probably do it in half the time. But where do I have to be that I can't be leisurely?" Cliff said as he walked in through one of the back entrances of the community hall.

"Well, it's annoying."

"Not as annoying as getting old. But sometimes I think people forget that, in not so very long, they are also going to be old. Then they'll have all the young people telling *them* to hurry up."

"Not me, I'll be fast."

"Then you, my friend, will be bored. That much I promise you. It's not like the days get shorter. Your time in them just gets longer."

"What are you on about?" Officer Thomas said as he directed Cliff down the hallway and around the corner into a giant hall.

Cliff spotted the arena off to the left side and was immediately brought back to his own days on the hockey rink, though he would hardly say he was ever any good.

"I'm just saying, right now, your day is filled with work and kids, if you have any, and friends...or, in your case, drug dealers, it seems. But then, one by one, those things start to go away. When was the last time you saw your parents?" Cliff asked.

"I don't know. Like, a month ago maybe. And I don't have any kids. Happily single," he said with a grin. "I got money in the bank and a new house, so I'd say things are good."

"Aww, a real bachelor. I know what that's like. Got my heart broken once and was too afraid to ever try again."

"That's not it at all."

"I'm talking about me, numb nuts. I'm sure you'll be happily alone forever."

"I don't want to be alone forever. I'm just not looking for anything now. How in the hell did this become about me?" Officer Thomas looked around the room as if he was expecting someone.

"It's not about you. Well, it is. Sort of. It's more about the world in which you get old. I mean, if you get old," Cliff said with a shrug.

"And why wouldn't I get old?"

"Well, for one, the company you're keeping. I'd hardly say they're in the habit of letting people live long and healthy lives. If they get crossed."

"Well then, it's a good thing I don't plan on crossing them." Officer Thomas forced Cliff into one of the small plastic chairs that had been lined up against the wall.

"Well, that's good to hear, Officer Thomas," Hurley said as he and a couple of the guys Cliff had seen at the barn, including both Tug and Hatchet, sauntered in. No one seemed happy about being in this place, as they looked around cautiously.

"Hurley, of course, I wouldn't cross you. How are things looking with the vote?"

"It appears that, despite our friend's interference, the good people of St. Marys are still fairly keen on all the green initiatives and improvements we plan on providing. At such a great rate to boot." Hurley laughed. The boys around him did the same.

"But you're not going to make any improvements," Cliff said.

"That, my friend, is debatable. I feel like this contract will greatly improve our bank account." Hurley laughed again.

"But you're going to destroy St. Marys," Cliff argued.

This received a scoff from Hurley, who waved away his comment like it was nothing. "So, a couple of potholes won't get filled. The important thing is that the town wants to make a change for a greener future."

"But there is nothing green about what you want to do."

"Says you. What could be greener than not doing construction?"

"Doing *green* construction," Cliff insisted.

"Agree to disagree. Only time will tell."

"And what does time tell you about all the other towns you've conned?"

"No one's said anything to me."

"Because they're afraid of you!" Cliff said, standing up.

"Maybe you should think before you say something you might regret," Hurley said, taking one big step in towards Cliff.

"You think you can scare me with death? I'm not a young student you can just push around." Cliff stepped defiantly closer.

"Oh, we didn't push him. We threw him off the train tracks," Hurley said, as almost a whisper, into Cliff's ear. The room grew quiet for a moment as Cliff stared him down. "You got balls, old man, I'll give you that." Hurley chuckled as he patted a now-fuming Cliff on the back. "Now, why don't you tell me what I'm doing here, and then we get the hell out of this place."

"What are you talking about?" Officer Thomas asked, stepping closer to Cliff and Hurley. "You're the one who told me to meet you here."

For a long moment, the whole room fell silent.

Cliff finally filled the void. "Well, I think it's safe to say *I* didn't call you all." He held his hands up in the air. "I've been in prison."

"Shut up!" Officer Thomas said, his usual bluster gone now, replaced with something akin to fear.

"I called you." Hans stepped out from behind one of the doors. "Or rather, I messaged you both to come here."

"But you can't be here. We have someone at your house, watching you," Hurley said angerly, slapping Tug, who quickly got on the phone.

"You're right. You have someone there, but they're not watching us," Hans interjected, clearly trying not to smile.

"Us?" Hurley asked.

One by one, Bunty, Sol, Kitty, and Jan stood up from behind a nearby half-wall that appeared to front a coat check room.

"I was afraid you'd all talk forever. My knees were starting to give out." Sol bent down and rubbed a knee.

"Wait, how did you get them all to come?" Cliff asked, equally surprised to see his friends standing around the room.

"It was Bunty's idea," Kitty said.

"I read about it in a book. We bought one of those pre-paid cell phones and got Officer Thomas's number from Lou. Then we got this man's number from Randy Gillis. Then we sent them each an urgent message to meet here and told Officer Thomas to bring you."

"And that worked?" Cliff asked, looking Hurley and Officer Thomas.

"I mean, now, in hindsight, the message seemed a little strange. Though the bit about the new phone number was a rather good touch," Hurley shrugged.

"There'd not really been an exact science to all of this." Officer Thomas shrugged.

"Wait, how did you know about him?" Cliff pointed towards Officer Thomas.

"Bunty again." Kitty smiled, causing Bunty to blush a little.

"Well, obviously we looked into Captain Marks first, but when we discovered he was planning on leaving his position, we couldn't really find any reason why he would be interested in helping them out. But we figured, at this point, it had to be someone in the OPP who was helping. So, with a little help from Lou, we managed to narrow it down. Officer Thomas seemed the obvious choice. He was vehemently against anyone investigating this murder and would miraculously turn up new information any time the investigation led anywhere towards Four Points or The Crimson Serpents. He recently purchased a new house, which he apparently doesn't stop talking about and finally, he seemed to have the most to gain from this investigation going away. Not only was he in line for a promotion with Captain Marks gone, but he would also be in the perfect position to tip off the Crimson Serpents about all the inner workings at the OPP and hold up investigations. With all the money they stand to gain from the contracts moving forward, I imagine his value would go up as well… So we figured it must be him," Bunty said with a shrug.

"How did you know he was up for a promotion or that he didn't want me investigating?" Cliff asked.

"Lou," Kitty added, matter-of-factly. "People talk, and apparently, they love to talk about our friend here."

"Of course they do because I'm awesome." Officer Thomas said smugly, "And also, you're bang on with that analysis, I will make a ton of money when this deal goes through.

"If this deal goes through." Bunty said coolly.

"Excellent work, all of you," Cliff said with a smile. "I was wondering if I was going to get the chance to tell you about there being no bribes on town council. Apparently, Captain Marks had already looked into it."

"You can't bribe people on a town council in a small town. The whole town knows about it before you can even manipulate the person," Hurley said with a laugh. "Law enforcement, on the other hand, usually have nothing to do with the town, and therefore, have no issues making a little extra money on the side."

This brought a few nods from some of the men behind him.

"Shut the hell up, Hurley!" Officer Thomas said, looking around at the unexpectedly full room.

"What are you so worried about? Okay, fine. They managed to get us here, so what? There are six of use with guns, and you're an OPP officer. They're five geriatrics and a child."

"I'm actually twenty-three," Jan said, raising a hand. The other one was holding his cell phone.

"What's that?" Hurley asked gesturing to the phone.

"This?" Jan said, frowning at the obvious question. "A phone?"

"I can see it's a phone, you idiot, but what are you doing with it? Stop pointing it at me."

"Sorry, I'm just facetiming this to the town council," Jan said with a smirk, which immediately vanished when all five of the Crimson Serpents, including Hurley, pulled their guns.

"I think it's time we leave," Hurley said, backing out of the room. "And I suggest no one follows us."

Everyone in the room raised their hands, except Officer Thomas who looked confused.

"You can't just leave me here."

"Of course, we can," Hurley said with a smile. "As for the rest of you, we should kill you right now," he said, pointing his gun.

"It feels like you'd be wasting some precious getaway time if you did that," Cliff said tapping his watch.

"Well, maybe I'll just shoot *you* then?" Hurley said, as the sounds of sirens could be heard in the distance.

"I think we should get the hell out of here, boss," Tug said, tapping Hurley on the shoulder. And to Cliff's joy, they all turned and ran.

"That was close," Cliff said, looking around the room and letting out a sigh of relief.

"Umm, I'm still here, and in case you haven't noticed, I'm completely fu—"

"Language, young man." Kitty said pointing a finger at Officer Thomas.

"I would argue you've found yourself in this position, son, because you did it to yourself." Sol stepped out from behind the counter where he'd been hiding with the others.

"I'm not going to jail," Officer Thomas said frantically.

"Then I suggest you make a run for it, 'cause you're running out of time," Hans said, pointing towards the door.

Officer Thomas looked around the room, contemplating what he should do.

"Or you stay and face the consequences," Cliff suggested. "You messed up. But I'm sure if you tell them what you know, maybe they'll knock some time off if you testify against Hurley and the rest of them."

"That's if they get them," he said, spinning around in circles. "I can't," he finally said, running out the door.

"Do you think we should have just let them all leave?" Cliff asked.

"Oh yeah. The sirens outside are Lou on the side street," Jan said. "She's been on the FaceTime as well."

"Wait, so there are no police coming?" Cliff asked.

"No. I hope you don't mind, but we called your friend Tom, who was with the boys and told him about the barn. He had a team go in after Hurley and his people left this morning. I suspect, when they get back to that hideout of theirs, there will be a bit of a nasty surprise for them," Kitty chuckled.

"Once they have Hurley and his men, they will take Randy and Marcus home. I'm not sure what the boy's punishment will be, but your friend Tom said they've been helpful so hopefully that helps." Sol said looking relieved.

"You thought of everything." Cliff smiled.

"It was all Bunty's idea. She's the real mastermind behind it all," Hans said, giving a big grin towards Bunty, whose cheeks flushed red.

"Anyone could have done it," said Bunty.

"Not anyone." Sol laughed. "I couldn't. Though I admit it was all kind of exciting."

"I particularly like the part where we tricked them into thinking we were home." Kitty grinned.

"How did you do that? And who is at the house?" Cliff asked.

"Bunty managed to get a few of her choir friends to go home in our stead last night." Kitty laughed.

"They'd always wanted to stay at the manor, and with the promise of Gerald's cooking in the morning, they couldn't resist." Bunty smiled.

"Genius!" Cliff clapped. "Where did you all stay?"

"Jan's." Hans laughed. "It was tight, but we made it work."

"I'm not sure we'll do it again soon," Jan said with a smile before he noticed his phone. "Oh, sorry. They're still on mute." He pressed something on the screen.

"Can you hear us?!" It was the sound of Mary Anne, who seemed to be dominating the phone at the moment, practically yelling, as if she couldn't be heard otherwise. "Are you safe?!"

"We're all safe, Mrs. Crawford," Jan said. "Did you get all that?"

"We did!" she said, continuing to yell. "I'm happy to say we managed to get the majority of the council here early enough to witness this!"

"That's great. I also have a copy of the entire event on video," Jan said, walking to the corner of the room, where he'd managed to hide a small video camera as well. "So, if anyone needs to see it for themselves, we can show them."

"Wonderful news! Hold on, we have the mayor here, who would like to say a few words!" Mary Anne stepped away from the phone, and the mayor's face appeared, though he, thankfully, had a slightly better idea of the concept of the video chat.

"It would appear this town owes a great deal of gratitude to the residents at the Limestone Manor. Without your assistance, we might never have realized what a terrible decision we were making. Mr. Shaw, I'd say we had the right man on the case after all!"

"That's very kind of you, Mr. Mayor, but none of this would have been possible without the help of Lou Polaski at the OPP, Jan VanDosen at the *Gazette*, and of course, everyone here at the Limestone Manor," Cliff said, speaking into the phone, getting smiles from all his friends.

"Particular praise should be given to Ms. Bunty Price, whose plan this actually was."

"Well, we are grateful to all of you, and we are very relieved that you're all safe. I won't lie. I had my reservations about the plan, and for all of you standing up to a group of possible killers, alone. All without the assistance of the police. Even now, I have to admit that was all rather dangerous." The mayor looked around at the other people in the room with him. "That could have gone much worse."

"People underestimate us, sir," Hans said. "Old people, that is."

"They find us disarming," Kitty agreed. She pushed her way into the camera feed to give a little wink into the phone. "That's why they always tell us the good stuff."

"Well, I'm sure, after this story gets out, no one will be underestimating you any time soon," the mayor said.

"I hope I'm not too late!" Mrs. Chen appeared behind the mayor catching the attention of the rest of the room. She peered into the phone. "Cliff? Jan? What are you all doing over there? You should be here." She narrowed her eyes. "No bother. I brought proof for the town of how bad Four Points is. I brought my niece and nephew, and also the mayor of Berlin. There was some resistance at first, but I can be quiet persuasive. They agreed to tell the town what happened to them." She smiled and gave them a thumbs-up. "So, problem solved, and you didn't even have to come."

"Mrs. Chen…" Jan began, but Hans put a hand on his shoulder.

"Great work, Mrs. Chen. You look like you could use some breakfast."

"Yes, I'm starving."

"Wonderful, we will pick you up in the Hearse in a few minutes. We just need to grab Gerald."

"Gerald's been eating all morning," Kitty said.

"He would also kill us if we went to the diner without him," Sol interjected.

"Hurry up, though. I hate town meetings. They're so boring." Mrs. Chen gave the mayor a thin smile. "I'll be out front."

"What about you, Cliff? Fancy a breakfast?" Hans asked, as Jan took the phone away and tried to talk Mrs. Chen through how to hang up the phone before realizing he could just do it himself.

"I would love to," Cliff said.

"It's only for house members," Kitty said, her eyes narrowing in on Cliff.

"You want me in the house? After all this?" Cliff asked, a bit surprised.

"You mean the most fun we've had in years?" Kitty smiled. "Of course!"

"It would mean you have to live in St. Marys, though," Bunty said, her brows raised.

"I think I could give it a year." Cliff smiled back.

"Wonderful. Then, I have something for you," Bunty said, leaving to go back behind the counter. She pulled out a large brown paper bag with white tissue coming out from it.

"Did you bring this with you?" Cliff asked surprised.

"Well, it wasn't just sitting back there, Cliff." Kitty laughed.

"We were a little pressed for time seeing as you were supposed to tell us yesterday if you wanted to stay," Bunty reminded him.

"I was a little preoccupied."

"We will forgive you for that." Hans chuckled.

"Here." Bunty handed Cliff the bag.

He took it gingerly and pulled out the tissue paper. He couldn't remember the last time he'd received a gift from anyone. Reaching into the bag and pulling out a hunter green, cable-knit sweater.

"Is this the sweater you've been working on?" Cliff asked. Bunty nodded. "You made it for me?"

"Of course. I make one for all the residents," Bunty said.

"How did you know I was going to stay yes?" Cliff asked.

"I hedged my bets."

"What's this?" Cliff said, looking back into the bag and pulling out a bundle of papers.

"The contract," Hans said. "Come on, you can sign those over breakfast."

He put a hand on Cliff's back. He was about to lead him out, but Cliff stopped and slipped on the sweater. It was a perfect fit.

He gave Bunty a hug. "Thank you."

"Welcome home, Clifford Shaw," she whispered in his ear.

"It's twenty-five degrees outside, though," Sol said, giving Cliff a pat on the back. "Just so ya know." He laughed.

But, for whatever reason, Cliff felt very comfortable in the sweater, despite the very warm summer's day. As the Hearse drove through town, en route to pick up Gerald and Mrs. Chen to go for breakfast, Cliff spotted the water tower as they drove past it. Suddenly, the message beneath it didn't sound so bad.

St. Marys, The Town Worth Living In.

The End

Acknowledgment

Acknowledgments The Limestone Manor.

As always, I would like to start by thanking you the reader! If you have made it this far it means you have likely completed the book in which case, I am eternally grateful for you giving this story a chance. As a new author, I am focused on putting out work that I find to be entertaining for you, and me to read. There are so many books out there that you could read, it means a lot that you would make this one of them. If you enjoyed the book please tell your friends, give it a review or simply let me know. You can find me online or email me at Jonny@jonnyonthepage.com. I appreciate your support!

I would also like to thank my family who has continued to support me throughout this journey. There are many of them and I am grateful for the gift of having them in my life. Although they may not always understand what I do, they are always there to read and encourage me to continue. So, thank you, J,G,J,S,H,L,R,D,J,L,A,H,B,K,A,L,L,N,G,K,G,R,H,T,H,D,P,G,R,J,K,C.

Mum and Dad, thank you for always encouraging me to follow my dreams. Not to mention my Mum, who has read this and every one of my stories a potentially unbearable number of times, as she is always the first and last one to read it before it gets shared with the world. She is also one of my editors and if you ever get the chance to see an early draft of one of my stories, you'll understand this is no easy feat. I appreciate you and everything you do for me. And I would like to thank my dad and his golf buddies who I was able to sit and chat with. I peppered them with questions about what life was like in St. Marys in the 50s and 60's so if you are from St. Marys and you remember things differently let me know so that I can build it into future stories!

I would especially like to thank Amy Cubberley at the St. Marys Museum and Archives for reading an early copy of the story and helping me fact-check some of the historical information in it. Although some of the facts are true about the history of the town, please remember that this is entirely a work of fiction and I as the writer have decided to take some liberties with this information to help better suit the narrative of my story. Think of this more as an homage to the Town of St. Marys rather than a biographical depiction. If you would like to know more facts about the town of St. Marys and its history, please visit the town and the Museum at 177 Church St. S., St. Marys, ON.

Continuing on, I would like to thank another Editor on this project with me, Shannon Cave, who helped tighten up the story. Her hard work and dedication to helping me get my story out there was greatly appreciated and I'm truly thankful for everything she did to help get it to where it is.

My Cover Artist, and dear friend Colleen MacIsaac. They are a rockstar artist, performer, and *very* soon to be parent who carved out some of their precious time to provide the rest of us with the eye-catching masterpiece we have all seen. Perhaps it was the reason some of you gave this story a chance. I'm so grateful for your work on this project. It means a lot to me to have your wonderful presence coupled with this novel. Thank you, Colleen!

Lastly, I want to thank my partner Hilary who has encouraged me from day one to work towards this dream of becoming a writer. She reads and edits all my stories and is always a helpful soundboard when I have to work through particular problems. She is my best friend and the one person I want to see every day. I feel honoured to have her as one of the many pillars of my life. So much love to you. And also, to Henry, our dog, who even now sits beside me while I write this and pretty much all my stories.

Thank you, again everyone for allowing me to write and share my work with the world. I hope you continue to find what I do entertaining. I look forward to bringing you more stories soon. Please feel free to check out my website www.jonnyonthepage.com where I occasionally share some short stories for free, sign up for my newsletter which I continue to work on. I promise it will not flood your inbox with stuff, but when I do try to keep people up to date on what I'm working on, as well I try to add in some exclusive short stories in there before they get posted anywhere else.

Best wishes and thank you for reading!

About the Author

Jonny Thompson is an award winning writer and performer living in Ponamogoatitjg/Dartmouth, NS with his partner Hilary and their delightfully entertaining dog Henry. Jonny was born in England and grew up in the traditional lands of the Anishinabewaki and Attiwonderonk nations now St. Marys, Ontario.

Jonny attended Dalhousie University, where he received a BA in Theatre. He's worked professionally in stage and film for over thirteen years, including five extremely exciting years travelling the world as a puppeteer.

Jonny's debut novel *Ash and Sun* was released in October 2022. He has written various novels, novellas and short stories which can be found on his website https://jonnyonthepage.com/.

He is continuously working through new projects and looks forward to sharing them with you soon. Thank you for reading!

You can connect with me on:

🌐 http://www.jonnyonthepage.com
f https://www.facebook.com/Jonnyonthepage

Also by Jonny Thompson

Ash and Sun

After a 200-day suspension, all that Sergeant Adam Jennings wanted was a win on his return to the Global Investigation Bureau (GIB). But when a simple warehouse fire begins to look more like a homicide investigation, he is forced to watch as the entire case begins to unravel, slowly revealing the dark underbelly of a world that should not exist. Saddled with an unwanted new partner, and a tarnished reputation, Jens is forced to tread a thin line between right and wrong as he tries to discover just what the truth really is.

Atlantis

With only twenty-eight days to find a weapon that could change the world as we know it, Master Sailor Clive Davis embarks on a mission that will take him to a place unlike anywhere else in the world. Atlantis is a technologically advanced city built in the middle of the Atlantic Ocean by billionaire philanthropist Grace Alice. Undercover as a civilian deep sea welder Clive must track down the weapon and destroy it before Grace and her team can unleash it on the world. As Clive discovers more about the mysterious city, he begins to question what his true purpose is. With just twenty-eight days to separate fact from fiction, it's a race against the clock for him and the rest of the world, whether they know it or not.

www.ingramcontent.com/pod-product-compliance
Lightning Source LLC
Chambersburg PA
CBHW061807190726
48289CB00007B/2111